A Tracy Brubaker Mystery

Book 1

The Big Nap

John Carter Stell

Midnight Marquee Press
Baltimore, MD, USA · London, United Kingdon

ISBN 978-1-936168-62-0
Library of Congress Catalog Card Number 2016916577
First Printing November 2016

Dedication

For my parents,
who put me here…
For my wife and kids,
who put up with me…
For the Svehlas,
who first put my words in book form…
And for Peter S. Fischer,
who put the idea back in my head
that dreams could come true…

I honestly think it is better
to be a failure at something you love
than to be a success
at something you hate. —George Burns

Chapter 1

It had been a particularly daunting week for attorney Tracy Brubaker, so she had crawled into her warm, comfy bed early this Friday evening, looking forward to a mostly event-free weekend. The poor economy and troubled real estate market of recent years had paved the way for a very busy time with respect to her practice's foreclosure protection department. She wanted to help the people who were at risk of losing their homes, especially those families with children. As was her nature, she had taken their stress upon herself. And it was wearing her down.

She could empathize with them—or at least their fears. As a child, her family had experienced tough times themselves, her father's paycheck being the only income. A career in law enforcement meant one had to keep an eye on every dollar spent, and that was during *good* economic times. But she was lucky because she was never without a home or had ever missed a meal. Nevertheless, she could still remember those occasions when her parents, thinking their daughter was out of earshot, sat at the kitchen table and, with hushed voices and shaking heads, prepared to pay the monthly bills. She also remembered how her father's worried expression would transform into a reassuring smile if Tracy happened to wander into the kitchen. Of course he did't want her to worry. But children are very sensitive to their parents' moods, no matter how many reassuring smiles they received. How could she not identify with the families that were going through this very same experience now? Some of her peers would say that made her a very poor attorney. But her heart said she was a very good attorney, she couldn't help it; she was who she was.

She felt a little selfish deciding that the next couple of days would be all hers. Time to relax: sleep in, do some cleaning in her condo, maybe watch a Bogart movie, make some phone calls to missed friends, take a stroll around the harbor and perhaps pop into The Cheesecake Factory. Other than church on Sunday morning she didn't even need to leave her home if she didn't want to. This weekend would consist of simple pleasures. She'd recharge her batteries and be refreshed and ready Monday morning to face the battle once again.

Her condo was located in downtown Baltimore overlooking the city's stunning Inner Harbor and Chesapeake Bay. The area had once been an industrial powerhouse, home to industries such as shipbuilding, canning and steelmaking. Gradual deterioration of the land, death of U.S. steel mills and residents retreat to the suburbs sparked a revitalization that in 1980 saw the opening of Harborplace, a stretch of sparkling buildings along the waterfront that housed numerous restaurants and specialty shops. The enterprise, along with the National Aquarium, Maryland Science Center, and of course, Fort McHenry, helped fuel a tourist boom that once again had the area thriving. The summers were especially wonderful, as one could sit outdoors and enjoy some of the best seafood the East Coast had to offer, while being entertained by the street bands and performers who were frequently present. And her condo put her in walking distance of it all. It was the one luxury she had allowed herself. Her law practice was profitable but hardly the kind that would make her a rich woman. Just entering her 30s, the five-foot-five, auburn haired lawyer was single and happy. And at present she preferred it that way.

The condo was smartly furnished and fit her perfectly. Her living room featured a sage sofa and loveseat, which allowed for comfortable viewing of the 35-inch wall-mounted television, which was a must for the classic movie fanatic. She had splurged and purchased a queen-sized bed with matching nightstand and dresser. Tracy had opted for a two-bedroom unit so she had room for her ever-growing collection of DVDs, which consisted mostly of old mystery movies, some film noir, a dash of suspense thrillers and some TV crime favorites.

The film room, as she referred to it, was something of a shrine to her late father, who had been a detective with the Baltimore Police Department. Growing up, she had spent countless hours with him watching the exploits of Charlie Chan, Sherlock Holmes, Mr. Moto, The Saint, The Falcon and any number of films starring William Powell (who was her personal favorite screen detective). Father and daughter often watched Perry Mason win yet another case against Hamilton Burger or another favorite Lt. Columbo, who somehow managed to always trick the suspect into incriminating himself. As she got older the two would seek out never before seen whodunits, and then challenge each other to figure out the villain before the big reveal. The loser bought the other an ice cream sundae or banana split. (She preferred the latter.) Initially her father had to loan her the money when she lost, which became less frequent as time passed. She was fairly certain she had settled her account with her father before his death.

The end result was that she had inherited her father's love of mysteries. She would frequently throw one in the DVD player to relax, especially during stressful times. There was something about the black-and-white images that instantly transported her back to those days when she had snuggled next to her father, asking him all sorts of questions as the film unspooled. "My, what a smart little girl I have," he'd tell her, as he kissed her forehead. Eventually that changed to, "You're too smart for your own good," but she still got her kiss. Now, her father's movie library was hers, and she could indulge her nostalgia at will, feeling once again, however briefly, the sense of safety and security of knowing that nothing could harm her with her father watching over her.

She would add to the library occasionally, delighting in finding a film that she remembered watching with her dad. In fact, before turning in this Friday night, she had spun a favorite of theirs, *Charlie Chan at the Opera*, part of a set she had purchased herself. The memories though had been warm, making her feel like that safe little girl again, and sleep, helped by the sound of the rain that pattered against her balcony door window, had come easily.

Her well-earned slumber abruptly ended when the phone beside her bed jarred her awake. She glanced at the clock radio and its big red numbers shouted 11:48 p.m. "Hello," she answered, not really attempting to mask the sleepiness in her voice.

"Tracy?" the voice asked. That voice was familiar, but one she had not heard in—how long had it been—about three years, maybe?

"Brian?" she asked in return.

"He's dead, Tracy. Someone killed Dad and I know they think it was me," Brian Shane stammered out.

She reacted instinctively. "Brian, I am so sorry about your dad." There was no immediate response from him so she asked, "Is there anything I can do?"

"Tracy, I don't know who I can turn to. The lawyer who's here thinks I did it. I don't want to deal with him. Could you please come over—just to help me get through tonight? I need to talk to someone I can trust. I know you don't get involved in murder cases, but..."

"Are you still at the house off O'Connor?"

"Yes."

"Give me about 30 minutes," she told him.

"Thanks, Tracy."

She hung up the phone, wiped the sleep from her eyes and moved toward her bureau. Once there, she couldn't resist opening the right corner drawer that contained memories of special events and happier times—including the time she and Brian Shane were in love. But that was years ago—college days. She found one photo with the two of them embracing but looking at the camera, her head leaning against his chest, a big smile on their faces, along with some sunburn. She could see the Boardwalk in the background so this must have been taken in Ocean City, Maryland, a favorite getaway of theirs because it was so close—about a three-hour drive—and they both loved the beach. It didn't hurt either that Brian's family had a vacation home there. Funny, but she couldn't remember who took the picture. A smile briefly crossed her face, but quickly disappeared. She stared in the mirror and thought about how things could change so dramatically in mere seconds.

Brian's father dead—murdered. She could empathize with him in a way very few people could. But it had been so long since she and Brian had had any contact. Was he drunk when he called her tonight? It didn't matter because he was clearly hurting and frightened. Not exactly the way she pictured their reunion. Still, she couldn't help looking forward to seeing him, even under these horrific circumstances. Quickly throwing on some clothes she ran a brush through her hair and then grabbed her trusty brief-case—and threw it over her shoulder. A quick glance in the foyer mirror and she was off to the garage to retrieve her car and make her way to the scene of the crime.

The Shane estate was off a private road in Baltimore City: more than 100,000 square feet of landscaped grounds, a main house, detached three-car garage, roundabout driveway, a gorgeous swimming pool and pool house, and sizeable garden in the back—just for starters. Large white-bricked walls encircled the whole property, which was further protected by a large gate in front that had 24-hour security. As Tracy's blue Audi pulled up to the gate the security guard on duty approached her. Even though the evening's rain had stopped by now, the guard that came toward her car was wearing a yellow poncho, which was reflecting the blue and red lights of the police vehicle parked in front of the gate. "May I help you, ma'am?" he asked after she'd put down her window.

She handed him one of her business cards and told him, "I'm Tracy Brubaker, Brian Shane's attorney. I should be expected."

He took her offering. "I'm sorry ma'am, no one told me," he said, his words occasionally snapping thanks to the incessant chewing of his gum. Peppermint, it smelled like to Tracy. "Just a moment please." He left her and went back to his booth, picked up a phone, read the name off the card to whoever had answered, and nodded. The gate started to open and he smiled as he motioned her forward.

The travel up the driveway was lengthy, just as she remembered, but the darkness masked the lawn and trees that were so beautifully maintained, at least they were in the years when she was a frequent visitor. She finally reached the large roundabout driveway, filled with a parade of police cars, emergency vehicles, and even a limousine, which seemed starkly out of place. Tracy parked in front of the limo and headed to the house's main entrance. The guarded front door was open. A familiar face greeted her.

"Hi, Tracy," Officer Theodore Banks said matter-of-factly, apparently aware she was coming.

"Hi, Ted," she greeted, smiling. She knew him from her many visits to the downtown police station to interview various clients, witnesses and the like. In spite of his uniform and daunting six-foot-plus frame, he was a welcoming sight. "Who's the big cheddar on this one Ted?" she asked.

"Detective Tanner," he responded, returning her smile.

"Great!" This was more good news. "Can you point me in his direction?"

"Follow me." He moved from the entrance and made a left at the large staircase that led to the second floor, and continued down the foyer halting in front of the main living room. Tracy followed. Banks motioned one of the officers, who was surveying what was no doubt the scene of the crime, over and briefly whispered in his ear. Banks smiled at Tracy as he returned to his post, while the other investigator moved toward Detective Tanner.

Detective Elias Tanner was a tall, African-American man in his mid-50s, married with a son of his own on the force, and the former partner of Tracy's father, who had been a decorated detective while serving with Baltimore City's homicide division. He was killed in the line of duty when Tracy was a junior in college. Since then, Tanner had become something of a second father to her, and one of her favorite people. He was standing in the large room that housed a 70-inch television, which seemed to preside over the whole area. When he realized Tracy had arrived, he ended whatever conversation he was having and moved toward her.

"Tracy! I'm surprised to see *you* here," he said as he joined her in the foyer, giving her a brief pat on the shoulder. "I thought you didn't get involved in murder cases." There was no irritation in his voice, just curiosity. Tracy figured Brian didn't tell every law enforcement member she was coming, but she nevertheless found herself smiling again upon seeing someone she considered family.

"I'm just here to help out a friend," she told him. "Can I see Brian Shane?"

"Sure," Tanner responded. "I didn't realize you two knew each other."

Tracy gulped. "You met him at my father's funeral."

Tanner just looked at her. He decided not to pry by asking any personal questions, and led Tracy back through the foyer, moving again toward the left side of the house. While en route he said, "I'm not sure what you've been told."

"Little. I know Brian's father is dead. That's about it," she responded.

Tanner shared some of the details. "Someone shot Stewart Shane in the back of the head between the time Brian Shane got home and the time the family attorney arrived; so we're talking sometime between just after 10 and 10:30. We questioned Brian about it of course. But we haven't charged him with anything yet. It's a little too soon for that." He stopped and turned to look at her. "But he probably should have the benefit of counsel, for obvious reasons." Their journey ended in the kitchen. Tanner silently turned and left her alone with Brian. Tracy found Brian seated at the large center table in the kitchen, a half-finished pot of coffee in front of him, black mug in his hand. He was staring intently at the table, unaware she was there. At first glance he looked awful. Bloodshot eyes, unkempt hair, his clothes a mess, as if he had slept in them. She suspected all of this was not solely due to his father's murder. She tensed a bit.

"Brian..." she said quietly.

Hearing his name, he jerked his head up and saw Tracy standing in the doorway. He rose to greet her. She moved toward him and the two briefly embraced. He kissed her cheek. "Thank you so much for coming, Tracy," he said. "I know I had no right to ask."

She was pretty sure she agreed with that, but their personal business would have to wait. And she wasn't sure letting him hug and kiss her was a good idea either. She had managed to move on with her life and thought she had finally ended the Brian Shane chapter. At least, she felt she had. She didn't want to give him the wrong idea about how things stood. They were old friends, once removed. But she was an affectionate person by nature, giving friends and family hugs and cheek pecks with regularity, or giving someone a gentle rub of the arm if she thought they needed comforting. Her father had been that way with her, and she couldn't help herself. But back to business; she moved toward the room's center and placed her briefcase on the table. As she pulled out her small notebook and pen, she said, "Just tell me what happened here tonight for starters. We can go 13 rounds over the other stuff later."

He had missed her sense of humor and her playful nature. Those facets of her personality, he noted, had remained intact. And he smiled, albeit briefly, for the first time since he arrived home that night. With her there he finally felt at ease, at least a little bit. The two sat down at the table, and Brian asked if she'd like something to drink. She declined, so he proceeded to relay the night's events. "I got home a little after 10. At least, I think that's what time it was based on what the grandfather clock in the hall said." He paused and took a sip of his coffee. "Anyway I came in, and Dad was sitting in front of the TV watching some ballgame, whatever ESPN was probably showing. I remember he turned to look at me but didn't say anything; went right back to what he was doing." Again he paused, sipped, and then continued. "I just headed upstairs to my room and crashed." Another pause, another sip: "I have to get up early on Saturdays to help at one of the warehouses—the only job Dad thought I could do—so Friday's an early night for me usually." He stopped to look at her. Her expression was sympathetic. He looked back at the table. "Next thing I know Kurt Barton and Bill Ryder are shaking me, asking me what happened. Of course I didn't know what the hell happened. They told me Dad had been shot— was dead." He couldn't keep his voice from cracking as he uttered those last words. "I could tell they thought I did it—the drunken punk finally off'd his old man. It was all over their faces." Another brief pause; "But I didn't, Tracy. I swear to you I *didn't*."

Tracy finished writing, quickly looked over what she had scribbled, and then said, "You're doing fine Brian." She put her hand on his arm and gave it a light squeeze. Then she asked, "There wasn't anyone else with your dad when you arrived?"

"No, he was by himself."

"Expecting anyone?"

"Yeah—he had a meeting with Kurt Barton tonight—10:30, I think it was supposed to be."

Well that explained why the family lawyer was here. She knew the name of Kurt Barton, a respected attorney whose firm represented some of the most successful business people in the state, as well as some of Maryland's most recognizable politicians, both former and present. "That limo I saw belongs to Barton, no?"

"Yeah, that's his." Brian then decided he wanted more coffee. "Are you sure you don't want some?" he asked Tracy.

But she just looked at him quizzically, ignoring his question. "Do you know what the appointment was about? I mean, 10:30 on a Friday night—that's a strange time for a business meeting."

Answering her he said, "All I know is that Friday a week ago Dad called Barton up and told him he had to see him tonight. I think Dad asked Barton to bring his copy of the will with him."

Oh boy, she thought—made to order motive there. "The two couldn't meet earlier during the week?"

"I don't know." He was about to take another drink from his mug, but he stopped, his facial expression indicating he had enough caffeine for the time being.

More jotting in her notebook: "You mentioned Bill Ryder—who's he?"

"He's one of the security guards. He watches the back at night. Does rounds every two hours or so. He probably let Barton in to see Dad."

"I see; anyone else here at this hour?"

"You probably already met Doug Stanz, he's the guard on the gate."

"Yes, I did," she confirmed.

"He's the only other person." Brian paused to rub his eyes and then added, "Doug's engaged to Crystal."

Tracy had almost forgotten about Brian's sister Crystal. She hadn't seen Crystal there yet, but no doubt she would arrive anytime now. "Crystal's marrying Doug?" Tracy asked. "How'd your father feel about *that*, the engagement I mean?"

"Probably just how you think he felt about it." He was looking at Tracy now, flashing back to when she used to have him grill her the night before an exam; the back and forth with its ever quickening pace, how angry she got with herself over the slightest mistake, the eventual belief it was all hopeless, his pep talk to her and the subsequent return of her confidence. Now *she* was asking the questions, and she seemed to have it down to a science. Shaking himself back to the present he continued. "But the last time Dad shared his feelings with Crystal regarding one of her lovers she ran off and married the guy."

Tracy was shocked. This was the first time she'd heard about this, a sad testament to how her friendship with Crystal ended when she and Brian broke up. Still, she had always felt Crystal was level-headed, not prone to rash decisions, not the eloping kind. "How long ago was that?"

"Must be almost 10 years now," he answered. "Crystal was just out of college when it happened. The marriage didn't last long though; big surprise there. I think Dad even managed to have it annulled."

Tracy had observed first hand, when she and Brian were dating, Stewart Shane's control of and influence over his children. Their mother had died of cancer when Brian was just starting high school, so Tracy had never met Lily Shane. But the pictures she had seen of her showed a beautiful, affectionate woman who always had a smile on her face. Eventually Stewart Shane's understandable grief turned him into even more of a control freak, something he had always been. At least, Tracy had it on good authority that he had always been. Brian's grades weren't good enough. Brian wasn't serious enough. Brian wasn't spending enough of his free time learning the family business. Stewart Shane pretty much said the same things about his daughter. And it was Mr. Shane's constant bullying of his son that ultimately led to that awful, awful night that had Brian seeking refuge in alcohol. Tracy had watched Brian sink deeper and deeper into the mire of the liquid drug, refusing to admit his problem and seek help. Eventually, after two-and-a-half-years of true happiness and nearly six months of increasing misery, it had become too much for her. And that was that—maybe. She had seen him a couple of times since the break up—spoken on the phone with him a few times more. But the meetings and conversations never went anywhere with respect to restarting their relationship. The drink that always seemed to be in his hand and the ever-present slur whenever he opened his mouth had seen to that. But she could never forget how happy she was during those first two-and-a-half-years.

"Where is Crystal tonight anyway?" Tracy finally asked.

"Dinner and a movie with some of her girlfriends," Brian answered.

"Ah." Tracy paused and flipped through her notes, making some small clarifications. "She still lives here I take it."

"Yeah."

Tracy paused, looked at Brian closely and then she said, "Then you think the police's theory right now is that you shot your dad after coming home; that's why you called me?"

"I didn't kill him," he said flatly, almost without emotion. "Although, I'm sure Barton and Ryder are telling the cops about those fights Dad and I had—as if fathers and sons never fought before."

She squeezed his arm again. "Do you know if the police might have anything else other than the fights?" she asked him. "Like, a witness that heard you actually threatening your dad recently in front of other people, or something similar?"

"I really don't know what the cops have," he answered. "I certainly never threatened him." Brian sighed. "Truth is, it took me a while to realize exactly what was going on. And when I finally did, and after a couple cups of coffee, I called you. Cops told me to wait here and haven't asked me anything since."

Tracy straightened up. "Good. Let me find out the extent of their case, if there really is one at this point." She rose to her feet, putting her notebook back in her briefcase. "One more thing: where were you tonight before you came home? The police will want to know so they can get an idea of your state of mind during the time just before the…crime."

He answered but couldn't look her in the eye. "Judds."

Judds, huh? She knew of it. She knew what they served. She could probably have guessed what he had there if she tried hard enough. Instead she just stared at him, feeling both sympathy and yes, some anger. But now was not the time to say anything about it. Now was the time for another conversation with Detective Tanner.

Tanner had relocated upstairs to Brian's bedroom. Tracy joined him there, again escorted by the super duper Officer Banks. She entered the room and took a quick look around. There was a pair of brown Rockports close to the entrance door, still wet and muddied thanks to the earlier rain. Brian's king-sized bed was expectedly disheveled. The room's mini-sofa served as a laundry basket. Stacks of books and magazines that sat atop the nightstand blocked the view of the alarm clock radio. There were more piles of clothes on his dresser, as well as some crumpled beer cans scattered about the floor. Didn't he ever let the maid staff in here? "At least nothing is moving around on its own," Tracy thought.

She approached Tanner, who was standing by the window. He heard her and turned. "We found a gun on the lawn just outside this window," he volunteered. "It overlooks the grounds to the right of the house. Brian may have shot his father, come up here and tossed the gun out the window."

"And then went to bed," Tracy said, finishing the thought. She felt a sudden sting when she recalled the last time Brian got into trouble for taking a nap.

"He was drunk, not thinking clearly," Tanner countered.

"Then are we talking some kind of diminished capacity case here?" Traced asked, slightly leaning in.

Tanner didn't respond. Tracy took his arm and started guiding him toward the doorway. "Come on, El." (El was her nickname for him.) "Let's you and I talk turkey—or ham, or salami, or whatever you want."

Tanner looked at her. She was slightly grinning. "How is it you manage to bring food into nearly every conversation?" he asked her rhetorically. "Downstairs, then," he said as they made their way out of Brian's sleeping quarters.

"I shouldn't be telling you any of this," Tanner began. The two were now seated in a small living room located to the right of the foyer staircase. "The investigation is just starting."

"I know," Tracy told him. "Let's call it a personal favor to your favorite mouthpiece and say I owe you one. And that it's off the record."

"Uh-huh."

"Pretty please…"

"I don't know."

"He's a close friend," Tracy pleaded, stretching the truth a bit.

Tanner sighed. "This is all very unofficial you understand."

"I understand."

Tanner sighed again, and started going through his own notes. "OK. For starters, Tracy, the time frame is pretty tight. Brian Shane got home at 10:05 p.m. That's when the gate guard, Doug Stanz, signed him in. This is corroborated by Bill Ryder who saw Brian enter the house just a couple minutes later—10:07 p.m.—while Ryder was making his rounds. Even Brian told us he noticed the grandfather clock on his way in. His father was alive—again, according to Brian himself. Barton and his driver arrive at 10:26 p.m., time confirmed by the guards, as well as Barton and the driver. Nobody entered or left the estate in that 20-or-so minute time frame according to Stanz and Ryder."

Tracy made some more notes, and then frowned. "I'm sorry, El, but this just doesn't make sense." She looked at him with the kind of expression she usually reserved for her opposition in court and continued. "Brian comes home, like he's done so many nights before, decides to shoot his father, then goes upstairs, tosses the gun out his window, and then takes to the sheets?"

"Maybe he thought he was going to be removed from the will," Tanner said flatly. "According to Barton, he was told to bring a copy to his meeting tonight and Brian told us he knew about that."

Brian must have given the police, or someone, his version of the night's events already, she thought, despite what he led her to believe. She could just see the scene in her mind's eye. The police saying gently, calmly, "Just tell us what happened, son. It will be alright." And Brian, not knowing any better, obliging. Then, "Did you know about the will?" and then, "Is that why you killed him?" Then Brian finally telling them he wanted a lawyer. Tracy pressed on. "So this criminal genius kills his dad to keep his inheritance, but contrives to make himself the only logical suspect, thereby negating said inheritance." She delivered this with some agitation. Old beau or not the police's theory of the crime just did not track for her.

Tanner returned her skeptical look with one of his own and said, "Then maybe Shane just got tired of the constant fighting with his father. Maybe it had nothing to do with the will."

Brian was right to be concerned. Stories of the fights were already in the air. But Tracy didn't want to buy that theory either. Tanner continued, "The short of it is: Brian came home, his father was alive. 20 minutes later, his father wasn't."

"What about the guards?" she countered. "Maybe one of them did it or they are in on it together. Do they carry guns?"

"What's their motive? Ryder's worked for the Shanes for over 10 years from what I've been told; Stanz only about two. They don't travel in the same circles. And yes, they have guns, which they turned over to us. Neither firearm appears to have been discharged."

Tracy frowned. "Couldn't Ryder have followed Brian in and then shot Mr. Shane? That seems as likely a possibility as Brian killing him."

"Ryder isn't about to inherit millions of dollars. He had no reason to kill Shane as far as we can tell."

"Maybe Stanz killed him then," Tracy offered. "He's engaged to Crystal, Brian's sister, as you may know. Father-in-law-to-be probably didn't like him. Stanz wants future pop out of the way so he can have the girl and the money."

Tanner continued their verbal tennis match. "Not likely. He'd have had to run up the driveway to the house after Brian Shane arrived, commit the murder, go around the house to ditch the gun, then run back down to the guardhouse to meet Barton on time—all in about 20 minutes based on the times we've been told. That's impossible. That driveway's gotta be more than a 10-minute jog just one way. And it was at night and raining." *30 Love*.

"Perhaps there was someone else already in the house when Brian left for the evening; someone who waited until after Brian came back, and then shot Stewart. He snuck out while everyone converged on the house." She didn't quite believe her own alternate theory, especially after she said it out loud. *40 Love*.

"There's no evidence of that," Tanner said diplomatically.

"What about burglary, anything missing?"

"There's no evidence of that, either. But like I said, this is all very preliminary stuff." However, before the back and forth could continue, their discourse was interrupted by the arrival of one very upset Crystal Shane.

"What *happened*?" Crystal asked, sobbing, clutching the arm of Officer Banks. Tracy and Tanner both heard this as they entered the foyer. Crystal turned as she heard their footsteps. "Tracy? Oh my God. *Tracy!*?" She was crying now as the two embraced.

"I am so, so sorry, Crys," was all Tracy could think to say as she hugged her old friend.

"Why are you here?" Crystal asked, starting to compose herself. "Not that I'm not happy you are," she quickly added.

"Brian called me."

"Why?" Crystal asked, sounding confused.

Tracy wasn't sure how to respond. But her hesitation gave Crystal her answer.

"*They think Brian did it?!*" Crystal asked, shocked. "No. No he would never…" Crystal again lost her composure.

"Crystal!" Doug Stanz called out as he now entered the home. He moved quickly to her and it was his turn to comfort the distraught daughter of the late Stewart Shane.

Crystal was still quite lovely, Tracy couldn't help thinking. Even through Crystal's tear-streaked makeup and tightly closed eyes Tracy could still see her exquisite features complimented by her wavy black hair that stopped mid-back. Why did their reunion, something Tracy had always hoped for, have to be under these circumstances? Tracy turned and gave a gentle stroke to Crystal's shoulder before Stanz led his fiancée toward the kitchen.

Tanner had remained quiet during all of this, just observing. Tracy turned to him, and then she gestured toward the living room—the murder room. Tanner nodded and the two headed to the crime scene, which was now much less occupied than when Tracy had initially arrived. Upon entering she could see the blood-stained cushion on the large L-shaped sofa. There was a nearly empty glass—of what, water?—resting on the table just in front of the couch where Shane's body was found. The universal TV remote was on the floor, which prompted her comment, "Brian said his dad was watching television when he got home."

"The TV was off when Ryder and Barton found the body," Tanner responded.

"How'd they discover the body?" Tracy wondered aloud.

Tanner explained. "Stanz radioed Ryder that Barton was on his way up the drive so Ryder could meet Barton at the front door and let him in. The two of them came in and found Shane dead."

Tracy and Tanner were interrupted. "We have the raincoat bagged, Detective." A member of the crime scene unit approached Tanner. Brian's green raincoat was now housed in an evidence bag. "There doesn't appear to be any blood on it," the man told Tanner.

"Test it for gunpowder residue," Tanner told him. "Even without any blood, maybe Brian Shane was still wearing it when he shot his father."

The impersonality of Tanner's statement stung. She was still standing next to him when he said it so matter-of-factly. "How can you be sure Brian was even wearing the raincoat?" she asked.

"The guards saw him wearing it. Brian admitted to wearing it."

"I see. And I suppose you already have the clothes he was wearing when he came home."

"Yes." Despite Tanner's insistence of everything being preliminary, it certainly seemed to Tracy the police had already made up their collective minds.

"So are you ready to charge him or what?" she asked with a hint of defiance in her voice.

"Not quite yet," he answered. "I told you, we're just starting. We'll check the gun we found for prints of course and will need to confirm if it is in fact the murder weapon, and to whom it's registered, and the like. There are still more people to talk to."

"Then unless you hear otherwise I'll be representing him," Tracy responded.

"Fine, Tracy," he said to her. "We still need to take an official statement from Brian Shane. I know you'll want to be there. Should we do it tomorrow?"

"I'll check with Brian, but tomorrow morning sounds good to me. Let's say 10 for now, at your office of course," Tracy offered.

"That will be fine with me too," Tanner said. "I think I better get back to work."

She briefly looked at him and then turned to make her way back to the kitchen. When she arrived she saw Brian was still there, and that Crystal and her fiancé had joined him. They all looked at Tracy as she entered.

"They're not ready to charge you yet, Brian," Tracy told him. "It's too early for that. But we need to meet with the police at their offices tomorrow morning at 10 to give your official statement, your account of what you did tonight. They'll probably want to ask you some questions too for clarification purposes. I will be here at your place around 9:00 and we'll drive to the station together. Don't say anything else to anybody in the meantime."

Brian stood up and went toward Tracy. "Whatever you say Tracy," he told her. The two hugged. Then Brian went to his sister, and as they embraced, Tracy turned from the scene, emotions starting to rise. She never did get to know Stewart Shane very well in the three years she dated Brian and was close friends with Crystal. But she knew his children. And she loved them. And she could identify with their pain. She had experienced it herself, a murdered father, a future stolen; not just the life the victim would have had, but also the times he would have shared with his loved ones: friends, family, children, grandchildren; all gone. Why? What had Stewart Shane done that someone felt he deserved to die and that they had the right to be his executioner?

But it was worse because here Brian was, for all intents and purposes, being accused of the crime. He wasn't being allowed to mourn properly. And neither was Crystal. Tracy ached for them, but she had no more words to offer. It was time to go and let them grieve; give them some modicum of privacy. When Tracy let them know she was returning to her own home, she received parting hugs from both Brian and Crystal. The latter volunteered to walk Tracy to her car, and the two exited the kitchen and made their way to the driveway. There were more words exchanged outside.

"Do you think they will arrest him?" Crystal asked.

"I don't know Crys," Tracy told her, getting into her Audi. But she *did* know. She knew, based on what Tanner had said tonight, that it was only a matter of time before Brian Shane would be charged with his father's murder. "Goodnight," Tracy said as she closed her car door and pulled away, leaving Crystal Shane alone to mourn her father and fear for her brother.

Chapter 2

So much for the free weekend; when all was said and done, Tracy didn't get back to her condo until almost three in the morning. She opened her door, turned on the lights, and just plopped herself down on her comfortable sofa. Humphrey Bogart was staring at her, gun in hand, from the framed *The Maltese Falcon* poster that hung on her living room wall. She stared back. "Shoot me now" she told him. Bogie didn't oblige. She kicked off her shoes and reclined on the couch's armrest nearest to her, and put her right forearm against her head. No point in making a formal appointment with the bed for the rest of the night, she thought. She wouldn't be getting lucky with sleep. So she just lay there, drifting in and out of consciousness. Flashes of the past occasionally made an appearance on the ceiling: Brian smiling, Brian pouring another one, Brian apologizing, Brian smiling again, Brian yelling…the good, the bad, and the ugly. She preferred mysteries. But western movies were the more appropriate genre for the last days of their relationship she thought as she drifted off again.

Fade in…

"Are you sure you want that?" Brian asked.

"What you do mean?" Tracy countered.

"That would be your second ice cream cone of the afternoon."

"I'm hot so I want something cold."

"But…"

"But what? Are you *implying* something?"

"No," he said quickly, mildly alarmed at how she took his question. "I just remember the last time you had too much junk food."

"Oh," Tracy said. "That was weeks ago."

"It's just that we're two hours from home if you start feeling sick."

She grinned at him. "I'll be fine. I think it's too much grease that gives me trouble."

He grinned back at her and then put his arms around her waist, pulling her toward him. He kissed her, and then helped himself to some of her soft serve. "Hey! Get your own," she teased.

He laughed. "I should know by now not to mess with you when you're eating."

"You got that right."

Brian moved to her side and took her free hand. "I guess we need to wait before we get on another coaster."

"We could see a show," Tracy suggested. "It's so hot out here."

"And noisy. Everyone's screaming."

"Yeah but they're having a blast." She turned to look at him. "Want another bite?"

"Not of your ice cream cone." And he moved in and kissed her again; so much pleasure in their silence. But the screams kept getting louder.

Tracy's eyes popped open. The sun was coming through the blinds, nudging her awake. Last night's storm had completely cleared out and the day was bright. But the wonderful memory of a day at Kings Dominion, a Virginia amusement park they frequently visited during the summer months, was being threatened. Were all the good remembrances now at risk of being sullied? She hoped not.

What time was it? She shot up from the sofa as if some icy hand had suddenly grabbed her leg. A few quick steps to the kitchen to view the stove clock—7:42 a.m. She had told Brian she'd be at his home by 9:00. She quickly showered and then dressed in a gray business suit with knee-length skirt. She picked up her briefcase from exactly where she had dropped it last night and gave Bogie a wink. She was at the door when she remembered to turn and grab something for breakfast—a bagel would work. "The Shanes better have coffee ready and waiting," she thought.

It was almost 9:00 when Tracy arrived at the Shane estate. An unfamiliar face was tending the guard station—Robert Billings his name was—and he came over to her as she dug out another business card. When he saw the name on the card he went back and opened the gate without question. The climb up the driveway made her feel a little anxious. Seeing the estate in the daylight was bringing back more memories. She and Brian had had some wonderful times here: picnics, movie nights, playful games of tag and hide-and-seek in the garden, evenings gazing up at the heavens while lying next to each other—STOP. She couldn't do this now. Detachment had to be the word of the day. She cleared her mind as she parked in front of the house, and made her way to the front door and rang the bell.

Brian Shane welcomed her with a hug. All he said was, "Tracy." They went inside. "Can I get you something, Tracy: Some coffee, or something to eat maybe?"

"Yes to the former, no to the latter," she answered. "I had a bagel in the car that will suffice for now."

"Sure. Why don't you follow me?"

He led her to the kitchen, and grabbed a black mug and poured from what smelled like a fresh pot. "Here you go," he said as he handed her what she needed most right now. "How did you sleep?" he asked her.

"I didn't really; you?"

He shook his head. He had on a different set of clothes than last night, and his hair appeared to be damp from recently showering. But his face looked just as haggard as it had last night. She looked at her watch—9:10 a.m. She took another sip and put the mug down on the counter. "How are you doing?"

"I don't know. I mean, I don't know how to answer that," he said. "But you've been through something like this before, so…" he trailed off.

She looked at him. She understood alright. How many times had she been asked by how many people how she was doing after her father's death—his *murder*? How do you find the words to adequately describe that hurt, that rage? Then she said quietly, "How's Crystal?"

"She's finally asleep, I think," he answered her. "Poor Crystal, that thing a couple of weeks ago and now this."

Tracy had started to pick up her mug but then put it right back down. "What thing a couple of weeks ago?"

"It might have been longer than that," Brian corrected himself. "She and Doug were coming back from a date, coming up Calvert Street when they got caught in some crossfire."

"*What?*"

"Yeah. A bullet came through the passenger's side back window."

"Oh my God…"

"Luckily no one was hurt."

"Did the police make any arrests?"

"Not that I'm aware of."

"They didn't see who did it, either of them?"

"No. They think it came from a passing car though, not the street."

"A case of road rage maybe?" Tracy asked.

"I don't think so. They were just riding along, the shot happened, then Crystal called 911 while Doug just started driving as fast as he could." Brian shook his head. "Last night was the first night she'd been back in the city since it happened."

Tracy was at a loss for words. She had lived in the city for two years now and never encountered the type of violence that frequently made local headlines. Of course she was very careful; single woman alone in the big city. She didn't own a gun. She had mixed feelings about them. Hearing stories like this, however, would no doubt have her reconsidering her decision. She took another sip of coffee, straightened herself up, cleared her throat, and said to Brian, "Okay. This is how it's going to work today." When he didn't acknowledge she was speaking to him she said, "Brian, are you listening to me?"

He looked up. "Yes, Tracy; I'm sorry."

"No 'sorrys' right now," she told him and repeated, "This is how it's going to work today. When we get to the police station on time for our pre-agreed upon meeting we will nevertheless be kept waiting, maybe 15 minutes, maybe 45, maybe more. This delay is hoped to make you more nervous, more jumpy, and more prone to making a slip. Someone will finally come to take us to the interview room while apologizing for keeping us waiting, but it won't be sincere. When we reach our destination we'll be asked to sit down, and probably offered something to drink. I suggest declining. No need to fill the bladder and make the interview any more potentially uncomfortable than it already will be. They are not making this offer because they are your friends. They are not your friends." She stopped and asked him, "Still with me?"

"Yes, Tracy," he answered flatly.

She continued. "We will then wait some more while the interviewing detective or detectives are en route. At this point you are being observed through the one-way mirror that you will notice in the room. They want to study you, analyze your body language, and the like. They know how criminals act when they've been caught, so to speak. Since you're not a criminal this will work to your advantage. Try to remain calm. It will be very difficult to do of course but do your best, okay?" She paused, waiting for an answer. He just looked at her and nodded.

"When they *do* start asking questions, answer them the best you can, be as truthful as possible. If you don't know the answer, tell them that. If you don't remember, tell them you don't remember. Don't make guesses. I will let you or them know if the question they ask is inappropriate. If they start badgering you I will warn them to stop. If they ask the same question one too many times I will warn them to stop. If I feel they are harassing you I will end the interview. In short, I am there to protect you. I don't anticipate much happening after you've given your statement other than follow-up questioning. Do you understand all of this Brian?"

He looked at her. She wasn't smiling. She was clearly serious. He just said, "Yes, I understand."

"Then let's go. I'll drive." She started moving toward the front of the house. Brian put down his coffee and followed her to her car.

There was mostly silence during their trek downtown. Tracy didn't feel like engaging in small talk. She asked him to tell her again what he did last night, step by step. His morning account sounded the same as last evening's. Then she asked, "Do you remember how much you had to drink at Judds last night?"

He looked at her but her eyes were fixed on the road. One-way streets with cars parked on either side made Tracy extra cautious. A car could suddenly pull out, or someone could rush into the street from between the cars, or worse some kid could just unexpectedly appear chasing a ball that got away. At least, those were the reasons she gave herself for not looking at Brian. "I'm not sure," he finally said. She made no sound, just kept looking ahead. "I had, maybe six or seven shots of bourbon; maybe more."

She said sternly, "They'll probably ask that, and they'll talk to the bartender at some point. As you said last night, the police know about the fights, and they'll be hoping you were carrying on at the bar about your dad. They will try to sell you on the idea that you had a lot to drink, weren't thinking straight, and shot your father. They'll say they know you didn't mean to do it. It was a horrible momentary loss of reason due to the alcohol. They'll say they know how sorry you are for what you did and that you'll feel better if you just tell them the truth about what happened. Based on how I think you're doing I'll decide if I let them keep asking such questions, or if I tell them that's enough. The advantage to letting them push you is that you could show them how certain you are of what occurred last night, that your account of last night is the truth. The other side of the coin is that they rattle you and get you upset, make you lose your temper, which they'll then say is what happened when you started arguing with your father again after you got home." She paused and then asked, "Do you understand?"

He was still looking at her, hoping she would just glance at him. No such luck. Then he answered, "I understand Tracy." Then he added, "I know I've said it already, but thanks for being here for me, for helping me."

"Don't thank me yet," she said. "You have no idea the size of the bill you're going to be getting for making me work this weekend." There was a slight grin on her face.

Tracy and Brian arrived at the Northeastern District office of the Baltimore Police Department by 9:50 a.m. They parked and then made their way to the front desk to check in and obtain their visitor passes. Tracy told Brian for now to let her do all of the talking. As expected they were told to wait, but the delay hadn't been as long as Tracy anticipated. By quarter after 10 they were seated in the interview room and Detective Tanner was coming through the door. Another detective was with him—Jim Lucas—whom Tracy had not met before. But she recognized him as one of the people she had seen last night moving about the murder room. After the introductions were out of the way, Tanner asked Brian to recount the previous night's events which would serve as his official statement. Brian's story to the police didn't sound any different than the one he had been constantly recounting to her since last night. Lucas, who must have been in his late 30s by Tracy's estimation, kept on his face a constant scowl that made him look like he needed to use the bathroom. He'd occasionally run his fingers through his thick brown hair and roll his eyes. He must be the Bad Cop, Tracy thought.

"So you didn't see or hear anyone else in or around the house or outside of the house after you got home last night?" Tanner asked.

"No," Brian answered.

"How drunk were you last night?" Lucas asked.

"I was buzzed but functional," was how Brian answered.

"Functional?" Lucas questioned.

"I could walk without difficulty," Brian explained. "I mean, I wasn't staggering all over the place. I knew where I was and what I was doing."

"Let's move on," Tracy said looking at Lucas.

"We recovered the bullet from your father's body early this morning," Tanner said. "Ballistics has already matched it to the gun we found on the ground just outside your window."

"But this doesn't surprise you, does it Brian?" Lucas added.

"Unless the Shanes keep guns scattered about their lawn I doubt this fact surprises anyone, including you, Detective Lucas," Tracy said; "Next question."

Tanner asked, "Have you ever fired your father's gun before last night?"

Brian looked at Tanner and answered tensely, "I've never fired that gun, or any gun. Not last night, not any night."

"Hey we're just asking questions here," Lucas told him.

"And he's answering them," Tracy interjected. "For now…" Then she added, "Besides, I'm willing to bet the paraffin test came up negative." Lucas and Tanner exchanged looks but said nothing.

"Did you have a fight with your father when you got home last night?" Tanner inquired.

"No," Brian said. "Like I already told you, I just went to bed."

Lucas said, "But you did fight all the time with him."

"I think the better choice here would be 'argue'," Tracy challenged. "I think 'fight' is too loaded a word, unless of course you have evidence of fisticuffs."

Lucas practically huffed when he said, "Fine, whatever word you want to use to describe your verbal clashes with your father is okay with me. But the fact remains you and your dad went at it quite a bit."

"Yes, we argued." Brian told him.

Tanner asked, "What about?"

Brian turned to Tracy and she said, "You can answer that, Brian."

"My drinking was the main thing," Brian started. "He wanted me to sober up and get on track so that one day I could help with the family business."

"And he was always threatening to throw you out if you didn't shape up, wasn't he Brian?" Lucas cut in.

"I call shenanigans on that question," Tracy scolded. "And you can start calling him Mr. Shane. He isn't your golf buddy, Detective Lucas." Lucas was a bit thrown by her jibe, but Tracy was starting to tire of his manner.

"Did you just say shenanigans?" Lucas asked her.

Tanner cut in. "Did you have a fight, I mean, argument with your father earlier in the day, Mr. Shane?"

Brian thought a bit. "No. He seemed preoccupied most of the day. I didn't really even speak to him at all yesterday."

"The lawyer, Kurt Barton, was coming over to discuss the will. Did your father talk to you about that?" Tanner asked.

"No we didn't talk about it."

"But you knew your head was on the chopping block Bri — Mr. Shane," Lucas stated.

"He said they didn't talk about it so he couldn't have *known* anything about it," Tracy said firmly. "Let's move on, gentlemen."

Tanner and Lucas again looked at each other. Lucas started again, "Look, Mr. Shane. We understand that you had been drinking, and that your dad made things tough on you day in and day out. So you came home, had another fight, and then you lost it. You're probably sorry you did it. You probably were in your bed wishing you hadn't done it. So just tell us what happened and we can make things easier for you; maybe a re- duced charge. You work with us and we'll go to bat for you with the State's Attorney."

Brian looked at Tracy. She was sitting there patiently, waiting for Lucas to finish his own at bat, already knowing he was about to strike out. "I think we're done here Detectives. You have Mr. Shane's statement, which he will gladly review and sign when it's ready. Otherwise I think our chat is over." Lucas gave her an exasperated look, while Tanner was a little more gracious with the defeat.

"Let's get his statement typed up Jim and send Mr. Shane and Ms. Bru- baker on their way," Tanner said. "I think we have all we need for now."

Tracy stood up and shook Tanner's hand, and offered to do the same with Lucas. He begrudgingly accepted and then turned and left the room. "Just sit tight a bit longer and someone will be back with your statement to sign," Tanner said as he started to leave too.

"Are we okay to talk in here, El?" Tracy asked before Tanner made it out the door.

"You're fine. No ears in the walls. We'll be in touch." Then Tanner shut the door behind him.

Brian turned to Tracy. "I'm impressed. You really called it."

"It's just the way they do things," she said matter-of-factly. "No magic involved."

After a brief silence, he asked, "So what next?"

"Unfortunately Brian, we now just have to wait. They may want an- other interview at some point. Or, they may just decide to charge you with what they have already. Or they may continue investigating and find something that will shift their attention away from you. It stinks, I know. But it's really their move now."

"Okay," Brian said. They waited another 10 minutes before Tanner brought in the now-typed statement. Both Brian and Tracy read over it and then he signed it, making it official. After dropping off their visitor badges Tracy drove Brian home.

As she drove to the estate Tracy asked, "So what are your plans for the next few days?"

"I think I'd like to just stay at home."

"And do what?" she asked.

"Not sure yet; read maybe."

"Do you still read those Ian Fleming novels?" she asked in a very pleasant tone.

He chuckled a bit. "Yeah; and I have all the Bond movies on DVD too."

"Blu Ray is the new thing you should be investing in, Brian," she said. "Especially with that beast you have to watch things on. You're lucky, most of the old black-and-white classics that I love are not likely to make their way to hi-def anytime soon. Not that it matters though, my TV screen is half the size of yours."

He laughed again, pleased that Tracy seemed to be feeling relieved now that the morning was almost over. Maybe she thought the meeting went better than she was letting on. So he asked her, "What are you doing now Tracy? Can you stay for lunch? We told the kitchen staff not to come in over the weekend. So it's just me and Crystal, and maybe Doug Stanz. I could put something together for us. I'd like to do that for you, actually."

She pondered his offer and then said, "To tell you the truth Brian, I am *really* tired. I think I'll just drop you off and then head home so I can catch up on my beauty rest."

He smiled. "Tracy, you may need rest but your beauty is just fine from where I'm sitting."

Tracy made a sour face and then said, "Brian I hope you don't use lines like that at the bar."

He blushed. "That bad, huh?"

"But I appreciate the thought," she quickly added. Then she said, "But I would like to come over tonight or tomorrow night and do some jogging."

Brian gave her a confused look. Tracy proceeded to explain. "Right now there seem to be two possibilities—either you shot your dad like the police say, or Bill Ryder came in the house after you did and shot him. The police are going for option one because they don't have any motive for option two."

"I still don't understand," he told her.

"Tanner said he didn't think Doug Stanz was a candidate because there wasn't enough time for him to check you in at 10:05, get from the guardhouse to the big house, shoot your father, and get back to his job before Barton arrived. Based on the time schedule he had 21 minutes from 10:05, your arrival, to 10:26, Barton's. So I just want to check the timing. I think I still know my way around the place well enough."

He looked at her and then realized what she was getting at. "Doug? Oh, I don't know Tracy."

"I don't know either. That's why I want to try it out for myself. Even if he could make it up and back in time that doesn't mean he did it, just that he *could* have done it. See?"

"Yeah, I see." Brian paused for a moment, and then offered, "Well why don't you do it right now and then we can eat."

"Dude, do you see what I'm wearing?" she asked incredulously.

"Oh, right," Brian said, sounding embarrassed.

She laughed and said, "That's okay. You're entitled to a brain fart considering the past few days. What I want to do is get some sleep, and then I'll call you to let you know which night works best. I want to do it at night so I'm closer to the circumstances of Friday night."

"I see," Brian told her.

"I'll just grab my sneaks and jogging sweats and head over. And *maybe* we can have dinner first."

"I hope so," Brian said smiling. "I'd just like to talk to you. It's been so long since we've talked."

"Whose fault was that?" she thought, but instead said. "I know Brian. But just so you understand I'm here as your lawyer for now. You have to let me focus on what I need to focus on, with as little distraction as possible."

"I understand." After a brief pause he added, "But it's been so great seeing you again. And I was blown away seeing you in action today. You have to let me know the next time you have a court appearance so I can come and watch."

A smile came over her face but left just as quickly. He may very well be getting that opportunity, front row seat included, a lot sooner than he was hoping. But she kept that possibility to herself. They were now approaching The Shane's Iron Guard gate and its trusty human sidekick, who quickly allowed their entrance. Tracy pulled up in front of the walkway leading to the main home and waited for Brian to open his door. He leaned over and gave her a quick peck on the cheek before getting out. "Thanks again Tracy. You can come by anytime for your jog. Just let me know in advance so I can have something edible ready for you by the time you get here."

"Deal, thanks Brian. I'll be in touch. And let me know immediately if something comes up, whether it's the police getting in touch or you remembering something from last night. Okay?"

"You bet Tracy." She smiled at him as he closed the car door, and she pulled away to head back to her homestead and her lonely bed, which she was sure must have missed her terribly last night. Hopefully it wouldn't hold her unfaithfulness with the couch against her. First, though, she'd have something light to eat to silence her now grumbling stomach. And then she would allow herself to close her eyes and enter a peaceful dream land.

Fade in…

"You know this stuff inside out, Tracy," Brian assured her. "You're going to ace this test tomorrow."

"I don't know," she responded nervously. "I'll probably get my dates jumbled."

"You'll do fine. You always do better than fine actually."

"But this time is different."

"You say that every time."

"But this time I mean it."

"You say that all the time too."

"Flapdoodle!"

Brian paused. "Okay, you got me there. I don't recall you saying that before. Is that a real word?"

She looked at him. She was sitting on her dormitory bed, her back against the wall, legs crossed, wearing a long sleeve shirt, jeans, and black socks. He was beside the bed sitting on her desk chair, a history text on his lap. "I'm not going to tell you. I'll use it when we play Scrabble and if you want to challenge me go ahead." She grinned at him.

"We've never played Scrabble."

"Why not?"

Brian looked at her quizzically. Finally he laughed and said, "You're yanking my chain again, aren't you?"

"Moi? Never!" She had that impish grin on her face that he found irresistible. And she knew it too. He decided to join her on the bed and the night's kissing began. After a while she said, "My roommate will be back from the library soon."

Brian gave her another kiss before responding. "Okay. Besides, you haven't eaten anything for dinner, have you?"

"No. My stomach's in knots."

"Tracy, you have to eat."

"Then I'll be nauseous all night and won't be able to sleep. Then I'll fall asleep in class, fail the test, and my future will be ruined."

"Flapdoodle."

Tracy started laughing hard and Brian soon joined her. Finally he said, "Well come back to my place and I'll make something for you. I'd love to cook for you, even if that means just making a salad."

"It's almost 9:00, Brian. If I did that who knows when I'd get back here?"

They were looking at each other now, eyes locked. Finally they moved toward each other so their lips could start Round 2. This time was more frantic and intense. The knots in her stomach were now untied, a very neat trick Brian had been able to do. "My roommate…" she started to say as Brian began kissing her neck.

"Do you want me to go?" he said as he started back toward her lips. She made her answer obvious by putting her arms around his neck and pulling him closer. "Never," she whispered.

Her clock read 8:20 p.m. when she awoke from her dream, now back in the present. It was completely dark in her unit. She pushed herself up and sat in the bed. Part of her wished she was back at her dorm. Some quick deductions — it was nighttime, she had slept more than six hours, and she could probably return her head to that pillow and fall right back asleep. There would be no jog tonight. At least she should call Brian and let him know tonight was out. He was understanding, and told her to be at his place at 6:00 p.m. tomorrow for dinner. Then she could run around outside all she wanted. She quickly accepted his proposal.

Her stomach grumbled, apparently not liking being teased about tomorrow's dinner when it hadn't even been supplied with tonight's nourishment. She remembered there was some grilled chicken left over from Thursday, as well as a tomato that should be eaten sooner rather than later. A can of vegetable soup also sounded good to her. So she warmed up the chicken and soup, cut up the former and mixed it with the latter, and then she sliced up the tomato into quarters, lightly salting each. She set everything out on her living room table, including utensils, and pulled a bottle of water from her fridge. Tonight's company, she decided, would be, appropriately enough, *The Big Sleep*. She never really cared who killed the chauffeur anyway so she went with the sexy version. The meal and movie went wonderfully together, and she was back in bed before 11. She giggled when the images of Brian as Bogart and she as Bacall popped into her head.

Her Sunday morning and afternoon went as they normally did. She slept in until about 8:30. For breakfast she had croissants with peach preserves and some chocolate raspberry coffee while skimming *The Baltimore Sun*, checking her email, and reading various blogs on her laptop. An orange won the fruit selection. She checked her office and personal voice mail messages—nothing urgent. Then it was off to The Cathedral of Mary Our Queen on Charles Street for 11:00 a.m. mass, followed by a visit to Whole Foods Market on Fleet Street for the week's groceries. She typically kept her unit tidy but she liked to clean her bathroom regularly, so she attended to that chore after putting her groceries away and having a tuna sandwich—light on the mayo—for lunch. There was still some time before she had to be at Brian's so she reviewed the notes she had made Friday, several times over, and added some comments with regard to yesterday's police visit. All that seemed clear is that the police had a circumstantial case against Brian, and she didn't believe their meeting yesterday did anything to alter the law's mind. Just after 5:00 p.m. she changed into her light blue jogging sweats and sneakers, grabbed her digital handheld timer and trusty briefcase, and headed to her car. She was looking forward to mixing some business and pleasure. But she was really hoping she'd leave Brian's tonight with another viable suspect to add to her list.

Someone new to her was on the gate this Sunday evening just before 6:00 p.m.. But Tracy didn't get to introduce herself because the bars opened almost immediately as her car pulled up. They must have all heard about her by now. Since she saw the guard pick up the phone as she started up the hill, she wasn't surprised to find Brian standing in the open doorway, arms folded, waiting for her. As she parked, Brian moved toward her in time to open the car door. When she got out he offered her his right arm, which she accepted, and off to the kitchen they went. But she could smell the delicious aroma as soon as she crossed the Shane threshold.

"It just got here," he told her. "It's from Isabella's. There's a margherita and what they call a saraceno to choose from."

She couldn't remember the last time she had brick oven pizza. She asked, "What's on the saraceno?"

"Uh, let me see," he said, consulting the paper menu. "Soppressata, capicollo, feta cheese, and some garlic and herbs—it sounded like something you might like."

"This is supreme Brian; thanks. But this can't be good for the ole waist-line," she said, hands on hips.

"But you're going for a run aren't you?" he pointed out.

"Yeah but I don't want to cramp up. Hope you offer your diners doggie bags."

He laughed at that. She *always* made him laugh. "Sure we do, at no extra charge even."

Tracy liked that price. Then, noticing Crystal hadn't come to say hello, she asked, "Where's your sister?"

"She had to get out of here for a while. She's with Doug at his place, I think."

"Of course," Tracy nodded.

Brian moved toward the pizza and grabbed a plate. "What will it be?"

"I'll try the one that starts with s," she told him.

He added her selection to the plate and handed it to her. He then did the same for himself while telling her, "There were reporters at the gate earlier today and yesterday."

Tracy looked up at him mid-bite. After consumption she said sympathetically, "Yeah. We knew that was coming. I don't suppose anybody got in, what with the high walls and the guards."

"No, but they still hung around for several hours. Just knowing they were there was enough to upset Crystal." He took a couple of bites and then said, "We saw the property on the news, cameras must have been outside the gate filming what they could. And they would flash stuff like 'Death House' and 'Murder Manor' across the screen. We turned it off pretty quick."

The reality of the situation suddenly hit Tracy. Here she was standing beside Brian, a murder suspect, enjoying a piece of pizza as if she hadn't a care in the world. Her appetite left her, not a common occurrence in Tracyville. Even though sunset was nearly an hour-and-a-half away, she decided she wanted to start her exercise now. "I'm sorry Brian. I'm suddenly full. Can we go outside?"

Brian gave her a concerned look but just said, "Sure Tracy."

"Walk with me down to the gate, would you?" she asked him as they exited the house.

"OK. Would you rather me drive you down?"

"No," she answered. "I want to reacquaint myself with the layout, just in case you've changed anything."

"Fine then. Let's go." And the two started making their way down the twisty driveway.

"Just how long is this thing again?" she asked him.

"Almost two miles," he told her. She groaned. "What are you going to do exactly?" he asked her.

"Well, I'm going to see how long it takes to run up the driveway, commit a murder, junk a gun, and then run back down."

"Right. See if Doug had time."

"Uh-huh." They walked a little further then she asked, "Do you have golf carts around here that people could drive around in if they needed to?"

"No, we don't have anything like that," he told her.

"What about bikes?"

"Nope."

"*Another theory bites the dust, hey, hey,*" she sang paraphrasing the classic Queen tune.

And Brian laughed again. It took every ounce of his strength not to reach for Tracy's hand.

When they finally reached their destination, Tracy stopped by the guard station just inside the gate. "Okay, you can wait for me here, or you can walk back up after I start," Tracy told Brian as she was warming up for her run: some stretching, some running in place. "But if you wait here you might have to carry me back up, whereas if you're back up there already you can just hop in your car and come and get me when you get the call about the collapsed female on your property."

Brian laughed. "Plan B, I think," he said.

"Perfect. The front door is unlocked, right?"

"Right."

"Well then, I'm off!" Tracy activated her digital timer, starting her run by the security booth door that opened up to the inside of the estate. She moved hurriedly back up the path from which she had just come, keeping an even pace as best she could. When she arrived at the front door she looked at her timer—just under 15 minutes. She then entered the house, moving to where Stewart Shane had been sitting when he was shot. Next, she went back out the front and around to where Brian's bedroom window overlooked the lawn; she tossed an imaginary gun from her hand. Finally she turned around, and headed back down the driveway to the security booth where she had started. Total time: 29 minutes, 38 seconds. She leaned against the interior wall next to the door, panting and trying to catch her breath. She rapped on the guard's chamber door, and when he turned and looked at her she made a phone symbol with her thumb and pinky. The guard nodded and called the house. Then he opened his door.

"Are you okay?" he asked her with great concern.

"Oh, yeah," she said mildly gasping, leaning forward with her hands on her knees. "I'm great."

Brian arrived via a motorized vehicle in less than five minutes, and asked the exact same question, and got the exact same answer. He gave her a skeptical look. "Here," he said, handing her bottled water.

"Oh thanks. That's—supreme," she managed to get out. Finally she straightened up, drained the bottle of its contents, gave Brian the empty container, and put her hands on her hips. "Almost 30 minutes," she said.

"So what does that mean?" Brian asked.

"A couple of things—one: I need to make more use of the exercise room in my building, and two: Unless Stanz is a super athlete I don't see how he could have done what I just did in 20 minutes, especially factoring in it was at night during a thunderstorm."

Brian nodded. "Can I take you back up now? Maybe feed you some more?"

She moved toward the auto's passenger door without answering. "Is this your Kia?" she asked.

"No, it's Donny's—he's the guard on the back gate tonight. I just borrowed his car."

"Oh." She got in and leaned her head back against the seat, where it remained for the journey back to the house. Once there, Brian offered her another bottled water and some more pizza, but she declined. "It's nearly 8:00, and it's a school night," she said. "I just want to go home, shower, and hit the hay."

"Well at least let me make you a parting gift plate."

She smiled. "Don't have to twist my arm for that," she told him.

Brian went in and soon returned with a paper bag containing three slices of each kind of pizza and a water bottle for the road. "If you get hungry later this should come in handy," he told her.

She accepted his offering, walked over to her car, and laid the bag flat on the front passenger seat. "Thanks for dinner and the workout, Brian," she said, now moving to the driver's side.

"Sure Tracy, any time."

She got in her car, gave Brian a quick smile through the window, and started for home, unhappy with the results of tonight's experiment. Tanner had been right. It didn't look like Doug Stanz could have killed Mr. Shane unless, maybe, he snuck a bike or something like it on the property that night. Or he had help. It would be interesting to learn if he owns a bike though, she thought. She would have to find that out.

Tracy arrived home, stripped off her jogging suit, showered, and put on fresh pajamas. She rested her head on the pillow but sleep wasn't coming like it did last night. The run had got her blood pumping and the case still had her mind searching for an alternate theory of the crime. She stared at her ceiling, wishing she wasn't seeing the writing all over the wall.

Chapter 3

Tracy arrived at her office Monday morning feeling exhausted. She had been unsuccessful at her game of alternate theories, and it had cost her much of the previous night in terms of sleep. No matter how optimistic she was trying to be, telling herself that the circumstantial case against Brian wasn't strong enough, she was still anticipating the call informing her of Brian's formal arrest, which she knew would probably be coming any moment now. And she was also well aware that she'd have to inform her staff they were about to take on a new client. But she hadn't decided yet just how much she should tell them about the past, lest they try to talk her out of representing Brian Shane. After all, this was a murder case, and, as a rule, she did not handle murder cases. She was today adorned in her blue power suit for her scheduled meetings. The color matched her mood.

Her law office was located just off of Falls Road, about a 20-minute drive from her condo, in a five-story building that catered to professionals: attorneys, accountants, marketers, dentists, and even a diagnostic testing lab were among the many tenants. She had leased a corner suite, 1,500 square feet of space which consisted of a waiting area just in front of the main desk, her associate's office, a small kitchen area, a file room which also served as a storage area, and her own office, whose window gave her a view of the side parking lot. Her private office was large enough so that it also served as the firm's conference room. Her floor's bathrooms were down the hall at the opposite end. The wall to wall gray carpeting and predominantly white-painted walls made the office a little too sterile for her liking. So she sprinkled artificial plant life liberally throughout the workplace; that, and some rather colorful wall art hopefully brightened up the digs for her clients.

It was just past 8:00 a.m. and her secretary, Rebecca Dietz, was already at the office of Tracy Brubaker, Attorney at Law, as she usually was. She had by now retrieved the voicemail messages left since the last time Tracy had checked them herself, and made notes on small pink sheets. The coffee had been prepared and the scent helped wake Tracy up a little.

"Good morning, Tracy," Rebecca greeted her, handing Tracy the sheets. Rebecca was tall, almost six feet. She was thin with angular features and a husky voice, and quite pretty. And she cut an intimidating posture when she stood up from behind the reception desk if a client or would-be client started getting impatient, rude, or otherwise out of hand. Tracy was glad they were friends. She would not want to mess around with this woman.

"Hey Beck," Tracy responded flatly, accepting the notes.

"A case of the Mondays?" Rebecca asked, noticing Tracy was not her usual chipper self.

"Huh? Oh, sorry Beck," Tracy said apologetically, and then added, "We may have a new client soon — criminal case. I'll tell you all about it later. Is Neal in?"

"It's Monday so he won't be here until after 9:00," Rebecca informed her, even though Tracy should have been very well aware of this already. "He's dropping his kids off at school since his wife works the early shift."

"Oh, right. Duh," Tracy said while unsuccessfully trying to force a smile.

"Tracy, what's wrong?" Rebecca asked her with concern.

"A friend's in trouble."

"Do I know him?"

"No. But I promise I will tell you more about it later." Tracy sighed and then asked, "I have that Wilson deposition at 9:30 a.m. and the meeting with Lewis and his accountant regarding the trust agreements at 1:00, right?"

"Righto."

"Please tell Neal I need to see him as soon as he gets in, okay?" Tracy hoped she hadn't inadvertently snapped at Rebecca with that question.

"Sure Tracy," Rebecca responded, not sounding offended.

Tracy made her way to her office that was at the very back of her rented suite. Her workspace was simply but effectively furnished with an L-shaped desk with a high-back black leather chair with two cushioned seats for clients facing the desk. The office also held a small conference table with matching chairs, a white wool sofa against the wall, and several oak bookcases containing the firm's law library. A small artificial tree stood in the corner — artificial because every time Tracy tried to bring living plant life into her office she inevitably managed to killed it. She imagined that every time she visited the flower shop for a replacement, the flora quaked in fear at the thought of being her next victim. Finally she showed mercy and settled for something that required no attention.

The other personal touch was the six-by-eight photograph that sat on her desk showing a six-year-old Tracy seated on the lap of her smiling father. Her mother had taken the picture when the family was vacationing in Ocean City. At that time in her life, her father was her best friend; in many ways he always was. She smiled at the photograph as she approached the desk, and reflexively touched the cross that hung around her neck, a Confirmation gift from her father. She rarely took the necklace off.

Tracy pulled out the laptop she kept in her briefcase, placed it on her desk, and booted up the box of technology. She still preferred taking notes by hand though; she wasn't a very fast typist. After pulling out the weekend's accumulated notes, she reread them several times, an activity that had consumed most of her free time during the past couple of days. (There, alas, had been no time for cheesecake.) But she gained no new insights from this umpteenth review. She brought the notes to Rebecca and asked her to type them up. "I'll tell you who to charge this to later."

"Sure: No problem."

"Oh, and Beck, see if you can get me a meeting with Kurt Barton of Barton, Lyons, and Rank, preferably sometime today after 4:00 p.m., or first thing tomorrow." Rebecca nodded.

Tracy had never met Kurt Barton but knew of his and his law firm's reputation. It was as solid as the proverbial rock. She knew Barton had, for many years, been Stewart Shane's attorney for both business and personal matters And he had come to the Shane's Friday night for—what, a week-old emergency meeting? It seemed odd. But she hadn't even considered trying to speak with him Friday night. The police would have wanted his attention, after which Barton would no doubt have wanted to get the heck out of there. Still, she *had* to talk to him, to at least confirm the reported details for her own satisfaction. Brian was probably right that Barton had leapt to the conclusion that he was guilty. That was the reason he'd called *her*, right? But she hoped the distinguished 57-year-old lawyer would make time for her regardless of what he thought or how he felt about Stewart Shane's only son.

As Tracy was about to make her way back to her own office Neal Bennett entered. Neal, like Rebecca, had been with Tracy for the four years she had her own practice. She had hired him mainly for his managerial and research skills, and for the fact that he *did* have a law degree. It also didn't hurt that he had worked briefly for a private detective firm. Book smart, he was a father of four, married to his wife for 12 years, and in his early 40s. He was, for all intents and purposes, her best friend.

Tracy said, "Neal, we need to talk. See me after you get settled. I've got a 9:30 so the clock's a tickin'. Oh, good morning." Tracy made way to her office.

Neal turned to Rebecca with a questioning expression but she just shook her head. This was obviously serious. Tracy usually came into work very happy and enjoyed a good verbal joust in the morning almost as much as winning a case. Neal was a worthy opponent. But she was clearly in no mood for such frivolity today. Too bad — he had quite a few new barbs prepared that would now have to wait.

"At your service," he said as he entered her office. "What do you need?"

She said without hesitation, "Rebecca is typing up some notes I made at some previously unscheduled weekend meetings. There are some names, among them Bill Ryder and Doug Stanz, in those notes that I'd like you to get backgrounds on. Also, the victim, Stewart Shane — see if he's annoyed anyone lately. Shane's the namesake of The Shane SnackFoods Company. They make the kinds of foods that no part of the body except the tongue appreciates. I'll give you a full report as soon as I can."

The Shane SnackFoods Company had been a publicly traded firm for over 10 years now, but it had started as a small family enterprise, while Stewart Shane was in his late 20s. He had obtained bank financing to purchase several small local food-related businesses that were on the verge of bankruptcy, and then consolidated them into one enterprise, picking and choosing the more tasty offerings sold by the individual businesses. He specialized in spicy products in a variety of snacks: pretzels, potato chips, tortilla chips, and crunchy cheese-flavored snacks. Eventually he added traditional and tangy dips to the output. With colorful packaging and aggressive advertising Shane SnackFoods quickly became a local success story, expanded to most of the East Coast within a year, and then spread throughout the rest of the United States. Shane's business had weathered the occasional economic downturns throughout the years — people still enjoyed and/or needed junk food regardless of the fiscal outlook. It had made him millions — millions that would now be going elsewhere.

Neal looked at her. "Victim? As in *murder victim?*" he asked.

"Yes," she answered curtly.

"I thought we don't handle murder cases." Neal said, perplexed.

She was looking down at her desk when she said, "This is a special case. Please just do as I ask. I'll tell you the client to charge it to later."

"Okay," he said flatly. As he was leaving the room he added, quite seriously, "But Tracy I want to know what's going on here — soon."

"You will." And with that she grabbed her briefcase and headed to her morning appointment. While waiting for the elevator to arrive at the third floor where she was located, she turned and saw Rebecca and Neal staring at her through the glass office windows with worried looks on their faces. She decided to use the stairs, and avoid those looks that threatened to break the composure she was struggling to maintain.

The morning deposition lasted nearly two-and-a-half hours. Tracy was grilling a bank loan officer on his application and acceptance practices, which she believed to be discriminatory. It was a joint suit with other plaintiffs, whose counsel was also present.

"You are aware, Mr. Van Ness, that current census data shows that more than 60% of Baltimore City's population is made up of African-Americans and other minorities, are you not?" she asked.

"If you say so," Van Ness answered.

"Are you aware that more than two-thirds of loan applications to your bank last year were submitted by minorities?"

"I'll take your word for it. But we are a *city* bank."

"Does it surprise you, then, to learn, given what I just told you, that only 12% of the loans you approved last year, with respect to *city* housing, were awarded to minorities?"

"Well, I guess not."

"Why not?"

"There are many factors in approving financing: length at present job, income, credit rating, previous rental history."

"And the bank's and/or loan officer's discretion," Tracy added.

"Well, yes, we have that ability."

Tracy pulled out a stack of loan applications from her satchel and placed them on the table. "I notice your bank has a policy of accepting only face-to-face initial applications, that is, the people need to come in and complete the initial paperwork. Why don't you offer online or phone call application processes?"

Van Ness squirmed a bit. "It is in line with our philosophy of wanting to have personal relationships with our customers."

"So you want to get to know them personally before they're your customers."

"Well, that's not quite right."

Tracy paused. "Would it be better to say, you want to know with whom you're dealing?"

He squirmed in his seat a bit more. "I don't like the implication of that."

"What implication?"

"That I want to see how they behave, or something. I mean, even if we did the online thing, the application asks questions about race so I wouldn't need an interview to determine that. Heck all you have to do is look at their name."

Tracy tilted her head a bit and asked, "You think you can tell a person's race by their name?"

Van Ness felt a tug on his sleeve by his counsel. There was a quick exchange. "Of course not. What I meant is…well you seemed to be suggesting the meetings were so that I could tell if the applicant acted black or something. All I was pointing out is that if I were a racist I could just look at applications and deny them without ever having a meeting."

"Acted black? What does that mean?"

Another quick talk with his attorney: "Poor choice of words. A person's demeanor, their poise and bearing, could be helpful to them in borderline cases."

"The discretion factor…"

"Exactly."

"These applications in front of me show how this discretion was applied. In the cases we sampled we found for every seven applications by minorities, you denied six of them, even though they had the same or near-same qualifications, based on your own written standards, as white applicants whose loans you eventually approved. Furthermore, the sample of applications by whites showed for every 10 applicants you approved 8."

Van Ness said nothing. Instead he looked down at his hands.

"Basically Mr. Van Ness, if I'm white I have an 80% chance of getting a loan with you. If I'm nonwhite my chance drops to about 14%. That's a pretty wide discretion gap."

"I can't help it if they don't qualify."

"Who are 'they'?"

"The people we turn down."

Van Ness' attorney, James Franks, spoke. "Ms. Brubaker, stop trying to put words in Mr. Van Ness' mouth."

"My problem, Mr. Franks is that I don't think Mr. Van Ness has satisfactorily explained the approval discrepancy with the words he's chosen."

"He did explain — discretion," Franks offered.

"You're not serious," Tracy countered.

"It's my bank, I can loan money to who I want to," Van Ness cut in, sounding indignant.

"Not if your decisions, especially your denials, are based on race."

Van Ness had had enough. "Look, I run a business. I can't help it if they are more interested in having babies or doing drugs than going to a job so they can pay their debts. Let them rent and go on Section 8. But I'll be damned if I'm giving *them* any of *my* money!" Van Ness went on like this a bit more, his own attorney unable to calm him down. But it was at the point that he uttered a racial epithet, which was now on the written record for all to see, that Tracy said she had no more questions. She suspected a settlement offer was in her client's near future.

She was sorry that the 21st century was a place that the Van Nesses of the world were still making decisions. But she was satisfied that the morning's events would effectively end at least one such practitioner. And, truth be told, the meeting had let her channel some of the frustration and anger that had been building since leaving the police station Saturday morning. Now that the morning was over, she felt a little better, and she was rewarded for her performance with an expensive lunch courtesy of the counsel for another plaintiff in their joint case. The shrimp salad was very, very good, Tracy thought. Unfortunately she had to leave the festivities in time to make her 1:00 o'clock. She made her apologies and expressed her thanks to her lunch companions. Now all she needed was to find a waiter to get a to-go box for her unfinished meal. That shrimp was going to travel.

The cell phone call from Crystal Shane came at 1:47 p.m. while Tracy was headed back to her office. "They're here," she told Tracy. "They showed us an arrest warrant and they're reading Brian his rights. Tracy, they're putting handcuffs on him." Crystal was crying now.

"Tell Brian to be cooperative, but stay silent. The officers should already know he's represented by counsel. Understand Crystal?"

"Yes," she managed to answer.

"I'll meet you and Brian at the police station. They won't let you ride with him, but grab your checkbook and let the police know you'll be right behind them."

"Okay."

"I'll see you there," Tracy said and ended the call.

Next she phoned Rebecca and said she'd be out of the office for the remainder of the day. "Were you able to set something up with Barton yet?" Tracy then asked.

Rebecca answered, "He couldn't or wouldn't swing it for today. But he'd be willing to see you first thing tomorrow. Eight in the a.m. — sharp — at *his* office."

"Please call him back and confirm."

"Righto.

"Thanks Beck. I'll fill both Neal and you in after tomorrow's meeting with Barton." Tracy rang off quickly. She didn't feel like answering any questions or offering any explanations. Now she was off to help Brian.

"We'll be seeing a District Court commissioner," Tracy told her new client. "It's what's called the initial appearance. The commissioner will make sure you understand the charges against you and what could happen if you're convicted. He or she will also decide if bail should be set. I will be there to make sure all the facts of the case are presented in the hopes you can get bail. Even if you don't get bail we can request a bail hearing, so don't panic too much if bail is initially denied. We won't enter a plea yet. Instead there'll be a preliminary hearing where the prosecutor will present evidence against you sufficient to support the charges, what's called having probable cause."

"When will that be?" Brian asked nervously.

"Since it's Baltimore City, one will automatically be scheduled. Make sense?"

"Yeah, I guess," he answered. "They're charging me with second degree murder, Tracy."

"They must be factoring in the alcohol," she told him. "Of course they may approach us with an offer to reduce it to manslaughter at some point, in return for a guilty plea. But we're getting a little ahead of ourselves. Let's just get through today."

"Okay."

"Hang in there," Tracy whispered as she held his hand.

At 3:45 Evan Stevenson, a District Court commissioner, read the charges.

"Do you understand you are being charged with murder in the second degree in the death of Stewart Shane?" Stevenson asked Brian.

"Yes."

"Do you understand that a second degree murder charge can mean a sentence of up to 30 years in prison?"

"Yes."

"Do you understand you have a right to an attorney?"

"My attorney is with me."

Stevenson nodded.

"At this time we would like to present our reasons as to why bail should be allowed in this case," Tracy added.

"Very well."

"The case is largely circumstantial. There are no witnesses to the crime, no real evidence Mr. Shane pulled the trigger. Mr. Shane does not have any prior arrests or criminal record. He is employed by his father's company, and has lived in Maryland all his life in the family home. He doesn't even own a passport, so he should not be considered a flight risk. There's no reason to think he's a risk to others or to himself, given the crime was unplanned and the gun used in the murder is now in police custody. Therefore we are asking for reasonable bail."

Stevenson reviewed the file in front of him. "Does the family own any other residences, inside or outside the state?"

"There is a vacation home in Ocean City, Maryland, but nothing else."

"Well, I don't see any objection to bail by the state's attorney listed here." Stevenson paused and then looked at Tracy. "Bail will be set at $500,000 in this case. Will Mr. Shane be able to post?"

The bail was high, but she did not feel like haggling now. She could request lower bail at his arraignment, if it came to that. "Yes. His sister is waiting and has funds available."

"Very well then," Stevenson said. Tracy mentally breathed a sigh of relief. At least Brian would be sleeping in his own bed tonight.

Tracy, Brian, and Crystal were making their way to their cars when Tracy spotted prosecutor Arthur Pankow speaking with Detective Tanner. She had little doubt Pankow would personally be presenting the State's case against Brian Shane when the time came. He had a good reputation among her peers as an honest, fair, and straight-talking SA. But he was no pushover, and he had an impressive conviction rate in murder cases. A wealthy businessman had been killed by, allegedly, his no-good son—at least, that's how she imagined it would read in the papers and play out in the media.

And because Shane was a generous political contributor — to both parties, depending on his mood — there would, unfortunately, be some politics involved here. The thought turned Tracy's stomach.

"Art," Tracy called out, as she, hand extended, approached Pankow.

"Tracy," he said, nodding, accepting her hand.

"Hi El."

"Hello Tracy."

"Thanks for not opposing bail," she told Art.

He gave her a slight grin. "That's the only favor you're going to get from me on this one, Tracy."

She looked at him returning his grin. "It's the only one I'll need, Art." She turned and headed back to rejoin the Shane children; business-face time.

Tracy told Brian, "Go home. Get as good a night's sleep as you possibly can under the circumstances, and wait for my call tomorrow. I need to meet with my staff to update them on your case. Continue not to talk to anyone about this but me." She was mildly surprised by her somewhat dispassionate delivery. This was Brian she was talking to — her first real love. As much as she tried she could not manage to let herself forget that fact. It was a fool's errand. How could she not remember? But if she was going to be any good for him she would have to play stoic. Any and all remembrances would have to be boxed, wrapped up, and stored in a freezer — solid ice, no slushy. Thawing could take place when the case was history; and then what…? Never mind. She could tell Brian wanted to say something to her, but he chose just to nod instead. She said goodbye to him and Crystal, and she watched the two of them leave together in Crystal's car, their nightmare getting even worse.

Tracy arrived home just after 6:30 in the evening. She hoped last night's troubled sleep would aid in tonight's attempt. She wanted to be fresh when she talked to Barton in the morning. And she would also have to face the looks of Neal and Rebecca when she told them about their new client. Feeling lazy, she just warmed up the pizza Brian had given her last night. She had polished off three pieces before she even realized it. Better stop now or there will be no sleep tonight either, she thought. She debated turning on the TV and maybe channel surfing for an hour or so, or at least trying to find a news report on Brian's arrest. No, she wasn't up for that. She wanted today to be over. Tomorrow she would begin preparing her defense in earnest. But instead of being morose or upset thinking about the coming days, she was starting to feel, dare she admit it, excited, because, to her mind, in this particular case, she was going to have to do more than just practice law. She was also going to have to play detective.

Chapter 4

Fade in…

"What's the matter Tracy?" Brian asked while rubbing her upper right leg.

She was staring at her lap. "My parents insist on meeting you."

Brian furrowed his brow. "Why is that upsetting to you?"

"It's not."

"Tracy, it's obviously bothering you."

She thought for a moment before responding. "I'm afraid."

"Afraid of what?"

She looked at him. "You know my dad's a detective right?"

"Yeah. So?"

"He means well and all but he has a habit of interrogating my suitors."

"He's scared some off in the past?"

"I think so, although no one ever came out and said that."

"So he's guilty of being a concerned and protective father."

"With a gun," she added.

Brian smiled. "Tracy, in all modesty, I'm a pretty good catch. And my intentions are honorable."

She didn't return his smile. "I know you are. But I don't know what you're doing with me."

The smile left his face and concern replaced it. "Tracy, what *are* you talking about?"

"I don't know. I mean: I guess I still wonder sometimes why you haven't broken up with me."

"Tracy! Why in the world would you think something like that?"

"I know I frustrate you when you're helping me study. I can't be much fun to be around."

"But you *are* fun to be around Tracy. So what if I have to lift your spirits every now and again? There are always going to be things that stress you out. In fact, I like being able to feel I'm helping you in something. You're just so perfect in everything else."

Tracy gave him a surprised look. "I am *not* perfect."

"You're pretty close."

"No I'm not."

"Yes you are."

"Brian, that's not fair, to expect me to be perfect."

"I don't expect anything from you except for you to be yourself when we're together."

She looked at him for a moment. "Brian…I…"

"What is it Tracy? Tell me. Please."

"Brian I love you."

He looked at her, and then he put a hand on her cheek. "I love you too, Tracy. I have for most of the time we've been together."

She closed her eyes. "I wish you had told me sooner."

He started caressing her cheek with his thumb. "I was afraid to tell you."

She opened her eyes. "Why?"

"I was afraid of looking like some guy who tells women he loves them just so he can…Well, you know."

"I've never thought that about you."

"That's because I didn't tell you I loved you."

She laughed. "Oh Brian, what kind of logic is that?"

"Brian logic," he answered. Then he moved closer to her, so she couldn't avoid his eyes. "Tracy look. Now that this is all out, let me be absolutely clear. I love you. L-O-V-E. You are smart. You are funny. You are kind-hearted. You never have a mean thing to say about anybody—most of the time. And you are beautiful. You are so beautiful Tracy."

"I'm not."

"See, you're modest too. Let me ask you this, are you calling me a liar?"

"I see what you're trying to do…"

"Are you calling me a liar, Tracy?"

"No, you're not a liar."

"Then that means I'm telling the truth when I say you're beautiful, right?"

"Brian, stop it." She was sobbing softly now.

"Why is this so upsetting to you? I don't understand."

She was looking at him again. "Because for most of my years all I heard from boys was how ugly I was."

Brian pulled back a bit and gulped. "Oh, Tracy. I'm sorry. I guess I never thought of you as anything but lovely. I'm honestly not teasing you, Tracy."

"I know," she whispered.

"I *want* to meet your parents Tracy. I want them to like me but even if they don't I hope *you* don't dump *me*."

She gave him a surprised look and then embraced him. He returned the gesture and began stroking her back. "I love you Brian. I'm not letting you go anywhere."

"I'm *not* going anywhere, Tracy. I promise you that."

Fade out...

When she opened her eyes it was still dark out. After staring at the ceiling a few moments, she sat up in her bed, put her hands to her face, and started sobbing. "What a lonely swan am I," she thought.

Kurt Barton's law offices were located in a 20-story office building that overlooked the Inner Harbor. It was a prime location for a top-tier law firm, one that had been in existence in one form or another for over 25 years. The view from the top must be staggering, Tracy thought. One would be able to see out into the Chesapeake Bay, or view M&T Stadium, home to the Baltimore Ravens and Camden Yards, ballpark for the Orioles. Heck you could walk to the stadiums from there if you wanted; lunch at the harbor every day if you so desired. Tracy observed the towering structure as she negotiated the jam-packed city streets—it was Tuesday morning rush hour after all. She was able to pull off of Pratt Street and take advantage of the building's valet parking. She boarded the elevator that took her to the 15th floor, which was, as it turned out, leased entirely by Barton, Lyons, and Rank, LLP. She moved through the tinted glass entrance doors and headed for the officious-looking young lady who was now watching Tracy approach.

"Good morning. How can I help you today?" she asked Tracy. The name plate on the welcome desk said Shanna Greene.

"I'm here to see Kurt Barton. Tracy Brubaker. He should be expecting me."

Shanna picked up her phone, which looked to be part of some giant command center that one would more likely find on a typhoon-class submarine, and input Barton's extension. He must have picked up almost immediately. "There's a Tracy Brubaker here to see you Mr. Barton." Shanna then hung up the receiver and rose from her desk. "This way please." She guided Tracy down the long, quiet hallway to Barton's office; their trek occasionally paused to make way for a passing associate who needed to be elsewhere. Bookcases and bookcases of law books, legal journals, various magazines, *Michie's Annotated Code of Maryland*—all probably out-dated since most could be easily accessed online—decorated the walls. It was meant to look impressive, and she had to admit it was. The expected office artwork was also present. She never really knew if her clients were impressed one way or another by her own wall art. She liked it because it looked nice.

"Can I bring you something to drink: coffee, tea, or bottled water?" Shanna asked as they entered Barton's office.

"No, thanks," Tracy answered. She was too busy taking in the size of Barton's personal domain. "My whole office suite could fit inside this room," she thought. She entered and saw Barton seated at his desk. He rose and motioned to a small conference table located therein. Barton was a strikingly handsome man with a full head of white hair that topped off a pale face best described as intense, with gray piercing eyes as a bonus. He was above average height, about 5'11", the managing partner of the firm, and not a man to suffer fools. Tracy quickly moved to seat herself at the table, and then pulled out her trusty notebook.

"Thank you so much for seeing me, Mr. Barton," she began, trying not to sound as impressed by him or his kingdom as she really was.

He nodded slightly. "What can I do for you?" he asked, quickly adding, "Being an attorney yourself you know I can't tell you anything that falls under privilege."

"I understand, sir, although I'm sure Crystal and Brian would authorize you to discuss such matters with me if it came to that." This was going to be *fun*, she thought sarcastically.

Barton nodded slightly again. Tracy continued. "If it's okay with you I just want to get some quick background. How long have you been the Shane attorney?"

"Nearly 30 years," he answered. "Stewart and I went to college together so we knew each other prior to the start of our business relationship, which began when we were both in our 20s."

"So you were really good friends then, I guess," she said.

"Yes," he said, although Tracy thought there should have been more emotion in his answer. His friend wasn't even in his grave yet.

"And you and Bill Ryder together discovered Mr. Shane Friday night," Tracy said trying to sound sympathetic, although the looks and attitude he was giving her were making it very difficult to do so.

"Yes. It was so awful."

She thought he might say something more. But that was it regarding the loss of his long-time pal. Then she continued, "And you didn't see anyone while coming up the driveway, or at any other point during your time there Friday, other than Doug Stanz, Brian and Bill Ryder?"

"No. I didn't. Of course, I really wasn't paying attention as I came up the driveway. I didn't know I was going to find a body."

A "body!" That sounded so cold, Tracy could almost physically feel the temperature in the room drop. She continued. "I'm most curious about how your meeting was arranged. Brian said his father set up the appointment a week ago."

"Yes, that's true," Barton agreed. "Stewart called me the previous Friday and was pretty adamant about seeing me. We agreed the meeting would be this past Friday. But I had a previous engagement—a dinner where I was to give a brief presentation—and I told him I couldn't be there until about 10:30 p.m."

"By which time you did arrive," Tracy broke in.

"I like to be punctual for my appointments, Ms. Brubaker."

She wondered if this was a dig at her since she arrived a few minutes after 8:00 a.m. But she didn't dwell on it. She said, "It sounds like the meeting was very important."

"Yes, I assumed so."

"Makes you wonder why he didn't schedule it earlier in the week." She let that stand a bit and then asked, "Why the long wait?"

"I wouldn't know."

"I should have brought my scarf and gloves," she thought. "Anything else you can tell me about the phone call? Did he mention anything about the meeting other than to bring the will?"

"No."

New thought: Tracy Brubaker: tooth extractor. Next tug: "How about *when* he made the call?"

He thought a moment and then said, "I do remember the call came just as I was about to leave for the day. I like to be out of the office by 5:00 p.m. on Fridays. So the call must have been shortly before or just after 5:00." She thought he was done, but he then added, "And, not that it means anything, but he must have been having trouble with his phone."

Tracy perked up. "What do you mean?"

"He was shouting," Barton answered. "Not angry really—the kind of shouting you do when you want to be heard. I assumed he must have thought I couldn't hear him, probably because he couldn't hear me. Mobile phones can be frustrating sometimes, you understand."

"Interesting..." Tracy wondered if this *did* mean something. But her reflections were interrupted.

"Is there anything else, Ms. Brubaker? I have someone coming in at 9:00 and I'd like some more time to prepare for my meeting."

Is that frostbite on my fingers? "Sorry, Mr. Barton. No, I think that's it for right now. Again, I really appreciate your time."

"You are welcome," he said politely but without warmth.

Tracy stood up, shook Barton's hand, and made her way to his office door. She looked back and saw Barton again behind his desk. "How did your presentation go Friday?" she asked him.

"Excuse me? Oh, it went just fine." He looked at her curiously.

"*He's mister cold miser...*" from the animated RankinBass *The Year Without Santa Claus* started playing in Tracy's head. She smiled at Barton but didn't stay to see what his reaction was to that. Shanna Greene was already walking toward her as Tracy entered the hallway. "This way, please," she called to Tracy. Ah, the warm air...

"Do you validate, Shanna?" Tracy asked.

Shanna smiled and handed her a small piece of paper. "Just hand the attendant this and you'll be set."

"Thanks, Shanna," Tracy told her.

"You're welcome," Shanna said kindly. Tracy made her way to the building's garage, turned over her ticket and get-out-of-garage-free card, and handed $10 to the attendant as she got into her Audi. ("Thank you, Ma'am!") The city streets still closely resembled a parking lot, but it was time to head back to the office.

Tracy knew what the rest of the day entailed. She would meet with Neal and Rebecca and fill them in on the case, and then visit Brian to see how he and Crystal were holding up. Perhaps another review of the previous Friday's events would yield something, *anything*. Regardless, Brian was now truly a client who needed her legal abilities. But she presently had no idea how she would crack such a seemingly airtight case.

Tracy returned to her office, which now seemed awfully small, just after 9:00 a.m. She reemerged almost immediately and motioned for Neal, who was parked in his own room, to follow her to where Rebecca was seated at the main desk. Tracy took a deep breath and began.

"Okay, team, here's what's happening. Our new client is Brian Shane—son of Stewart Shane, a wealthy man thanks to his junk food business—The Shane SnackFoods Company. Brian has been arrested for the murder of his father, which occurred last Friday night. The assumption the police are making is that Brian was about to be disinherited. That, or Brian and his father finally had one argument too many. So Brian arrived home, drunk, and shot his dad. Brian was arrested and released on bail yesterday afternoon. The case against Brian is purely circumstantial." She looked at them and then added, "He didn't do it."

Neal and Rebecca just looked right back at her. She knew they wanted some of the back story, so she continued. "Brian and I dated in college. Well, I guess it was more than dating—by that I mean it was serious, at least for me, and I thought for Brian too. Obviously it didn't work out. But he called me Friday asking for my help. And here we are." She wasn't comfortable sharing anything else, even though she trusted Neal and Rebecca. Tracy believed she had told them all they needed to know. They were both older than she was and they probably worried about her more than most employees fussed over their bosses—they were more big brother and big sister. At least, that's the impression Tracy had.

Neal spoke first. "What do you need us to do?" he asked, managing a slight smile.

She looked at her secretary. "Well, Rebecca, put together our boiler plate engagement letter and I'll get it signed. Just email it to me when it's ready. You can just put zero in for the retainer paid. The family is well off, so I'm not worried about us getting paid or anything. Still, given the circumstances, I need to keep in mind this a business arrangement with Brian, if that makes sense."

"You don't have to offer any explanations to me Tracy," Rebecca said. "I'll take care of it."

"Thanks Beck. Go ahead and set up a charge code for Brian too." Tracy looked at her associate. "Neal, were you able to find out about any of those people we talked about yesterday?"

"Have my notes right here," he answered holding them up.

"Beck, I'm going to meet with Neal and go over his notes with him. Please call the Shane estate now or after you're finished with the letter, get a hold of Brian, and tell him I'll be there around lunchtime." Tracy leaned over the desk and jotted the Shane number on a sticky note, and then handed it to Rebecca.

"You bet," Rebecca said as she reached for the phone.

Tracy was feeling better already. At this moment, in spite of her hesitation to disclose all, she nevertheless felt especially close to these two people who she considered more family than employees. "Thanks bunches, Beck. Neal—to the trenches." Tracy's associate followed her back to her office, seated himself in front of her desk and proceeded to share the fruits of his research. Neal had built up relationships over the years via his private detective days with various employment agencies, bank officials, and even Department of Motor Vehicle employees. His polite phone manner always helped. And it was truly amazing—scary even—what could be found through basic internet searching, especially the myriad of social sites.

"Okay, let's start with William Ryder." Neal began.

"Sure," Tracy agreed.

Neal continued. "He's worked for Stewart Shane for 11 years—always in security. He used to be at the entrance gate before shifting to what he does now, by that I mean he patrols the estate—every two hours I think. I took the liberty of calling and speaking to some of the Shane security staff yesterday."

"What did you tell them?" she interrupted.

"That I was just doing a standard background check on the security employees. That was enough. I didn't really lie or anything." Tracy just gave him a skeptical look. He continued. "Anyway, before Ryder went to work for Shane he spent 15 years employed at a company that contracts out security services—like at construction sites that might need watching at night if they have valuable building materials on hand—stuff like that. Samaritan Security Services is the name of it. They're still around. But when I called they told me even if they were at liberty to discuss an employee file it wouldn't matter since he had been gone so long. His file is in storage, or maybe lost."

"Hmmm," Tracy said nodding, her chin sitting atop her folded hands. "He must have been hired shortly after Brian and I broke up. I don't recall ever meeting him when I was a regular fixture over there. What about his personal life?"

"No criminal record—48 years old, married with two kids in college. Wife works at an elderly care facility in Baltimore County. The Ryders rent an apartment at Castle Landing, which is about 10 miles from the Shanes' if I'm not mistaken. They got financial aid to help with their kids' college costs. But I didn't find anything to suggest that the family is having financial troubles."

"Doesn't sound like much there, does it; and Douglas Stanz?" Tracy queried, ready to move on to the next subject.

Neal shuffled some of his printouts, "24 years old, no criminal record. He's been employed for almost two years at the Shanes. Before that he spent a year-and-a-half at an advertising company. He was a marketing major in college; rents an apartment off Roland Avenue. But he's a frequent visitor to Pimlico Racetrack from what I learned."

"Really? He likes the horses, eh?"

"The person I spoke with at the Shane estate says you can tell when he's had a good day or a bad day at the race track. And he mostly has bad days. He also visits casinos too. Not sure about exact numbers of course. I get the impression he lives paycheck to paycheck. I'd really love to get my hands on his credit reports."

"Mmm, no wonder Crystal's father didn't like this guy," Tracy said. "A gambler: I wonder if he owed any money to the kind of people that would have him hurt."

"Not sure about any of that yet; I'd have to pursue other avenues for that information. Think the elder Shane knew about all this?"

"*Absitively posolutely,*" Tracy quickly answered. "No offense, Neal, but whatever you found on Stanz, Stewart Shane found out more."

"I am deeply hurt," Neal responded. "You think Stanz is our guy?"

"Not sure," she replied. "The way things look right now he couldn't have done it without Ryder's, or someone else's, help and I can't work up a scenario yet where the two guards would come together to plot a murder. Still, keep poking around with respect to any debts Stanz may have had." Tracy turned in her chair to look out her office window.

"What about Crystal Shane?" Neal asked her. "Should I do any digging on her? Is she a suspect?"

Tracy returned her chair so she was again facing Neal. "No, I don't think so. She left the house early because she had plans with some friends. She got home late — I was there when she arrived and was told everything. Besides, I know Crystal. She wouldn't kill anybody, least of all her own father."

Neal frowned. "Well, I can at least talk to those friends she went out with, if you want, just to nail down her alibi for the record and see what they told the police."

"Thanks, Neal. That's a good idea. I'd hate to find out she said something that night against Brian. The law would jump on that. I'll get the
names of her friends when I'm over there later today. Is there anything else
to report?"

"Just that Stewart Shane had no immediate family other than his two
children. So I figure they'll split the estate right down the middle, except
for some small bequests to various parties—the help, certain charities,
maybe."

"You're probably right." She paused, leaning back in her chair. "I think
I'll go meet with Brian now, see if there's anything new he's remembered
about last Friday. Maybe I can get a line on some other possible names
worth looking into."

"And as for me?" Neal asked.

"Well, work with Beck regarding what we had originally planned for
this week. There were some tentative meetings, I think. See if we can jug-
gle some of the times, if need be, or, if we can't, if you can go in my stead.
Otherwise, see what can be moved to next week. Basically I want to clear
the decks so I can focus on this case."

"Got it. But there were a couple matters you wanted me to research
regarding non-compete agreements in Maryland," Neal reminded her.

"Do your best to work it all out." Tracy was now smiling at him. "I
know you can do it."

"Yeah, I know. 'I'm the man,'" Neal said, returning her smile.

Tracy got up from her desk and gave the still-seated Neal a pat on his
head. She then gathered her papers and headed out for another sit-down
with Brian Shane—one that would hopefully yield a suspect other than
Brian in the murder of Stewart Shane.

Billings opened the Shane gates for Tracy, and it was Crystal who greeted her when the door bell demanded attention from someone inside. They
hugged, and then Crystal led her to the kitchen where a deli platter and
various fixings and sides had been set out. This was clearly done for Tracy's benefit. Brian knew of her fondness for sandwiches, especially their
construction: selecting the bread, the meats, the cheeses, the condiments—
endless possibilities, some new variation each time. And she *was* hungry.

"You can just help yourself, Tracy," Crystal told her. "Brian will join
you shortly."

"Don't go yet, Crys. Let's talk a bit and catch up."

"Hey, that'd be great." Crystal and Tracy took their seats.

"What are you doing now in your father's company?" Tracy started.

"For the past year I've been the CEO."

"The CEO? Crys, that's supreme! Congratulations, I didn't know."

"Yeah, well, I earned it," she said, laughing a bit. "Dad had been teaching me the business for a long time. You remember the summers I'd work in the corporate office. After college I got a Masters in finance; I've had little time for anything but the business ever since. When Dad wanted to step down, I was pretty much it if he wanted to keep it in the family so to speak."

Tracy nodded. "I guess Brian wasn't in the running."

Crystal looked at her. "No, he never liked the office life too much. Dad bounced him around from accounting, to marketing, to personnel; it never worked out. For the last couple of years Brian's been working in the warehouses; manual labor. At least it's a job I guess."

"He's capable of more than that," Tracy remarked.

"Yeah, and Dad knew that. That's one of the reasons Dad was…well, always giving Brian a hard time."

Tracy nodded. "How did some of the others feel about your appointment? Any hard feelings?"

Crystal grinned. "Well, if there are any, people are keeping them to themselves. Nobody's quit since I took over and nobody's given me a hard time. In fact most people were telling me to ask if I needed anything. It's actually been a good year."

"So, no shouts of nepotism."

"Nope. Now if Brian had gotten the job, then that may have caused some problems."

Tracy's eyes widened. "Hey: Brian told me what happened to you and Doug—the shooting."

Crystal straightened up. "Oh God, that! Tracy, I was so freaked out."

"What happened?"

"I wish I knew, really. We were coming back from dinner, just driving along. We hear this loud crash—turned out to be a back window. We see this car that must have been next to us speed up and run the red light. It was only later after the police looked over Doug's car that we learned the window had been shot out. The bullet lodged in part of the ceiling."

"I can't imagine. When did this happen?"

"It was April 15th. I remember because I had spent the day working with our tax accountant to prepare extension payments. I never file on time."

Tracy smiled. "Me neither. Have the police had any luck tracking down the shooter?"

"Not that I know of. They're pretty sure it was a random thing, maybe just someone out to scare somebody else. That's the way things are today sadly."

Tracy shook her head. "You never had anything like that happen to you before or since, right?"

"No, thank God."

"How'd your dad take it?"

"He was very upset; you can imagine. He didn't want me going out at night for a while, and I can't say I argued with him. But things calmed down and life went back to normal." Crystal went pale and said, "Until Friday night."

"Okay, I think that's enough," Tracy thought. "Well, we can talk some more later on. Why don't you go check on Doug?"

Crystal nodded. "Okay. But if you need me or Doug, we'll be upstairs." Crystal smiled, got up from her chair, and started to leave the room.

"Hey, Crys," Tracy called out.

"Yeah Tracy?"

"Could you make me a list of the people you were with Friday night? The police are probably going to be talking to them and I'd like to find out what's being said. I'm just taking precautions." Tracy was a little nervous about asking this. Crystal might not like the implication.

But Crystal just said, "Okay Tracy, if you think you need it to help Brian. I can put together a print-out that will have their names, phone numbers — anything else you need."

"Supreme! Thanks Crys." Tracy turned her attention to the table that held the mouth-watering feast, rubbing her hands together she plotted her lunch. Contrary to her mother's belief that she never ate, Tracy had a perfectly healthy relationship with food (others might called it obsession) and the willingness to indulge it. Metabolism was the villain with respect to her outward appearance — she was perfectly within the acceptable weight range for her height. Her mother never saw it that way of course — she would always be too thin for mom. Still, her calorie burning capabilities weren't what they used to be. She was more cautious now about her diet. But she could still get away with a sinful meal now and again. There *was* that fitness center in her building she could use if she needed to.

And then the memories started coming back again—the hour or so she would spend debating with herself what her lunch would be for the picnic that particular day, the beautifully landscaped backyard that would serve as the dining hall, what came after the meal. He had been so handsome—sandy hair and a boyish face that made him look younger than he was, before the drinking quickly reversed that attribute. Theirs was an old-fashioned courtship that seemed to be leading to a happily ever after.

Her thoughts of what were and what may have been were interrupted when she realized she was no longer alone in the room. She turned around and saw Brian standing in the doorway. He was smiling. But there was something else. He looked much better than when she saw him last. He was clean shaven, neatly dressed. In spite of it all he even looked rested. The sadness in his eyes was still there, of course. But, she thought, he had cleaned himself up nicely.

He had been observing her surveying the table's offerings. "I couldn't resist, Tracy. I had our cook order this in—told the kitchen staff not to worry about preparing any lunch."

She smiled at him, a warm smile that he had been longing to see again, and now had. "Thank you, Brian," she said quietly.

Brian moved forward, practically charged to the other side of the table opposite Tracy. He leaned in her direction. "So what will it be, Tracy: white, wheat, or rye? Toasted or untoasted? Mayo, ketchup, mustard, or a combination thereof? Lettuce, tomato, onion? Oh—I almost forgot." He now went to the refrigerator and pulled out a jar of dill pickle spears. "And of course you'll want at least one of these."

The two of them completed their ritual. She opted for turkey and Swiss on toasted wheat with mayo, tomato, and lettuce. A pickle spear and spoonful of potato salad completed the masterpiece. Brian went for roast beef and cheddar on rye with mustard, tomato, and onion. Two pickle spears for him as he passed on the potato salad. He pulled two Evian water bottles from the fridge, grabbed some napkins and a fork for Tracy's salad. They then sat down across from each other at the table. Their eyes met briefly before they made their first assaults on their creations.

"That's so incredible about Crystal being CEO," Tracy began.

"Yeah, and she deserved it. She's smart and knows the company. At least Dad had one of his kids he could trust with it. And she seems to be enjoying the job too." Tracy was looking at him, but he was unable to tell what was on her mind. He decided to change the subject. "So, Tracy," Brian started in between mouthfuls, "I thought you were going to be a detective like your father was. What happened?"

She and Brian had broken up before she graduated from college. And their subsequent meetings had resulted in little more than clichéd exchanges. It always seemed to her he went out socially only when he had a buzz on. He would call her once in a while, but his words were always slurred. She wanted none of it, and ended what Brian attempted to start as soon as she could. Now here they were, all these years later, and she was being asked about a decision—a very difficult and emotional decision—that seemed like ancient history. But for whatever reason she found herself not hesitating to answer his question.

"It would have killed my mom," she answered, no hint of exaggeration in her voice. "Each and every day of my life Mom started worrying as soon as Dad walked out the door. She tried in vain to hide it but I could tell, even when I was small. If he was ever late without letting her know in advance that he wouldn't be home by dinner time, she'd be saying *Our Fathers* and *Hail Marys'* until he finally did get home. Then she'd scold him from the time he arrived until the time they went to bed, probably until he faked falling asleep." She laughed at her last comment.

Brian smiled at her and reached for her hand. She let him take it. "Anyway, our worst nightmare was realized when he was killed. Well, you were with me when I got *that* news."

He suddenly felt terribly guilty and pulled his hand away, although she didn't seem to notice or care. He had started drinking by that point—her junior year—and he wasn't there for Tracy as he should have been during an excruciatingly painful time for her. God what an awful sight it was to see her break down like that, right in front of him, without any warning. It rattled him so much he dealt with it in the only way he knew how at the time. That awful night was most likely the beginning of their end.

Tracy continued. "So I knew if I joined the police academy, hoping to follow in Dad's footsteps, that Mom wouldn't be able to handle it. I really do think it might have killed her. She has a hard enough time coping with what life normally throws a person's way."

"Yeah, your mom was always the stereotypical Italian mother from what I remember," Brian chimed in. "Neither of us ever ate enough. And you always had to call her if you were going to be late."

"Yeah. And you there tickling me and doing other inappropriate things while I was trying to talk to her on the phone; naughty boy." She was smiling again.

"Guilty as charged."

Tracy paused a moment and then said, "So I went to law school."

"Why law school?" he asked her earnestly.

She took a bite of pickle, had a sip of water, and continued. "I never did tell you this, did I? It happened before we met and I didn't realize until much later its significance with respect to my future." He was looking intently at her, hanging on her every word it seemed. "Anyway, when I was in high school—a senior—Dad was working on this case that was really bothering him. I had never seen him like that before, so preoccupied when he was home. Not being able to sleep at night; raising his voice way too often." She took another sip of water. "I finally found out Dad and his partner—Detective Tanner, as a matter of fact—had gathered sufficient evidence against someone to turn the case over to the States Attorney for Baltimore City—or SA as they say. They got their indictment and a trial date was set. But Dad didn't think, in spite of the evidence, the person they arrested was guilty, at least not of the murder charge against him. His gut told him something was wrong. When he opened up to me about it I asked if I could look at the evidence they had. My Dad and I had been watching old murder mystery movies together since I can remember—you know, like all those Sherlock Holmes, Charlie Chan, and William Powell movies I used to make you rent for us. I guess I fancied myself something of a Nancy Drew in training." Brian smiled at her, nodding.

Tracy continued. "He blew me off initially but thanks to my constant nagging, he—probably breaking every evidence rule in the book—brought me to his office one night and let me read some of the notes and reports. I noticed a discrepancy in one of the witness' statements. He had told two slightly differing versions to two different officers. Long story short they re-interviewed that witness, found he had been paid to lie, and ultimately got the real killer."

Brian smiled at her, impressed. "All due to you."

"No, due to my dad's experience and instincts, along with some help from his obstinate daughter."

Brian was not sure if this was a case of false modesty or Tracy's habit of underestimating herself. She had been a great student for those school years he had known her, but fretted every paper and test like they were the most important things in her life, and she was doomed to failure. Exam weeks — lordly lord how high strung she'd get. Of course there was only one letter of the alphabet — the first one — that ever appeared on her report cards. And she always seemed surprised when she learned the outcome. He was looking at her now, this beautiful, smart, good-hearted woman that, at one time, would have done anything in the world for him — would have accepted his ring, shared his bed, bore his children. He reached out and this time put his hand on her free arm, slightly massaging it.

She looked at him, and then, another bite of the sandwich, some potato salad. "It really bothered him — the possibility an innocent man might have been convicted. And I remembered that when I was looking at my options. So I figured I might be able to help people if I were an attorney. 'It's all about helping people,' he always told me when I asked why he did what he did, risking his life every day, driving Mom crazy. His own father had been on the job too. But Granddad passed away of natural causes."

Tracy let out a brief sigh and continued. "Of course, the other thing that grated on my father was when a defendant he *knew* was guilty got off because a 't' hadn't been crossed somewhere along the way. He had some rather unpleasant names for my fellow lawyers. My mom would have to calm him down sometimes. Some of those dinner table discussions…" She trailed off. Resuming she said, "So the last thing I want to do is be too good at my job and let some guy walk that everybody knows is guilty. I wouldn't want my mother to read about her daughter doing exactly what her husband loathed so much."

"But the system needs that kind of scrutiny, Tracy" Brian opined. "Everybody involved with our system of justice has to do their job and cross those 't's. Mistakes like that *do* send innocent people to prison."

"I understand that," she told him. "But that doesn't change how I feel about it. You should know better than anyone that my dad was the world to me when he was alive, and even, for a time, after he died, I guess. I know it sounds strange but I feel I'd be betraying him somehow if I got murderers off for a living."

Brian didn't respond. He remembered that at one point during their arguments leading to their break up blaming her father — or at least her saintly image of him — for his own drinking since he couldn't live up to that ideal. She expected too much from him, wanted him to be perfect like her blessed pop. It was all a lie of course, and his accusations were even more cruel given that her father had recently been killed trying to protect a witness, whose life he did manage to save. Brian removed his hand from her arm.

Tracy then said, "So, I try to help people who have been taken advantage of, need legal advice, like if they have been threatened with lawsuits by people and companies who should know better. And then there's some business related work—wills, estate planning, non-compete agreements when employees leave companies—exciting stuff like that." She looked at Brian and gave him a small smile. "And every once in a while I'll take on a client who's been accused of or arrested for a nonviolent crime—they may or may not be guilty. Sometimes it seems they deserve a second chance. Admittedly it's a judgment call on my part. But I've been able to make a decent living at it. I've had my own practice for four years now. I have two employees—Neal and Rebecca—who have been with me from the start. They are some of my favorite people. And together we've done solid enough work that we get referrals all the time, and the client list keeps growing. But I try to stay away from the violent stuff...and the ugly stuff."

"And that's why you don't handle murder cases," Brian said. This was about the only thing he knew about her with respect to her career. Crystal and Tracy would still talk on the phone once in a while, at least in the earliest years after the breakup. Tracy and Brian had met thanks to Tracy and Crystal's friendship. The ladies had both attended a summer orientation for the college they were going to attend in the fall, and hit it off. But it was hard for Tracy to talk to Crystal during the time just after the end, and then the two became more like acquaintances than friends, occasionally chatting but little more than that.

"As a rule, no," Tracy said.

"And I'm an exception," Brian said, sounding more guilty than flattered.

Tracy did not initially respond. The two had finished their plates at this point. Tracy wiped the remaining mayo from the side of her mouth and drained the rest of the water bottle. Then she continued. "Well, you know me, never say never to anything. But the way I see it I'm helping someone who needs my help, or at least asked for it. We haven't even had the preliminary hearing yet much less set a trial date. I hope it doesn't come to that."

"And you're getting to play detective," Brian said, his spirits rising.

She looked at him smiling at her. Yes. Yes it was true. She was getting, in a way, to live out what she had planned nearly all her young life to be doing as an adult. And there were many times that, despite her success in her chosen profession, she wished she had an office downtown, a Detective shield hanging from her pocket, to walk the hallways her father once walked — to continue the family legacy. But she had made her decision and she would live with it. She was helping people, wasn't she?

She returned his smile. "Speaking of which," she said, "we should start discussing this fine mess you've gotten yourself into." She paused a moment, looked around, and then added, "Although, if you have something to offer for dessert, I guess we could stay here a *bit* longer."

Toward the back of the Shane home there was a study where Tracy and Brian moved to continue their post-lunch discussion. They took a seat together on the room's brown suede sofa. Tracy pulled out her notes — both her handwritten ones and the notes Rebecca had typed up for her — and placed them on the oak table that was centered in front of the couch. She handed Brian the typed copy and asked him to look it over.

"This sounds right, Tracy," he said after his read-through. "I can't think of anything to add."

Tracy frowned. She was hoping a few days might yield some new details, that some cobwebs might have been dusted from the mental attic. "So it was business as usual Friday then," she said. "Have dinner, go to the bar, come home, and call it a day."

"Pretty much," Brian confirmed.

"Did something happen at the bar that upset you, maybe?" she asked.

"No, I don't remember anything like that," he answered.

"Are there people there you confide in? People the police or SA have talked to or will be talking to that might tell them something they could use against you?"

"No — nobody like that," Brian answered her. "I keep to myself. Maybe some chatter about current events with the bartender once in a while; some nods of recognition to the regulars who know my face. But I'm the proverbial loner when it comes to Judds."

Then Tracy asked, "Do you drive yourself home all the time after drinking all night?"

Brian hesitated. He could tell she was getting agitated. She did not like his answers. But what was he supposed to tell her? Clearly her tone was different here in the study than it was in the kitchen where he thought they had just shared a pretty nice meal and some warm moments. "Yes," he said quietly.

"That's pretty stupid, Brian, not to mention illegal and dangerous."

"Tracy, I know," was all he could think to say.

"But you do it anyway," she said, her words coming to a boil. He nodded. She asked, "Don't you at least carry a cell phone with you in case you need to call somebody, just to be on the safe side?"

"I don't usually carry one of those things. Don't like that people think I should be at their beck and call 24/7."

She made some noise with her throat. She was clearly getting angrier, or maybe frustrated was the better word and she wanted to take it out on somebody. Brian put up his own defense. "Look: I know the way to and from Judds like the back of my hand. I go out, have a few drinks, and usually make it back before the Friday night partiers hit the streets. No problems."

"What does 'usually' mean?" Tracy asked, her glare fixed on him.

So is this how she conducts her cross examinations, Brian wondered. He answered her. "Well, I usually get home about 9:15 or so. I leave Judds around 9 and it's a 15-minute ride home give or take. I'm pretty sure I left there at 9 on Friday too, but…"

"But you didn't get home until just after 10," she finished.

"Right," he answered, pretty much mumbling.

"Where did you go for that 45 or 50 minutes?" she demanded.

"I'm not sure," he offered.

"You're not *sure*?"

"I don't remember."

Tracy stood up. She was looking down at him. He did not look up at her. Her temper was rising. "You had a blackout, didn't you?"

"I've never had a blackout—at least not for quite a while. I mean, I didn't drink enough that night to have a blackout." He now felt like the proverbial kid caught with his hand in the cookie jar.

She wouldn't let up. "Why didn't you mention this to me Friday—the time loss I mean."

"I didn't think it mattered."

Tracy looked at him in disbelief, maybe shock. She of course had dealt with clients who withheld information before, be it willfully or ignorantly. So she should have been used to this, maybe even seen it coming. But this was a murder case—and a very personal case at that. Suddenly she was ready for an argument—hell, a fight. "You didn't tell me because you thought if I knew you were blacking out I wouldn't help you," she growled.

"No, that's not true, Tracy," Brian pleaded.

Unacceptable answer: "Then where did you go—another bar where maybe you told someone you were thinking of killing your old man?"

"Tracy—I didn't go to another bar!" Brian shouted.

She shouted back. "Are you sure? I mean that's the difference between you and me Brian: I can pass a bar!"

Brian snorted, stood up, turned his back on her and moved to the rear of the study, then turned again to face her. "That was pretty damned cold, Tracy."

She glared at him. "No, Brian! *You* don't get to lecture *me* about cold. *I'll* tell *you* about cold. Cold is telling someone how she means the world to you, how you want to someday marry her and all that goes with it, and then throwing her aside because a bottle is more inviting!" She was surprised that she said what she said. She did not want a repeat of the night they broke up. But she was angry: angry at him for the promising life he was squandering, angry at him for destroying the life she thought they would have together, angry at the police for jumping to the most obvious, simplest conclusion, angry at herself for taking this wretched case—just angry.

Brian finally let out what had been on his mind since he saw her on Friday. "Yes, Tracy, you're right: I screwed up. I screwed up big time. I let the most wonderful woman I've ever known get away from me. I couldn't admit to myself then that I was drinking too much and too often. And I paid the price. And I'm *still* paying the price; I always will be. After all these years I still love you. And I know we'll never be together because of *me*, because of what *I* did." He was close to tears now. But he had said his piece, and so he slowly moved back to the sofa and sat down. Quietly he said, "But I didn't kill my father." He paused and then continued. "If you want to go, then go. I can get someone else to represent me."

Tracy sat back down. This was the first real apology Brian had offered since she terminated their romance. And she believed he was being sincere. Kicking a man when he's down was not her style. As a result, she felt guilty now. Not so much for her feelings—no, she was justifiably entitled to those—but about the timing of their expression. She had let the business and personal mix, always a risk when defending someone you know, someone you care about. He was grieving, but couldn't do so properly because of the situation: accused of a loved one's murder. And he still loved her. That's what he had said, right? The anger was leaving her, leaving her quickly. She took his hand and put her head on his shoulder. "I'm sorry, Brian. I really am." She then added, almost chuckling, "This isn't usually how I am with my clients."

"It's my fault, Tracy" he said, starting to feel relieved. "I shouldn't have called you. It wasn't fair of me. I put you on the spot. I knew Barton thought I did it. So I didn't relish the idea of having him, or his firm, defend me, if it came to that. But I guess I took advantage of the situation. Truth is I've wanted to see you again for so long…" He trailed off.

She hugged him, kissing his cheek. But that was as far as the making up was going to go—for now. "I'm not going anywhere yet, Brian. I believe you're innocent even if no one else does." She released his hand and picked up her notepad. "I'll see if we can find someone who can tell us where you went after Judds. Maybe it will help us. What are you driving now?"

Having regained his composure, he said, "Same car."

She couldn't help but smile. "You still drive that '75 Mercury Cougar XR7?"

"Still runnin'." It pleased him that she remembered.

She told him, "I want to go for another spin in that bad boy. Crank up some Boston tunes."

He laughed; she laughed; friends again.

"I'll want to snap a few pictures of the Mercury." She pulled out her phone and then told Brian, "Smile, you're on Tracy's Camera."

"Fromage!" he grinned.

"Got it. After I photograph your car I'll email pictures of you and it to my associate so he can show them to anyone he may talk to."

"Okay."

Tracy paused a moment, and then said, "Now, time for some more questions. To your knowledge, was your father having any problems with Kurt Barton, business or personal?"

"No, at least Dad never said anything to me about it. I mean, those two go back a ways. They played golf together at least once a month when the weather was right. He'd have Barton and his wife over for dinner a couple times a year. I think they were pretty tight."

"Huh. Barton didn't seem that upset when I talked to him," Tracy said.

"That's just how he is. I don't know that I've ever seen the man smile, come to think of it."

"I know the presumption regarding Barton's visit is that it was all about the will. But maybe there was another reason, pertaining to Barton himself. Can you think of any?"

"Sorry Tracy."

Tracy shrugged her shoulders. "Oh, well. Next, would you mind giving me the name and number of your father's accountants so we could contact them?"

"Sure Tracy. Let me grab one of their business cards off the desk here." Brian quickly flipped through the rolodex that was on the study's desk, removed what he was looking for, and handed it to Tracy. "Here you are."

"Thanks Brian. Could you call at some point and let them know someone from my office will be calling and that it's okay to answer our questions?"

"Consider it done."

"Great. Now: What about Ryder—anything going on with him and your dad?"

"No. I know Dad liked Bill. Bill sat right by him at dinner anytime he was there and the two of them talked mostly to each other."

Nothing to see here, move along. "And of course your father was no fan of Doug," Tracy continued.

Brian shook his head. "Dad hired him on Crystal's recommendation. I don't think Dad knew he existed. But once Doug and Crystal let it be known they were an item Dad had no use for him. Started having Doug join us for dinner when he worked though, probably to keep the peace with Crystal. Maybe said 'hello' and 'goodbye' to him. But that was about it. Dad never liked any of Crystal's boyfriends. Never; not one."

"Hmm…So it was just Bill and Doug on duty Friday then. And you're sure there was no other staff left over after dinner."

"Pretty sure; I didn't see or hear anyone."

"How is your house usually staffed during the day?"

Brian scratched the back of his neck. "Well, there's basically kitchen and housecleaning. The kitchen is staffed seven days a week. There are four of them. They get here around 6:30 in the morning and are out of here by the same time in the evening. I think they rotate the people so it works out that one group works four days and the other works three. They also serve as the wait staff. It's a pretty informal arrangement, nothing fancy: just cook, serve, and clean up afterward. The cleaning people come in two days a week, Tuesdays and Thursdays. Three people who work 8:00 to 5:00 each day. Then there are the gardeners and lawn people. They're here a couple times a week, more during the summer, and their numbers vary. But they don't usually stay past 4:00 when they're here."

Tracy looked at him with a slight grin. "Where's your personal maid been lately?"

He looked at her for a moment confused. "Oh. That. Well, if I'm in my room when they're mulling about I tend to have my door closed, and they know to keep out and not bother me. I just haven't had the chance to make a trip to the laundry room in the last couple of weeks to deposit my stuff. Since I'll be here in hiding I guess I should tackle the ever-rising piles."

She gave him a curious look. "When did you become such a loner Brian?"

"I don't really know," he mumbled. "Just happened, I guess."

She couldn't help feeling sorry for him although she was sure his loneliness was his own doing. "So you just hang out here; work at the warehouse a few times a week; go to bars when you feel like it. Is that your life?"

He hesitated and then said, "Pretty much."

"No one special?"

He looked at her wondering why she even asked that when he had made no secret about his feelings for her. Just wanting confirmation? "No Tracy. There's been no one like that in my life for a long time."

She could empathize. Working as hard as she did hadn't left her much time for companionship, not the kind she wanted anyway, the long-term kind. The dates she *had* had were rarely encouraging; mostly with guys who talked about themselves all night, and then expected things they had no right to expect. But dwelling on their romance-challenged lives wasn't helping matters, so she asked, "And what about security?"

"We have three shifts on the front: 6:00 in the morning to noon; noon to 6:00; and then 6:00 to 6:00. We have two people who rotate through the week on each shift. There's no one on the back booth during the day. So it's just Bill and Donny splitting the week."

"No cameras?"

"No. We're fairly low tech; never had any trouble that I can recall, so Dad never considered getting them."

"What about your alarm system?"

"Pretty basic. You enter a code to turn it on and enter the same one to turn it off. We rarely have it on, unless Dad knows—knew—that we were all in for the night when he turned in, or if nobody was home. And then each security station had a panic button which would sound the alarm if need be."

"Who knows the code?"

"Me, Crystal, Dad, and the security people; I think that's it."

"But the alarm wasn't on when you got home Friday."

"No. Dad probably would have turned it on before he went to bed. I think Crystal was supposed to stay with her friends that night and not come home."

"Okay Brian, tough question. Can you think of anyone who might want to hurt your dad: employees, former employees, business associates—any-one?"

Brian looked at her. "No Tracy. I can't think of any reason why anyone would want to hurt him. He got on well with everyone at the house; at least, I never heard different. He was mostly out of the business now; just a meeting every once in a while. Crystal let him know what was going on. He'd stop by the corporate office now and again just to say hi to some of the people he missed. He may have been hard on me and Crystal—well, not so much Crystal anymore—but he wasn't that way with anyone else. I just can't figure it."

Tracy squeezed Brian's hand, and decided he had had enough ques-tions for now, so she finished up her note taking for the moment and said, "Well, I may want to talk to members of the day staff at some point so it'd be great if you or Crystal could get me a list. Like I mentioned, I've already talked to Barton. So I guess the people I'd like to talk to next are Stanz and Ryder."

"Bill doesn't get here until about 5:00 p.m.. Same with Doug usually except he's been here quite a bit lately to comfort Crystal. So you can talk to him now if you want."

"They both go on duty at 6:00?" she asked.

"Right; but they usually have dinner with us before starting. Dad insisted on that since they were going to work a 12-hour night shift starting right at dinner time. It was kinda nice, actually."

"Okay. I think Crystal told me that they'd be upstairs. Tell you what, let's go to the garage so I can click some pics of your hot rod, and then I'll go track down Doug."

He nodded and they both stood up looking at each other. "I'll get to work on that employee list," he told her. "Why don't I just email it to you at your office?"

"That'll work," she answered. "Oh, and I'll be emailing you some paperwork regarding our legal business together."

He smiled, "What are you charging me for this?"

She playfully admonished him, "Hey, I got two mouths to feed in addition to my own at that office, buddy." He hugged her again. And she thought, in spite of everything darn it, is it possible that maybe she still loved him too?

Chapter 5

Crystal Shane and Doug Stanz were no longer upstairs. They were now in the kitchen enjoying the spread that Tracy and Brian had partaken of about an hour earlier. Tracy heard them laughing when she returned from the garage photo shoot, so she made her way to the kitchen. When Tracy entered, Crystal turned and smiled. "Oh Tracy, hi; here's your list." Crystal picked up a piece of paper from the table handed it Tracy, and then asked, "How did it go with Brian? Is he okay?"

Tracy accepted the list, folded it and placed it in the inside pocket of the light blue jacket she was wearing, and then thanked Crystal. "I think he's doing fine under the circumstances," Tracy said, not really quite sure how accurate her assessment was. "It's good he's here with you and you believe in him."

"Of course I do," Crystal said. "I know he wouldn't hurt Dad, or anyone else for that matter. There has to be another explanation for what happened."

Tracy instinctively turned to Doug, who was coming back from disposing of the trash. He moved toward Crystal and made a shocking discovery. "Darling you seem to have missed some mustard." He reached around behind him and pulled out a handkerchief which he utilized to remove the offending yellow blob from his betrothed's visage. She kissed him for his act of heroism as he shoved the kerchief back into his front pocket. Tracy grinned at this edition of Lover's Games of the Rich and Famous. She said, "Crys can I borrow Doug for a few moments? I just want to go over a couple of things with respect to Friday. I promise I'll return him safely."

Crystal looked at her and gave Tracy a wink. "I guess I can trust you."

Doug looked at the two of them. He could certainly understand how they had been close at one time. Crystal had told him how she and Tracy were friends first, and that's how Brian met her. And then the two started going out. Crystal thought the world of Tracy and lamented on several occasions how she wished Tracy was her sister-in-law. No doubt about it, Crystal needed a friend right now and Tracy fit the bill perfectly.

When the two ladies finished their round of bargaining for Doug's time Tracy moved toward him and took his arm. "Shall we go out to the garden?" Tracy asked.

"How can I refuse?" Doug responded.

The Shane garden was located in the back of the estate and consisted of several dozen types of colorful flowers: rows and rows of pansies, yellow trillium, lilac, various irises, and others. But Tracy was no expert on their names, rarity, or worth. She just thought they looked awfully pretty. Doug and Tracy made their way through the flora, finally sitting down on some oversized wicker furniture that rested under a large awning erected to protect, from sun and rain, potential occupants who wanted to admire the estate's beauty.

"When are you getting married?" Tracy finally asked him.

"I don't know. We were originally talking early fall this year. But, this thing with her father—I mean, that will all have to be sorted out first. I don't mind the wait."

"Of course," she said sympathetically. "You've been here, what, two years?" Tracy asked him.

"Almost," he answered her.

Tracy took on the tone of a nosy Nelly looking for gossip when she asked, "So tell me Doug, how did the two of you meet?"

Doug smiled. "I met Crystal while working at my old marketing firm. I was on the team that was trying to develop a new way to sell Shane's Salty Snackers and Shane's Sizzling Spud Spears."

Tracy laughed. "Good grief."

"Yeah," Doug said, chuckling himself. "I think the company was seeing what was out there. They had been using the same advertising firm for years. Crystal was part of the team evaluating the new proposals. We hit it off, even though she was like seven years older than I was. When my firm didn't get the account, Crystal called me to tell me personally that we lost out. She was very nice and regretful about it. We talked a while, and somehow I got offered a job doing security when I hinted I didn't like this marketing thing anyway. Truth is, though, I took the job just to be near Crystal. I guess I fell for her pretty quickly."

Tracy decided to do some sharing, or rather, some pushing. "I can certainly understand that. Crys and I hit it off pretty quickly ourselves when we first met. We have a similar sense of humor and a similar drive. But I also remember when I went from being Crystal's friend to Brian's girlfriend. Suddenly Mr. Shane didn't seem to like me as much."

"I hear you," Doug told her. "He just gave me intimidating looks every once in a while that told me where I stood. He wasn't outwardly hostile. But I wasn't kidding myself about how it looked, a paid-by-the-hour security guard romancing the daughter of a wealthy junk food king. It wasn't really that bad though."

Enough about that, Tracy thought. What did she think he'd say: "Yeah I killed the guy to be with Crystal"? So Tracy asked, "Can we talk about last Friday now? Can you tell me who came and who went and everything in between?"

"I'll certainly tell you what I know. Let's see—Brian left a little after 7; then he got home a little after 10. The lawyer showed up a few minutes before 10:30 p.m. That was it. Nobody else came or went between 7:00 and 10:30 p.m.."

Nothing new there, so she said, "Brian told me he usually gets home on Fridays closer to quarter after 9:00. What did you think when he didn't show up as usual?"

Doug pondered the question a bit. He looked at Tracy. "To be honest, I thought he may have had an accident. Or got pulled over and arrested. There's only so many times you can drive the same route intoxicated like that without tempting fate."

Tracy grimaced slightly but hoped it didn't show. "So I guess you were relieved when he finally did show up."

"Sure was."

"Did you ask him why he was so late? Where he'd been?" Tracy asked hoping Brian may have made some kind of comment upon his return.

Stanz hesitated. "Well, I don't remember asking him. I mean, I saw his car approach and just let him in. I guess I assumed he stayed at Judds longer, watching the game or maybe getting lucky with some…" He stopped himself, suddenly remembering to whom he was talking.

"It's okay," Tracy assured him.

"Yeah, well, okay," Doug stammered. "Why are you asking me that? Do you mean he wasn't at Judds all that time?"

She didn't mind answering. "Brian thinks he left Judds around 9:00 like he always did. But I'll visit Judds myself at some point to confirm that either way."

"Oh, I didn't know that. I wish I had seen someone else that night."

"Me too. So Doug, are you telling me you just let Brian in when you saw his car?"

"Right."

"You didn't even leave your booth?"

"Uh, no."

A new thought occurred to Tracy so she asked, "I know this may sound like a strange question but how can you be sure it was Brian driving the car?"

"Well, I saw he was wearing that bright green raincoat of his." Doug's eyes suddenly got wider and he straightened up. "Hey: You think maybe someone hitched a ride in Brian's car? Killed the father and managed to sneak out?"

Suddenly Tracy was thinking of all kinds of new scenarios. Could someone else have been driving Brian's car that night? Could Brian have had more to drink than he realized and passed out at some point? Could he have been slipped something at the bar to knock him out? But that didn't quite track with Brian's version of events that night. He had told both her and the police he remembered driving home. Maybe he was drugged and passed out, the killer following him and then entering the car. Brian wakes up and continues home without realizing he has a passenger. That would account for the lost time. Far-fetched? Wasn't it Sherlock Holmes himself who said, "Once you eliminate the impossible, whatever remains, no matter how improbable, must be the truth?"

"It's a distinct possibility," she finally answered. "While everyone was converging on the house the killer could have made his escape."

"Wow," Doug responded. "And the cops think this whole thing is a slam dunk against Brian."

Tracy grinned at him. "But they don't know Brian like we do, right Doug?"

"Hell no, they don't," he said in agreement.

"Doug, when Barton arrived, did you approach his car at all, or did you just open the gate since you recognized the limo, like you did for Brian?"

"I just opened the gate," he told her. "I knew he was coming. I didn't see the need to bother him or the driver."

"So you pretty much just let Barton's car through anytime he shows up; I mean, without leaving your booth to check anything," Tracy said.

"As long as he has an appointment, I just open the gate. You know how he is."

Tracy nodded and then added, "And I bet he never shows up without an appointment."

"You're right about that," Doug told her.

Tracy got to her feet. "Then I'll take my leave now. Thanks so much for talking to me, Doug."

"Hey, whatever I can do to help," he told her as he too arose.

Tracy left him standing under the awning as she made her way back to the house. She wasn't ready to ask about his financial situation quite yet. He'd be easily available for more questions. And the talk hadn't been a waste of time. The idea that someone who knew Brian's schedule could have contrived a way to hide in his car to gain entrance was intriguing alright. But how did the unwanted passenger then get off the estate? Sneak out through the gate when Doug went up to the house at some point? Suddenly Tracy wished she or the police had had the chance or a reason to look inside Kurt Barton's limo that night. There was plenty of room in there to hide out after committing a murder. And maybe even have some refreshments.

Tracy re-entered the Shane home through the rear entrance and made her way to the living room in which Stewart Shane had been killed. If it had been *her* father shot there she wasn't sure she could continue to live in the same house, at least not for a while. But the Shane children had lived here all their lives. This was all they knew, a guarded fortress protecting them from the rest of the world. Their age difference was just over one year apart, Brian being the older one, so the siblings were very close. Perhaps they were able to just ignore the one room where Tracy was standing now. Still, she didn't want to ask Brian or Crystal to join her; she saw no point to that. She could handle this part of her investigation herself.

Stewart Shane had been sitting on the far right side of the room's expansive L-shaped sofa, which was now covered over, when he was shot in the back of the head. His back would have been to the room's entrance. What had he been doing when he was shot? Watching television like he was when Brian got home? No, the TV was off when the body was found. Was he reading? There didn't seem to be any reading material nearby. Using the phone? The nearby portable phone was resting on the table when Shane was found. She remembered there was a glass on the square-shaped glass table around which the sofa was centered. Maybe he was just sitting there waiting for Barton and having a drink, pondering what he would say at their meeting. But if he was doing that, wouldn't he have had a copy of his will nearby? He had asked Barton to bring his own copy. What Stewart Shane was doing there was still unclear.

Regardless though: wouldn't he have heard someone come into the room? Turned to see who it was; probably not, if the killer was very quiet.

That suggests the killer must have had a key to the front door. Or maybe he or she was able to make a copy of someone else's key. It seemed to her the murder had to be an inside job.

Tracy remembered too that the universal TV remote was found on the floor. Did that mean something? It could have just fallen off the sofa as the result of Stewart moving around to get more comfortable, or reaching for the drink on the table, or putting the drink back on the table. She had certainly done the same things before to cause her remote to slide off the seat. She had plenty of questions; but really no sure way of finding the answers. This was frustrating. She left the living room and went toward the hall closet where Brian had seen his father alive when he hung up his raincoat. She opened the closet door, no squeaky hinges. If only his father hadn't turned around. She could have at least put forward the theory that Stewart was already dead when Brian got home. Could Brian have been mistaken maybe? He was drunk after all. Maybe he confused a motion from the television program that was airing at the time with his father's movement. It was a sporting event his father was watching after all, people running around; possible, but not likely.

She found herself looking at the foyer that led from the closet to the front door. The housekeeping staff must have done a pretty good job cleaning up the mess of mud and grass that had covered the floor during the night of the murder, tracked in by Brian, Ryder, Barton, and maybe Stanz. The rain had made everyone's shoes an accessory to that minor crime. The cops would have been wearing protective footwear over their shoes, but not anyone else. There was some mud still present in the area just in front of the grandfather clock. But otherwise top marks for cleanliness.

Tracy heard footsteps descending the stairs, looked up, and saw a small, dark-haired woman wearing a hairnet and holding what must have been bathroom towels in need of laundering in her hands. She couldn't have been more than five-feet tall, and was probably in her mid-60s. "Good afternoon, ma'am," Tracy said to her.

"Good afternoon to you too."

"I'm Tracy. I'm Brian's lawyer. Do you have time for a few questions?"

The lady looked at her, squinting a bit. "Sure, I guess. The name's Winifred. But everyone calls me Winnie."

"That's right. I remember you now; Hi Winnie. Do you remember me? I dated Brian about 12 years or so ago."

Winnie squinted at her again. "Can't say I do cutie. Sorry."

"Oh, that's okay. I'm guessing you've worked here a long time."

"Twenty-two years this September."

"Wow. So you were here when Brian and Crystal were just kids."

"Oh yeah; always fighting something awful those two. I'd have to give them what for every now and again. Of course, I was a lot younger then. They may have messed up the house but they knew better than to mess with Winnie."

Tracy grinned. "At least they're close now, no more fighting."

"If you say so, toots."

Tracy stifled a giggle. "And you knew Mrs. Shane then."

Winnie gulped a bit. "A beautiful lady and a beautiful person; never raised her voice, never had an unkind word for any one. She was the heart of this house. Why the Lord sees fit to take the good ones early I'll never understand."

Tracy paused. "How's Brian been getting along with his dad lately, Winnie?"

She didn't answer right away. "Don't pay attention to that stuff. That's why I've been here 22 years this September."

"Didn't the police already talk to you about this? I'm really just interested in what you may have told them."

Winnie snorted. "Yeah, they had the nerve to call on me Sunday during dinner. I like my dumplings hot, not cold. And I told them that. Did they care?"

Tracy was having a hard time keeping a straight face. Winnie was just so adorable. "I'm sorry about your dumplings, Winnie."

"Wasn't your fault, toots."

"Will you please tell me what you told them?"

"Didn't tell 'em much of anything. Mr. Shane was always asking the boy when he was gonna grow up and stop acting like he was still in college, start making a life for himself. Boy would tell Mr. Shane to get off his back, sometimes use bad language, which I won't repeat. Disrespectful is what it was. If he'd been mine he'd have been massaging pavement with his keister."

Tracy turned away to let out her chuckles, feigning a cough lest she unintentionally offend the dear woman. "Do you have kids Winnie?"

"Had one. That was enough. Trouble since day one."

"Sorry to hear that."

"No need to be sorry. I'm glad he's around. Even gladder he's not around me anymore though."

Moving on..."Brian and his dad never got physical though, did they Winnie? They never hurt each other?"

"Not that I ever saw. Would have brained the kid myself if he laid a finger on his father; a dear man really."

Good answer. "Anything else the police asked you about?"

"No, just how Mr. Shane and the boy got along. Since I wasn't here Friday I couldn't really help 'em much. Even if I were here, I would have been gone before all the action started."

"Did you see or hear Mr. Shane ever argue with anyone else: a member of the staff, a business associate who came over for a meeting?"

"Once in a while he'd start raising Cain with someone over something. Maybe holler at someone on the phone. That's just how he was; had to blow off his steam then and there instead of saving it for later, out and over with. Only the boy got it regularly."

"Winnie, do you think Brian killed his dad? After seeing them together for almost 22 years you must have your own idea about it?"

Winnie gave her a squint. "No, I doubt it. Mr. Shane wasn't telling the boy something he didn't already know himself."

Tracy gave her another smile. "Well thanks for talking to me Winnie. Maybe I'll see you later."

"No problem girlie." And with that Winnie moved toward the basement steps which led to the laundry facility downstairs. Winnie had confirmed what Tracy had feared, that the two Shane men did not keep their battles closed to the public. Probably everyone on the staff would confirm what Winnie had witnessed. Angry son got tired of it one night and killed his dad. Not much you can do to dissuade the police from that scenario toots.

On the other hand, if the other staff felt as Winnie did, then at no time did anyone working at the Shane household believe the elder Shane was in danger from his son. And that was something Tracy could use for her defense. Thank you, Winnie.

It was about 3:30 now and Tracy didn't want to hang around waiting for Ryder's arrival. She could see him later. It was time to go back to the office and put Neal on the hunt for Brian's car to see if anyone spotted it after he had left the Judds' parking lot. And the possibility that Barton's limo may have been the killer's escape vehicle made Tracy want to take another look at Kurt Barton, whom she hadn't really considered a possible suspect—until now. She found Brian and Crystal, as well as Doug, downstairs gathered around the billiard table that monopolized a large section of the finished basement. They weren't engaged in any kind of game, but rather reminiscences of childhood times when Brian and Crystal used to grab pool cues and engage in battle. And those sore bottoms they subsequently had if either parent had discovered their duel.

"Is anyone down here?" Tracy called out. After finding the trio, she announced her intent to depart for the day, and they all said their goodbyes.

Brian left Crystal and Doug downstairs while he walked Tracy out. "I wish you didn't have to go just yet, Tracy," Brian told her.

Tracy touched his arm. "I'll call you, Brian. But I have to keep moving forward on this." She turned not giving Brian a chance to respond. The truth was she really didn't want to leave just yet either.

Fade in…

Brian and Tracy got out of the car which was now parked in front of the home of Tracy's parents. "Nervous?" she asked him.

"I'll be fine, as long as he doesn't start polishing his guns."

Tracy laughed. "I'm happy to tell you he's never done that before."

"If you say so..."

"Come on," she said as she smiled at him and took his arm. The front door opened before the lovebirds even made it to the steps. Peter Brubaker was standing there, a pleasant, warm smile on his face.

"Tracy! Come give me a hug, girl." Tracy released Brian and obliged.

"Hi Dad," she said while embracing him. "So good to see you again."

"You don't come home weekends too much anymore," he said as he looked at her, his smile unbroken. Then he turned his attention to Brian, who was standing behind her quietly. "And I suppose this is the person responsible for that."

Tracy backed up and took Brian's arm again. "Dad—this is Brian."

Brian offered Peter Brubaker his hand. Peter took it firmly and, after a few shakes, said, "Welcome, Brian. Please come in." Tracy and Brian obliged and moved toward the kitchen, where Violetta Brubaker was preparing the night's meal. At least, it was supposed to be for one night. When

Tracy saw how much food was ready and waiting she feared her mom thought Tracy would be there for the next month.

"Hi Mom," she said hugging her mother from behind.

"Oh Tracy, be careful. You'll get food all over you." Violetta turned and hugged her daughter firmly, kissing each cheek. "How are you dear child?"

"I'm great."

"You don't look good. You're not eating over there are you?"

"Three meals a day, Mom. Promise."

"Bah."

"Mom, I want you to meet Brian." Tracy turned and jerked her head a bit, motioning Brian to come forward.

"Ah, Brian," Violetta said as she gave Brian a hug. "I hope you are hungry."

"Famished."

"You don't eat either huh?" she asked him, mild reproach on her face. "I'll fix that."

Tracy and Brian both helped with transforming the Brubaker dining room table into a veritable smorgasbord. There were more than generous portions of steak, chicken, pasta dishes, sundry vegetables and other sides that extended from one end to the next. Peter brought bottles of red and white wine, a variety of soda cans, and a pitcher of ice water to the table. Finally the four sat down, Tracy's parents on either end and she and Brian next to each other between them. Tracy leaned into Brian and said, "You better make your own plate or you'll be sorry." Suddenly Peter started chuckling. She must have been overheard. The various serving platters and dishes made their way around the table, and when everyone was satisfied with their initial selections, Peter Brubaker made the sign of the cross and lead the gathered in grace. "And thank you Lord for bringing Tracy back to us even if it's for only a short time," he added. Tracy looked at him and then her mother. "So far, so good," she thought.

"So Brian," Peter started, "Are you going to eventually take over for your father when he retires?"

Brian finished his mouthful of steak before answering. "That's the plan right now, sir."

"Just call me Pete. What are you majoring in to that end?"

"Business administration. But the truth is I'll be getting most of my education by a lot of on the job training."

"Mm hm. So you're just biding time in school then?"

Tracy's eyes widened and she stopped chewing, looking at her father and giving him a nasty glare. Peter was looking at Brian, ignoring his daughter, waiting for an answer to his question.

"Oh, no, sir — I mean, Pete. An education is important so I'm taking my studies very seriously. But I'm nowhere near as smart as Tracy is." Brian surreptitiously started rubbing Tracy's knee and turned to give her a reassuring smile.

"I see," Peter finally said.

"Besides," Brian added, "one never knows what the future holds; nothing wrong with a college degree to keep your options open."

Peter liked that answer, so he resumed his meal. "Tracy, pass Brian the gnocchi," Violetta commanded. "He didn't try any yet."

"Yes he did," Peter said, coming to Brian's defense.

"He hardly had any. He wants some more." Violetta was forcing the dish that held the gnocchi into Tracy's hand. Tracy finally took it begrudgingly and passed it to Brian."

"It's very good, Mrs. Brubaker. I'll have some more," Brian said.

"You see," Violetta said looking at her husband. "You think you know everything."

Whether it was the mounting tension Tracy had been feeling or the way her mother had admonished her father, Tracy started laughing. Brian soon joined her. Violetta looked confused but Peter just smiled at his daughter and then at Brian. Then he looked at his wife. "That's why I married you dear heart, to learn everything I didn't already know." Violetta waved her hand dismissively at him, and that just kick started the laughter again.

"Stop that, you two," Violetta finally said. "You'll choke on your food."

"Sorry Mom," Tracy finally said after regaining her composure. It wasn't helping matters that Brian was elbowing her in the ribs. She tried to push his elbow away without being noticed but that just seemed to encourage him. There were a few more moments of silence as everyone resumed their meals. Then Brian wiped the corners of his mouth and looked at Peter Brubaker.

"Mr. Brubaker — Pete."

Peter looked over at Brian. "Yes?"

"I have a younger sister Tracy's age. And I know how my father feels about her."

"Crystal, right?"

"Yes. So I know fathers feel very protective of their daughters." Tracy had stopped eating, instead poking at her pasta with her fork. She had no idea where Brian was going with this. She started to feel tense again.

Peter leaned back in his chair. "Yes. That is very true."

"Well: I just want to tell you that your daughter is my world." Violetta dropped her fork on the plate, but it sounded more like a gong amidst the silence. Tracy was looking at Brian. She so wanted to reach over and embrace him but she knew she better save that for later. Everyone was looking at Brian now, but he continued to look at Peter. Peter met Brian's eyes for what felt like minutes but was in reality mere seconds.

"Well then, my boy," Peter finally said, "that's a wonderful world you live in. And you need to take care of it."

"Absolutely. I want to do just that." Brian then resumed eating his dinner. Peter looked at him a while longer, and then he looked at Tracy, who was looking at Brian in a way that told him just how serious it was between the two of them. Peter then looked at his wife, a warm smile on his face. She was, in turn, looking at Brian, smiling. She finally met her husband's eyes, and eventually the parents turned their attentions back to their own plates. There was silence for the rest of the meal.

Violetta started gathering plates and the leftovers when it was clear no one was going to accept her offers of fifth helpings. Peter rose and said, "Tracy, help your mother with the dishes. I want to talk to Brian." Tracy's horrified look started Peter laughing. "Don't worry Tracy. Just help your mother."

Brian forced a smile. "It's okay Tracy." Tracy wasn't so sure. Her father had never done this before.

"This way Brian," Peter finally said. "We'll go back here in the spare bedroom."

"There aren't any guns in there, are there?" Brian asked, only semi-jokingly. The question started Peter laughing heartily, and he slapped Brian on the back. But he didn't answer Brian's query.

Tracy kept looking in the direction of the meeting, and was not being very helpful to her mother. "Tracy, what do you think your father's going to do, huh?"

"I don't know."

"Tracy, he loves you. He's not going to do anything to hurt your young man."

"I know Mom."

"Come, help me make some plates for you two to take back with you."

"Mom, I live in a dorm. We don't have a refrigerator."

"Then Brian can keep the food at his house."

"He has a cooking staff that probably keeps their fridges full."

"They don't have me. Besides, you don't want this to go bad, do you?"

"Of course not."

"Well, then get me some plastic containers and stop your backtalk."

"Oh good grief."

"Listen to your mother, and I'll tell something. The secret to keeping a man happy is to keep his stomach full and his bed warm. That's kept your father coming home every night for all these years. But since you and that boy aren't married yet, you better just be concentrating on his belly for now."

Tracy looked at her mother mildly shocked. Did she just say what Tracy thought she said?

It was probably about 20 minutes before Brian reemerged from the interrogation room. Tracy was ready to go. She wanted a blow by blow description of the past 20 minutes—immediately. "We have to get going," Tracy told her parents. "Right, Brian?"

"Yeah. Studying to do," Brian said nodding.

"It's Friday night," Peter said chuckling.

"No rest for the wicked," Tracy quickly countered.

"Here," Violetta said moving forward, handing Brian a large a paper bag. "You take that home to your family."

Brian accepted saying, "Thank you so much ma'am. Your food was incredible; maybe the best and biggest meal I ever had. In fact..."

Tracy leaned into Brian and said out of the side of her mouth, "Quit while you're ahead, dear." Brian looked over at her and nodded. Tracy grabbed his arm and moved in the direction of the front door. Her parents followed and warm hugs were exchanged among them. Peter again shook Brian's hand, and Violetta gave him a kiss on each cheek.

"You will come back and dine with us again soon, when you can stay longer," Violetta told him.

"Yes ma'am. Absolutely." But Brian suddenly found himself being pulled toward the car, so that's all he managed to say. He yelled out "Thanks again!" as Tracy guided him away. She looked back at her parents, who were standing side by side in the doorway. Peter had his right arm around his wife, his hand stroking her shoulder. Violetta's head was slightly tilted in Peter's direction, her right hand stroking her blouse collar. They were both smiling. As the lovers reached the car, Brian opened the door for Tracy. As she was getting in she saw her father nod. And she couldn't resist giving him a slight wave and mouthing "I love you." Brian closed her door, put the leftovers in the back, and then sat himself down. Her parents were still standing on the porch as the car pulled away.

Neither immediately spoke. But they reached for each other's hand and rubbed their respective thumbs together. Tracy broke the silence. "So what did you two talk about for 20 minutes?"

"How many different ways you can get rid of a body without it ever being discovered."

"Oh hardy-har-har."

Brian chuckled. "Sorry Tracy. I couldn't resist."

Tracy was not amused. "Well?"

"He said it was important that we both finish school. We need to be focusing on our studies even though he understands that can be challenging under the circumstances."

"What else?" she asked after waiting too long for him to say more.

"He said if I was really telling the truth about how I felt that I needed to watch over you and make sure nothing happens to you."

"He really said that?"

"Yup. And he said…" Brian stopped again.

"What? What else did he say?"

Brian pulled the car off the road so he could turn to face Tracy. He took both of her hands and told her, "And he said that he wasn't going to be around forever and wanted to know that someone would be there to take care of his smart little girl." He paused a bit and then added, "I promised him I'd be there."

It was time to pay him back for his "world" comment so Tracy moved her hands to Brian's cheeks and then kissed him. The two moved closer and Brian started stroking her hair with one hand, her back with the other. Neither wanted this moment to end, but Tracy, always the responsible one, pulled away. "We better stop before some officer pulls over to see what's going on here." Brian looked at her, as if his life depended on it. "Besides," she added, "we need to get that food to your house."

"I love you Tracy," he finally said. Alright then, the food could wait a little longer, and they picked that moment right back up where they left it.

Fade out…

Tracy turned her engine off as her car was now parked in its reserved spot in her office lot. She sat there a moment, and then leaned back in her seat. Sleeping and driving, the times when her mind wandered. She had no control over what she dreamed of course, but she usually could be making mental checklists when en route to one place or another. But now she was involuntary showing reruns of times past. "I've got to stop doing this," she told herself. She took a sip from the water bottle next to her. She knew she was kidding herself though. She just wasn't sure what and when the next trip down memory lane would occur.

Chapter 6

"Hi Beck: Any messages?" Tracy asked Rebecca as she passed through her office suite's doors.

Rebecca handed her a stack of the familiar pink message sheets. "Hi ya, Tracerino," Rebecca greeted. "Neal and I have been able to take care of almost everything. I made notes on the sheets and updated your calendar. You might want to call Larry Waters back though. He's getting — *nervous*."

"Tracy Brubaker: Babysitter At Law," Tracy said accepting the pink pile. "Thanks Beck." She continued to her office but stopped by Neal's and poked her head in. "Neal, got time for me?"

"Oh certainly," he said. "I've been sitting here *all day* longing for your return." She gave him a mock glare as he grabbed his notepad and followed her to her office. Sitting down he asked, "What's brewin'?"

"Time — up in smoke; Brian can't account for almost an hour the night of the murder."

"That's not good," Neal said, helming the good ship Obvious.

"I'm not sure if it means anything or not just yet. But I'd like you to see if you can find anyone who may have seen Brian or his car between, say, 9 and 10 last Friday night." As she spoke she was writing something down in her small notebook that Neal couldn't make out when he tried to read the text upside down. "He drives a red 1975 Mercury Cougar XR7. Here's the license plate number." She tore off the sheet and handed it to Neal. She continued, "I emailed you some pictures of that as well as some Brian photos that you can pull up on that smart phone of yours to show around. I'd start at Judds — Brian thinks he left there around 9 — and then just follow the trail to the estate, seeing if there's anywhere along the way where he may have stopped — or *been* stopped."

"Got it."

Tracy pulled out the list Crystal had given her, and handed it to Neal. "Here's the list of people Crystal was with Friday night. Their phone numbers, business and cell, are listed so you could just call them I guess. But I don't really think anything will come of it, so it's low priority." Neal scanned the list and then Tracy added, "And we might want to take a closer look at Kurt Barton."

Neal stared at her. "He wasn't even there yet when the murder happened."

"I realize that. But Doug Stanz told me that he didn't personally check Barton's car when it arrived. Doug just opened the gates and let it through. Now, suppose Barton wasn't in the limo. Suppose Barton was in Brian's car hiding when Brian got home. Stanz didn't check Brian's car either. So maybe Barton kills Shane after Brian's gone to bed, then he hides outside somewhere, maybe in that garage. Or Barton meets the limo at some point as it's coming up the driveway, and then gets in, making it appear as if he just arrived."

Neal stared. Then he smiled. "Hey, that's pretty good."

"Thank you," she said smiling, a little proud of herself. "But the truth is I can't see Barton twisting himself up like a pretzel kissing floor mats. So my ingenious theory is actually pretty cray cray."

"What?"

"What 'what'?"

"What is cray cray?"

"Neal, haven't any of your kids educated you in the new vernacular. It means crazy."

"Crazy, huh? It sounds pretty stu stu to me."

Tracy laughed. "Now you're getting the hang of it." Neal chuckled. Then Tracy said, "Of course, if someone else was still in the house when everybody left, they could have shot Mr. Shane and then hid out in the Barton limo."

"You really think Barton had something to do with it?"

"Who knows? The main problem is I have no motive for him, at least not yet. But I still want you to check out Barton's alibi. When exactly did he leave that function he was attending? Does the timing work out from the time he left to the time he arrived at the Shanes'? When did he actually deliver his remarks? Stuff like that."

Neal nodded as he jotted. "What about talking to the driver?"

"I don't think that will be helpful at this point so that's on the back burner for now," Tracy answered. "The driver no doubt corroborated Barton's version with the police, so unless we can find something to contradict Barton's story, there's no reason for the driver to tell us a different tale."

Neal, still smiling, said, "You're right. Of course, you're right."

"But if someone *is* going to talk to the driver I'd like to take that one myself," Tracy said. "I do want a look inside the limo."

"Is that all with regards to Barton?"

Tracy paused and then said, "There *is* something odd about that phone call Stewart made to Barton to set up the meeting."

Neal, intrigued said, "Do tell."

"Barton said Stewart was shouting, but not as in arguing, but rather like they had a bad connection. Now maybe Barton was covering his bases in case someone heard Stewart shouting at him over the phone."

"So Barton already has his own version on record, so to speak, if the question ever comes up," Neal said nodding.

"Exactly. We should find out who would have been in earshot of the phone call, heard what Mr. Shane was saying. We—or rather the police—may be wrong in assuming that the meeting was about changing the will to Brian's detriment. If Barton is the executor of the estate, then there's still money to be made from Shane's Salty Snackers."

Neal snickered. "Okay—I'll see if there was any bad blood between Barton's law firm and the Shane people. Anything else?"

"Yes. Here is the contact information for the Shane accountant," she said, handing Neal the business card Brian had given her. "Brian said he'd let them know we'd be in touch. Also, he's going to email me a list of the house staff. I'll send it to you and if you could do the standard background checks on them, just to be thorough, that'd be most appreciated."

"No problem."

"As for me, I'm debating whether or not to try and talk to Bill Ryder tonight at the estate, or wait until tomorrow and try to talk to him at his apartment. I think the latter option might be better. He wouldn't have to worry about being overheard. And I can ask him about the aforementioned phone call too."

"You sound like you think he knows something," Neal observed.

"Well, he's worked there quite a while. Probably seen some people come and go. I'd think he'd have some stories to tell." She paused while she mentally planned out the rest of her day. "I think I'll go talk to El to make sure I'm up-to-date on everything, return Larry Waters' call, and then call it a day."

Neal nodded. "I'll start my canvas of Judds and the surrounding establishments tonight. It doesn't make sense to do it during the day since the shifts who work the day probably don't work the night. And if I can I'll find out where Barton's Friday soirée was and nail down his schedule. But that might have to wait until tomorrow."

Tracy smiled. "Are you sure Sara will be all right with that, leaving her to deal with four sleepy but no doubt rowdy kids at bed time?"

"She'll be fine, just as long as this doesn't become a habit."

"You're the best Neal. Get yourself some nice takeout and it will be my treat."

Neal rose to make good on his plans for the evening. She told him goodnight as he left her office. She stood up to gather her belongings and head out to meet Tanner when Rebecca entered. "How are you holding up, Tracy?"

"I'm fine, Beck."

Rebecca wasn't sure. "Do you want to talk about it? You look like you're carrying the weight of the world on those shoulders of yours."

Tracy just looked at her for a moment. There had been times that Rebecca had played big sister, and she was obviously offering to essay the role again. Tracy was about to take a rain check when instead she sat back down. Taking that as her cue Rebecca shut the office door and took a seat in front of Tracy's desk.

Tracy spoke first. "Oh Beck: I don't know what to do."

"What do you mean?"

"Maybe I should tell Brian to get another lawyer. This is becoming too hard."

Rebecca gave her a slight smile. "Reliving times past, are we?"

"Oh my yes."

"Good memories?"

"So far. But, that's the thing. They're just making me sadder. I just don't understand how it could have happened. I mean: I know how it happened. I was there after all. But, it really wasn't all Brian's fault. He just handled it badly." She stopped herself a moment. "I'm not making any sense, am I?"

"Why don't you tell me about it, Tracy? Get it off your chest."

Tracy looked at Rebecca a few moments. "You realize this is privileged communication, don't you?"

Rebecca grinned slightly. "Absolutely."

"I'm not sure where to start." After a brief pause Tracy continued. "I met Brian through his sister Crystal. She and I were attending a retreat in June that our college was offering to incoming freshman. We became fast friends and she hosted a July 4 party at her house and invited me. That's when I met Brian. He's only a year older than her. Anyway as the night went on I found myself by his side a lot, just kidding around, making stupid jokes. He was so nice and good looking..." She stopped talking, finding herself slightly embarrassed by that last admission, feeling like an infatuated schoolgirl.

Rebecca was smiling at her. "Go on, Tracy."

"Uh, well, as I was getting ready to leave he asked if he could call me. I remember him laughing when I answered 'yes' way too quickly."

Rebecca chuckled. "Sounds like a violation of the rules to me."

"Well, what can I say? He wasn't like one would expect a handsome, wealthy 19-year-old male to be. I mean, a guy like that would have every reason to be arrogant, wouldn't he?"

"I have no experience with wealthy people myself, Tracy."

Tracy nodded. "I guess I was guilty of stereotyping him before I even knew he existed. But I realized when I got home after the party that I never felt nervous or self conscious around him. We were just hanging out, you know?"

"Sure."

"And it got even more interesting when he suggested our first date be a visit to a diner for burgers and shakes and then a movie at the Bengies Drive-In."

"No kidding?"

"Yeah; real old fashioned—right out of the '50s."

"A nice night I bet."

Tracy laughed a bit. "Uh-huh, until my stomach started bothering me after eating too much popcorn."

"After the greasy burger and ice cream?" Rebecca asked in mock horror.

"I was being bad. Up until the college years when I started the dorm life I always ate home, and my mom always served healthy stuff. No junk. So I overdid it."

"Oh, Tracy...what happened?"

"Brian couldn't have been sweeter. He put his arm around me and of-fered to take me home right away. I tried to brave it but eventually I had to take him up on his offer. I thought I'd never see him again. But as he was dropping me off he promised from there on out he'd only take me to places that offered healthy food. Then he kissed me on the cheek and said good-night." Tracy stopped for a moment. She wasn't sure anymore if saying all of this out loud was a good idea or not.

Rebecca leaned in, sensing what must have been going through Tracy's mind. "Pretty special night then."

Tracy looked at her. "Yeah, very special. I know it will be hard for you to believe, but this suave and sophisticated woman you see before you wasn't always this together. I mean, in high school I was something of a, um…"

"Nerd?" Rebecca finally chimed in.

"Intellectual," Tracy corrected her. "Plus my sense of humor doesn't always come across, and well, I guess I always felt like an outsider. And everybody knew my dad was a cop. I think that may have scared some guys off. And the guys that did take me out were given the third degree by my father. I didn't have many second dates. I guess that's why I waited so long before I let my parents meet him."

Rebecca nodded. "But none of that bothered Brian."

"No. For lack of a better way of putting it, he just liked me. And we hit it off right away. He was always the perfect gentleman. We did picnics; double dates with Crystal and whomever she was dating at the time, would take weekend trips to the beach or Kings Dominion, weather permitting. And Brian was a great study partner whenever I needed one. What can I say?" Tracy paused. "And I fell in love…hard." Tracy rose from her chair and turned to look out her office windows.

Rebecca straightened up and gave Tracy a few moments. "What happened, Tracy?"

Tracy cleared her throat and then turned to face Rebecca. Still standing she continued. "Sometimes Brian would go out with his buddies on the weekend doing what college guys do. I mean, he partied a little but he never drank in excess when we were together." Tracy paused again, and found herself staring at her carpet. "This one particular weekend I was visiting my parents and he went out like he sometimes did. And, well, he ran into an old girlfriend of his." Tracy decided to sit back down before continuing.

Rebecca was looking at her now. "Did he cheat on you?"

Tracy met Rebecca's eyes. "No." There was more silence, and then she continued, "She said he sexually assaulted her."

Rebecca's eyes widened. "Oh my God."

Tracy nodded. "I know, right? Brian denied it of course, said he never laid a hand on her, just said 'Hello' and moved on. And I believed him. We had been together more than two years by this point and he never, not once, did anything like that. He put no pressures or conditions on our relationship. I knew he'd been drinking that night. But I still couldn't believe what this girl was saying." Tracy paused. "This ex of his had approached someone in the school administration and filed the, uh, complaint. They talked to Brian of course, and it boiled down to a 'he said, she said' situation. Obviously Brian was crushed."

Rebecca nodded. Then Tracy added, "But it got even worse. I was there with Brian when he told his father about what was going on. And I'll never forget what his father said to him before Brian got a chance to tell his side: 'How could you do something like that? What were you thinking?'"

"His own father thought he was guilty?"

"Yeah. The look on Brian's face. I'd never seen Brian cry before that night but he came awfully close at that moment. He was so hurt, and I felt terrible. I think I blurted something out like, 'Brian didn't do it' but his father just ignored me. Then Brian just turned and left."

"That poor guy."

Tracy nodded. "And that's when it started. He was drinking almost every night. He started telling me that the only reason he was majoring in business administration was so that he'd one day run the family business. Brian really didn't know what he wanted to do but he knew it was important to his father to keep everything in the family. Of course all of that was shattered now. 'Why would my dad want a rapist running things?' he'd ask me. His hurt had turned to anger and since I was the one he was spending time with I was the one listening to it night after night."

Rebecca interrupted. "Did he ever hit you?"

"No, never," Tracy answered immediately. "He was angry but not violent. And what should have made things better only made things worse."

"What do you mean?"

"Well it turned out this ex of his accused another old boyfriend of hers of the same thing a few months earlier, and that she offered to forget about it if she were compensated. When the school found out about it she withdrew the complaint and tried to blame it all on her current boyfriend, said it was his idea."

Rebecca shook her head. "But the damage had been done."

"That's putting it mildly. I know his father felt terrible and tried apologizing but Brian felt so betrayed that it didn't matter by then. I tried to be understanding and sympathetic. But then..." Tracy trailed off. Her eyes moistened. She cleared her throat again. "And then I got the call that my father had been killed."

Rebecca immediately stood up and came over to where Tracy was sitting. She kneeled down beside her employer and put her arm around her.

"I really needed Brian, for him to be there for me. And he wasn't. He was so full of self-pity and anger that what I was going through was an annoyance to him." Tracy wiped her eyes and turned to look at Rebecca. "So one night soon after — it was near the end of my junior year — he came over for a simple dinner I made. We sat there, barely saying anything. Finally he asked if I had anything to drink, and he wasn't talking about soda. It must have been the way I said, 'No,' that set him off. After he finished, I stood up and told him that I'd had enough. He'd have to decide between me and his booze. I would help him anyway I could. If he agreed to get help I'd stand by him. But there was no way I was going to let things continue as they were."

"You were very patient with him, Tracy."

Tracy smiled. "I tried to be. But, like most people I guess, he didn't like being given an ultimatum. He just looked at me, and after a while he finally turned and left. I figured after a couple of days he'd call, apologize. But after a week or so without hearing from him I realized he wasn't going to be calling. Now it was my turn to be devastated."

"Oh Tracy, I'm so sorry about all of this. It's just so awful."

"I know. We went from Cinderella and Prince Charming to Juliet and Romeo. I lost my love and my father just like that." Tracy paused again briefly. "I later found out from Crystal that Brian did actually try to stop drinking, intending to present himself to me clean and sober. But he just couldn't manage it on his own. He'd call occasionally to check up on me, saying he was sorry. But I wasn't about to start anything again as long as he was drinking. And sadly, Crystal and I drifted apart too. I guess it was just too painful for both of us." Tracy managed to smile at Rebecca. "And that's my sad story."

Rebecca remained silent for a bit and then said, "But, after all that, you didn't hesitate to help him."

Tracy smiled again. "What was I gonna do? Play the vengeful female? I don't think I could forgive myself if I turned Brian down and he ended up getting convicted. I mean: I loved him, really loved him, the kind of want-to-get-married-and-have-a-bunch-of-kids-and-grow-old-together love."

"Oh Tracy…"

"I know what he was like before the alcohol took hold. I really believe he could set his life right again if he just tried to get help. Regardless: I can't see Brian killing his father. Maybe if this had happened a few years ago I would have just blown him off. But I guess enough time has passed, even if the wounds haven't completely healed."

Both Tracy and Rebecca stood up and shared a cathartic hug. Having shared everything with Rebecca, she did feel a little better. There was a time when she wondered if she should have tried harder to help Brian. But over the years, replaying everything in her head, she realized, if anything, she should have said something sooner. Either way she now could accept she did all that she could have at the time. "Thanks for caring, Beck."

"Hey Tracy, anytime you need to talk to someone I'm here." Rebecca soon returned to her desk as Tracy prepared for her visit with Elias Tanner. Returning her thoughts to the case, she hoped a talk with Tanner would prove helpful, that something came to light over the last few days that she could use to help her former beau. Despite the evidence against Brian she had the feeling she might be on to something with Kurt Barton. And she couldn't deny to herself that she felt a certain excitement at the prospect of not only proving Brian innocent, but also providing the police with the true guilty party. Tracy said goodnight to Rebecca, thanking the receptionist again as she left the office.

Fade in…

Brian pushed through the front door with enough force that had someone been standing on the other side they'd have been knocked out cold with a cracked skull. Tracy was close behind him. As he approached his car he stopped suddenly and opened the passenger door, waiting until Tracy sat herself down. He then slammed her door shut and moved to the driver's side. He fed his key to the ignition switch and the engine roared to life. The car jerked forward as it started to make its descent down the driveway. Brian hadn't said a word since he left the house. Tracy stared forward, her hands folded on her lap. She wanted to say something, but she knew that there really wasn't anything she could say. She had no idea of how to relate to what he was going through. She was about to ask him what he was thinking when he finally spoke.

"My own father. My own father thinks I could do something like that." He was shaking his head. "I wish Mom were still alive. She wouldn't think her son was a monster."

Tracy spoke softly. "I'm sorry Brian. I wish I could do something for you."

"I mean, Tracy, if you came home and told your father that someone said you beat them would he ask, 'Why did you do it?'"

"No."

"Of course he wouldn't. I thought parents graded their kids on a curve, you know? Most parents would say how their kid couldn't have done such a thing. But my father? Noooo…God I hate him sometimes. I mean what kind of chance do I have if my own dad thinks I could hurt a woman that way?"

Tracy reached out for his free hand, and felt tremendous relief when he took it and entwined their fingers together, squeezing hard. "Thank God I have you, Tracy; that you believe me. If I didn't I don't know what I'd do." He stole a quick look at her and then returned his eyes to the road. "Lord. There's a reason Brenda's my ex-girlfriend. Hell, lots of reasons. She's everything you're not Tracy — conceited, selfish, vain, manipulative, the kind who thinks she deserves anything and everything she wants." He stopped speaking and brought Tracy's hand to his lips, kissing it firmly. "But I never thought she was so rotten that she'd do something like this."

Tracy was looking at him. "I love you, Brian."

He turned to look at her, and then he suddenly slowed the car down and pulled off the road, putting the vehicle in park but leaving it running. He turned to her, looking directly into her eyes. "I love you too, Tracy." And then he reached for her and they embraced. He then kissed her with more passion then he ever had. He pulled away and put his hand on her cheek, stroking it gently. "Ya know, I'm almost glad this happened. Now I know what my father really thinks of me, so the hell with him and what *he* wants. After the both of us finish school we're going to get married and then it will just be you and me."

Tracy continued looking at him, and they both now had tears in their eyes, water streaming down their cheeks. He kissed her again and then said, "Boy I could really use a drink right now."

"Are you sure Brian? I'll stay with you as long as you want me to."

"Just a beer or something to relax — that's all. And of course I want you to stay with me."

"Okay Brian." She paused and then added, "I know this will work out. I know this will turn out alright."

Fade out…

Tracy shook her head. She hated replaying that scene in her head but she couldn't help it. Autopsy of a relationship—the beginning of the end. Dr. Brubaker, please report to the morgue again and again and again. But maybe the patient had some life left. Maybe with a lot of therapy there could be some resemblance to what it used to be. But the self consultation would have to end for now. Tracy had arrived at her destination.

Tracy entered the Baltimore Police Department, obtained her visitor's pass, and made her way to the office of Detective Tanner. She knew her way around the place, and many people knew *her*, especially the older officers who were there when her father was alive, and would occasionally bring his daughter in to show her off. She loved it here, even though she could never explain exactly why, even to herself. Important things were always going on, these men and women were doing something that really mattered, affected people's lives. Despite the fact they could be intimidating when they wanted to be, not to mention that they had guns dangling from their belts, Tracy felt the officers and detectives she had met throughout the years were some of the nicest people she knew. As odd as it may have sounded to others, she felt at peace here.

When she finally reached her destination, she rapped on Tanner's door. He was on the phone seated at his desk, but looked in her direction, and then motioned with his hand for her to come in. She took a seat while she waited for him to finish his call. She observed the picture of El's family—him, his wife Rita, and son Elias, Jr.—on his desk, as well as a smaller photo of him and his former partner. If her father were here, he'd prove Brian innocent. When Tanner finally hung up the receiver, he smiled and asked, "How's your case going, Tracy?"

"Just peachy. How's yours?"

He grinned. "Let me get the file." Tanner got up from his chair and went over to a table in his office that, despite appearing cluttered with files of all types, was actually quite organized. He quickly found and picked up the folder he was looking for and returned to his chair. He began, "The SA's office has all of this of course. But I'll give you a break and save you the trip over there."

"You're the best El." She smiled at him and took out her small notebook—ready for action.

"Nuts and bolts: Cause of death was a single gunshot wound to the back of the head from a .38 caliber pistol. Ballistics identified the gun we found on the lawn as the murder weapon. But there were no fingerprints on the gun handle. The fingerprints we found on the cartridges all belonged to Stewart Shane. Not surprising considering the gun was registered to him."

Tracy interrupted. "Where did Mr. Shane keep the gun?"

"According to the family and staff we talked to Shane kept the gun in his upstairs bedroom bureau." Anticipating her next question, Tanner quickly added, "And yes, the drawer was unlocked."

"So the murder weapon was kept in an unlocked drawer and several people knew about it," Tracy repeated, not looking up from her note taking.

"Correct. Brian Shane being one of those several people, of course."

She looked up at him. He continued. "Powder burns on the sofa cushion indicate Shane was shot at close range."

"Did you find any powder traces on the clothes Brian was wearing?" she broke in. "I remember you took his raincoat in for testing."

"No, we didn't find any traces of powder on either his clothes or the raincoat."

Tracy liked that news. She liked it very much. "What about time of death?"

"Consistent with the time frame established by the security guards and Brian Shane himself," Tanner told her.

"But could Mr. Shane have been killed earlier?"

"In his statement Brian Shane said he saw his father alive when he was hanging up his raincoat," Tanner said.

Tracy again looked up. Why hadn't Tanner just answered the question? Wondering if she was on to something she said, "I realize that. But Brian's father didn't say anything when he turned to look at Brian. And there's that colossal TV hanging on the wall overlooking the room. Brian had been drinking. Maybe he mistook the movement of someone or something on the screen for his father turning toward him."

"That's pretty thin, Tracy," Tanner said as he consulted the medical examiner's notes. "Let's see, coroner lists the approximate time of death between 9:00 p.m. and 10:30 p.m."

More good news she thought. "I don't know, El. There seem to be some chinks here in the circumstantial armor."

"We think it's a pretty solid case Tracy," Tanner countered, not seeming offended. "I've already explained the guards' situations. Several people would have to be lying for someone else to have somehow entered the grounds, shot Shane, and then vanish. I can count on one hand without using all of my fingers the number of murder cases I've been involved with in the last 30 years that turned out to be conspiracies."

Tanner's level-headed sounding explanation did not dampen her spirits. She understood that he was viewing this murder as just another case, calmly and rationally reviewing the evidence, and reaching the most obvious conclusion, as wrong as she felt it was. Still, she couldn't be angry with him. She loved him almost like a father. He used to be her dad's partner which made the two of them family. He was merely playing the role of the voice of reason as far as she was concerned. And that was a good thing.

"Well, the one advantage I have here is that I know Brian," she told him. "Drunk or sober, I don't think he could kill his father."

Tanner didn't immediately say anything. He knew she must be hurting on some level and he had no interest in adding to her pain. Tanner had eventually recalled the name Brian Shane from the years he and Tracy's father worked side by side. His memory told him she had met Brian in college, or maybe before. At one point Tracy had told her father she was in love with him, and Peter Brubaker started wondering aloud if a wedding was in the cards. It must have been serious. It was also about the time Peter asked Elias, should anything happen to him, if he could take care of her, and give her away on her wedding day on Peter's behalf. A wave of melancholy came over him as he watched Tracy, Peter Brubaker's little girl, finishing her note-taking. Then he said, "Anything else I can tell you, Tracy?"

"Did you check Mr. Shane's phone records that evening? Follow-up on any calls he may have made or received?" she asked.

"He made one call and received two in the early evening after dinner. They were all quick and concerned with the same thing; he and some friends were planning a golf outing on Sunday. The friends were at home with their spouses the whole night." He paused and then said, "Next."

"Am I correct in assuming Barton's firm will be handling the estate, and that Brian and Crystal are the chief beneficiaries?"

"Perfect score. There are some allowances for staff, some charitable donations. But the children will be coming into almost four million dollars each right away in addition to the estate land and increased ownership of the business via the stock they'll be inheriting. That's the preliminary figure anyway."

Tracy gulped. Four million? Each? "It's my understanding that Stewart Shane hasn't been involved in the day-to-day operations of the company for a couple of years and that Crystal took over as CEO last year. Did you look at anyone else involved in running things at the company now?"

"We did check the alibis of the current COO and other key employees just as a matter of procedure: rock solid across the board."

"And I guess you talked to the limo driver and confirmed Barton was the only one in the car."

"Yes. The driver—his name is Bernard Cubbins—said he brought Barton from the restaurant where he was speaking directly to the Shane estate. They left the restaurant at approximately 10 after 10. No stops. No one else was in the limo at any time according to Cubbins."

Tracy pursed her lips. Did that account just knock down her recently built Barton-did-it theory? She asked, "So you're *still* thinking Brian killed him either for the money or for the bad blood between them?"

"Or both." Tanner leaned in a little and continued. "Tracy, you may have a diminished capacity case here. Brian was drunk, not thinking clearly. Maybe he and his father had another argument and Brian lost it for a few seconds. I know you don't want to hear that. But it happens."

Tracy just looked at him. Of course she had run this scenario through her brain already. Detective Lucas had already presented it on Saturday. She could see how this theory made sense to *them*. But Brian seemed so sure he was innocent. Could he be lying? Could he have changed that much in the ensuing years after their intimacy ended? She couldn't believe it. Evidence and motives be darned. It just wasn't possible. She gave Tanner a small smile to let him know she understood his position and his concern. "Thanks, El. But I still stand by my belief in Brian's innocence."

Tanner returned her smile. To him she seemed to be handling this just fine—at least for now. "Very well then—are we done?"

"Not quite yet."

"What else then?"

"Are you aware that someone took a shot at Crystal and Doug last month?"

Tanner raised an eyebrow. "Yes we are. I have a copy of that report too. Let me grab it." Tanner returned to his seat as quickly as he had left it. "If I recall correctly the investigating officer felt it was a wrong-place-at-the-wrong-time incident."

"That's what Crystal said about it too. Which back window did the shot enter, driver or passenger side?"

Tanner scanned the file. "Passenger."

"Crystal's side then."

Tanner nodded. "Yes, according to the report Doug was driving."

"Does it say if Doug's car had tinted windows?"

"Let me see. Here—the windows weren't tinted."

"So the shooter could probably see there was no one in the back."

"That's the thinking."

"Did you think to see if the bullet came from Stewart Shane's gun?"

Tanner furrowed his brow. "No need to: Different calibers. The shooter in the drive by used a 9mm."

Tracy paused a moment. "Were either Doug or Crystal able to give a description of the car, maybe a partial plate number?"

"No; they were both too upset by the incident to be observant." Tracy started scratching her chin with her pen. "Any more questions, Tracy?"

"You are free to go," she answered. She rose and Tanner got up to open the door. She hugged him and thanked him, and started out the door.

"Tracy," Tanner called.

"'You rang?"

"You didn't call your mother this weekend did you?"

Tracy gave him a mildly horrified look. "Yikes—no; I was a little pre-occupied."

"Well she called me yesterday to find out if there were any unidentified young ladies in the morgue answering your description," Tanner said grinning.

"Oh good grief," Tracy said, somewhat embarrassed. "Thanks El. I'll call her from the grave tonight."

Tanner let out a good laugh and she couldn't help chuckling herself. So now she had another call to make. Who would be first: Larry "the worry wart" Waters or Violetta "my daughter must be worm food" Brubaker? It was a tough choice. Maybe she should just go home and go to bed. Or put on a James Cagney or Edward G. Robinson movie—hang out with some real tough guys. Or maybe she could call Brian. She found herself smiling at that thought. But she knew that wasn't a good idea—at least, not right now. Decisions, decisions. So she applied her usual scientific method when faced with evaluating equally unpleasant options. "Eeny meeny miny mo," she mumbled to herself as she opened her car door.

Neal Bennett arrived at Judds just after 6:00. It was a corner bar that was located in a mostly residential area and looked as though it must have been a local fixture for years. The outside was definitely in need of several coats of paint, and the black letters that spelled out the tavern's name could have used some adjusting too. Two heavy, brown doors with small rectangular windows served as the entry.

While there was a gravel parking lot just across from the bar, Neal chose to park on the street. He grabbed his small notebook, exited his Honda Accord, and then made his way inside, having to give the doors an extra hard push to move forward. He next headed toward the bartender on duty, noticing the looks he was getting from some of the clientele. He didn't pay them any mind, and they quickly went right back to their drinking.

"Excuse me," Neal said to the tall, pale fellow who was chatting with another patron.

"I'll be right with you," he responded, not even looking at Neal. He continued his conversation with someone who must have been a local, and was, this night, sharing with the barkeep his theory on why electric cars were the worst idea in the history of the world.

"See, if you run out of gas," Neal heard him saying, "you can leave your car and bring a can to get the gas you need to be on your way. But what the hell you gonna do when you run out of electricity? You can't put *that* in a can, now can you? No—you gotta get a tow or push your damn car to the nearest electric station. That's crap. And what the hell happens if the tow truck runs out of electricity on its way to pick you up? Then what'll you do? I tell you Marcus, the whole thing is a conspiracy between the electric company and those environmentalists to make us all walk everywhere so we then have to stop at air conditioning stations."

"What air conditioning stations Louis?" Marcus asked.

"The ones they'll start putting up as soon as they get their electric cars everywhere. And they'll charge you a pretty nickel to come in and cool off, too."

Marcus chuckled at Louis' discovery of the nefarious plot against all, and then went to grab him another Miller Lite. After dropping off Louis' drink he turned his attention to Neal. "Good evening. What'll you have?"

"How about a Coke," Neal said, putting $20 on the counter, "and maybe some conversation."

Marcus looked at him, and then at the $20, and then moved to add Neal's request to an ice-filled glass. He grabbed a straw on his way back.

"Thank you," Neal said. "That $20 is all yours if we can talk for just a couple of minutes."

Marcus picked up the $20. "What's our subject?"

"Brian Shane. He was arrested yesterday for his father's murder."

Marcus nodded. "We've all been talking about it. Cops came in asking about him too. What's your interest?"

"I work for the law firm that's representing him. He was here last Friday, the night his father was shot. Were you on duty that night?"

"Nope," Marcus said quickly. "I work nights Sundays through Wednesdays. The guy you want is named Ernie. He works the other nights, 4:00 p.m. until close."

"Oh, I see," Neal said. Then he leaned in a little and asked, "Do you think anyone who's here now knew Brian and could I maybe talk to them?"

"Never saw Brian talk to anyone when he was here during one of my shifts," Marcus told him. "And I don't want you bothering the customers."

Neal didn't take offense. "Perfectly understandable," he said. "So Ernie will be here Thursday at 4:00 p.m. then?"

"He should be here, unless he gets sick or something."

Neal began enjoying his soda. "Did Brian ever say anything to you about his dad, about their relationship?"

Marcus looked at him and answered, "Nothing specific. I know they didn't get along because he said his dad was always ridin' him about something. But he always stopped himself before he said any more than that. And I never asked for more details."

"So there's nothing you can tell me about him then?"

"Sorry fella; he was pretty much just like that guy over there," Marcus said while pointing at Louis, "except without the vocabulary. He came in when he wanted, drank what he wanted, and left when he was done."

"I got it," Neal said. He then remembered the photographs Tracy had sent him, and decided to pull up one of the auto photos on his Samsung Galaxy. "Ever see Brian's wheels?" Neal asked, showing Marcus the screen.

Marcus leaned in and smiled. "Hey, that's pretty sweet. I knew he drove some sporty antique but never actually saw it."

Neal asked, "Do you know where he'd park it while he was here?"

"We have the lot across the street and then there's street parking. Not sure if he had a preference."

"So, Brian couldn't keep an eye on his car while he was inside."

Marcus' eyes widened. "Hey, you're right about that. I guess he's lucky no one ever broke into his car, tried to steal it. At least, I never heard that anyone ever had."

Interesting, Neal thought. Could Tracy have been right after all? Could someone have snuck into Brian's car, unobserved, when Brian was inside Judds? He kept that to himself as he thanked Marcus, finished his soda, and then left the bar. He went to his own car, unlocked it and, before getting in, looked in the backseat for intruders: Nobody there. Could Brian have said the same had he checked last Friday night?

Neal started the journey toward the Shane estate, keeping an eye out for places Brian may have visited. First stop was a 7-11 just a block away from the bar. Neal entered, grabbed a 20 oz. Coke from the store's refrigerator, and went to pay for it. He told the cashier who he was, and then showed pictures of Brian and the Mercury.

"Ever seen this guy or his car before?"

"No sir," the attendant said, not looking at the pictures.

"Please take a look. This is very important."

The employee handed Neal his change and looked at the images Brian showed him on the small rectangle-shaped phone. "No, sir," he said again.

"Do you have a manager on duty I might speak to?"

"No, sir. Just me."

"Were you here last Friday?" Neal continued.

"Yes, sir."

"And you were alone then too?"

"Yes, sir. Next customer please!"

Neal thanked him and opened up his purchase on his way out the door; back on the hunt. When Neal came to a McDonald's a few miles later he pulled in, went inside, and asked one of the order-takers if he could speak to the store or shift manager. A young lady who couldn't have been older than 21 emerged smiling and asked, "Yes sir?"

Neal explained the situation in much the same way he had at Judds and the 7-11. But he got lucky this time in that *three* people, including her, were there Friday night. "Could I briefly talk with the three of you? I'd like to show you all some pictures of the man and his car."

She looked at him strangely. "Why would we want to see his car?"

"He may have been a drive-through customer," Neal told her.

"I should have thought of that," she said flatly. She told Neal to take a seat near the Employees Only entrance and that she'd be with him as soon as she could. It wasn't long before she came out from the back with two people younger than she, and they all sat down, somewhat squished together, opposite Neal in the booth where he was seated. He showed the manager Janie, and the two others, Lance and Carly, the photos of Neal and his auto. "Cool," they all seemed to mouth when they saw the Mercury. But no one remembered it or Brian inside or outside of the restaurant that night, or any night. He thanked them all for their courtesy and left, but not without first purchasing a few chocolate chip cookies which he told himself were for his kids.

A few miles further down the same street, but on the opposite side, Neal noticed a bright yellow sign with a red-headed, pig-tailed girl who went by the name Wendy, inviting passers-by in for something to eat. He pulled off and went through the same ritual there as he had done at the clown's eatery. Lucky again in that there were people there who were working Friday, unlucky again in that none of them recognized Brian or his — this time the adjective used was 'awesome' — vehicle. Neal resisted the temptation that was the Chocolate Frosty.

Just before turning into the residential area that would have taken Neal to his ultimate destination he noticed a strip shopping center off to the right. The tenants consisted of a Laundromat, florist shop, Hair Cuttery, and Chinese restaurant. The first was a 24-hour self-serve business so there'd be no point in going in there. He checked the store hours listed on the doors for the second shop (closed at 7:00 on Fridays) and the third business (closed at 9:00). As they were both still open, he entered each anyway to confirm they closed when the posted hours told him they did. The humans he talked to agreed with the doors.

But the Chinese place was open until 10 p.m. on Friday. Did Brian get hungry and stop for a quick bite? Neal went in to find out, repeating his by-now familiar routine. "No we didn't see him," a kind lady behind the cashier desk told him. "I don't think he's ever been here."

But before Neal left, he thought he'd look at a menu. The overwhelming smell emanating from the kitchen was too much for his hungry self to resist. He checked his watch. Not even 7:15. "I'll eat in." While awaiting his meal Neal pulled out his Galaxy and typed "Kurt Barton Friday Event" into the search engine. A news article caught his attention about Kurt Barton being one of the presenters at a function honoring local attorneys who scored the highest on the February bar exams. Marcelo's Ristorante Italiano on High Street was the location. Their kitchen didn't close until 10, so Neal decided he'd make one more stop before heading home for the night.

Marcelo's Ristorante Italiano was located in Baltimore's Little Italy, an area east of the Inner Harbor. The area was founded in 1849 to accommodate the influx of Italian immigrants and their families who arrived to take advantage of the growing local railroad industry. The new population had been large enough to claim this part of the city as their own. The resulting neighborhood was a frequented attraction due to the fine reputation of the numerous restaurants offering authentic Italian cuisine. It also hosted several events throughout the year such as film festivals, the Christmas tree lighting, a Columbus Day parade, and bocce tournaments, among other things. And it was one of the city's safest regions. If Neal had known he'd be stopping here later tonight, he would have waited to eat dinner.

There was a parking garage about one block from Marcelo's in which Neal chose to park. It wasn't completely dark yet so he enjoyed the walk. Neal entered and made his way to the hostess. She smiled and greeted him. Her name was Gabriella

"Good evening, Gabriella," Neal said smiling back. "I was wondering if I could briefly speak with the owner regarding a function that took place last Friday. One of the attendees was an attorney whose client was involved in some bad business Friday." Neal took out a business card and handed it to her. She was very serious now, and told him to wait. A few minutes later she returned with who Neal would shortly learn was Matteo Altomare, son of the owner. Matteo introduced himself and led Neal to a private dining room that was not in use.

"Mr. Altomare," Neal began, "you had a dinner here Friday where one of your guests was Kurt Barton, an attorney. One of his clients was killed late Friday night, and I am working for one of the law firms involved in the case." Neal was deliberately vague in describing the situation. Hopefully Matteo would not want more specific details.

"How can I help?" Matteo asked. His Italian accent was obvious but not so heavy that Neal had trouble understanding him. Neal used his Galaxy to show him a photo of Barton. "Do you recognize this man?"

Matteo looked briefly and nodded. "Yes, he was here Friday at the lawyer dinner."

"What time did the function start and end?"

Matteo said, "The room was reserved from 7 to 10. We started actually serving the meal at close to 7:30."

Neal made some notes and then continued. "I wonder if I could briefly speak to someone who was working that dinner. I promise my questions will be brief."

"Of course," he said smiling. "Please wait here." Matteo turned and left Neal alone for what must have been less than 10 minutes. He returned with a lovely young woman named Siena who looked a little apprehensive. Neal smiled at her hoping that would put her at ease. Matteo introduced her only by her first name and then asked if he could stay during the interview.

"Yes, that would be fine, Mr. Altomare," Neal told him. The three sat down at one of the small round tables covered in white linen. Neal showed Siena the Barton photograph. "Do you remember seeing this man Friday?"

She nodded. "Yes."

"Are you able to tell me what time he left the dinner?"

She shook her head. "No. I am sorry."

"Could you then tell me the last time you remember seeing him?"

She paused a moment and said, "He started talking just after we finished serving the cake. But I am not sure exactly what time that was."

Matteo added, "We brought the cake in at about 9:15." Siena nodded in agreement.

Neal looked at Matteo and then back at Siena. "So Siena, you didn't see him after he finished his speech."

"No," she answered him. "I did not return until we started cleaning up. People were all about. I do not know if he was there or not."

"And what time would clean up have started?"

"Close to 10," she told him.

Neal made some more notes and then said, "I want to thank both of you very much for your time. You have both been very helpful." They both returned his smile as the three prepared to leave the dining room.

Then Siena added, "Sir, we may have a copy of the program for that night. I think I saw some extras behind the bar."

Neal smiled. "That would be great, Siena. Thank you." She smiled in return and left the room first, followed by Neal and then Matteo. Siena arrived at the bar and then handed Neal the promised schedule. He thanked her and Matteo again, and then headed for his car. Outside Marcelo's he looked at the program and saw that Barton was the last speaker, scheduled for 9:30. Better still there were other names listed in the program. Now

Neal knew some people he could talk to that would hopefully help nail down Barton's movements. If Barton left immediately after his presentation, he might have his own unaccounted-for time to explain.

Chapter 7

It was now Wednesday morning around 8:30 and Tracy was not looking forward to sitting down with Larry Waters to go over his foreclosure case later that morning. She agreed to meet with him at 9:30 based on the previous night's phone conversation. "They're going to come in the dead of night and throw me out into the cold," he had whined.

"Larry, they can't and won't do that," she had told him, trying to calm him down.

"But I hear them outside," he had insisted.

"Are your doors locked?"

"Yes, of course."

"Then they can't come in."

"But they might have keys."

"Then put chairs or heavy items in front of the doors and go to bed."

"But what about the windows?"

"Lock them too."

"But they can break the glass."

Sheesh. "If you hear glass break, you'll have time to flee. Just keep a pair of shoes close to the bed."

After a brief pause he had asked, "But if they do manage to come in and evict me, can I call you?"

Finally after 10 minutes of arguing with him she had had enough and ended the call. Before she could hang up he asked her, "What can I do, Ms. Brubaker? What *should* I do until I can see you tomorrow?"

"Don't sleep naked," she had told him before showing mercy on her eardrum.

Of course that was nothing compared to the next call she had made. She could hear the worry in her mother's tired voice as soon as she picked up the receiver. But Tracy couldn't resist indulging her dark side given what she had been through the last few days.

"Hello," Violetta Brubaker had answered.

"Hello. This is the ghost of your daughter. *Ooooooooooo….*"

"You are NOT funny young lady!" had been the as-expected response. If Tracy had a dollar for every time her mother told her how un-funny she was, she wouldn't have to work a day in her life.

"As you can tell I'm fine Mom. I'm working a case and it took over my weekend," Tracy had offered.

"Well, I'm *not* fine. What's going on in your life that's so important that you can't spend just a few minutes talking to your own mother? You know how I worry."

Tracy had anticipated that question. "Do you remember Brian Shane, Mom?"

After a brief pause, her mother had asked, "That Irish boy who broke your heart and had you shopping for sleeping pills?"

Good. Freakin'. Grief. "Mom: Enough of that. He's in trouble and I've been helping him. I'm sorry I didn't call but I wasn't up to it. It's been a rough few days; some painful memories. I didn't mean to hurt you or worry you. I'm sorry, Mom."

There had been another pause. "Are you coming to visit this weekend?" The tone in her mother's voice had completely changed.

"I don't know yet. As I said, I'm helping a friend; maybe the weekend after this one." Tracy had started to feel a little guilty. Her mother had lost her husband of 23 years in a most horrible way, proving that the worry she always felt had been completely justified. Now her only daughter was making jokes at her expense. Tracy had found out when she was younger that the Brubakers wanted to have more children. But it was not to be. Being an only child has its advantages and disadvantages. So growing up she had had all of the attention, but the pressure of expectations. She had done her best to make both her parents proud. But now it was just her and her mother. She loved her mother, but there were times when Tracy needed some understanding from her, and she rarely got it. At least, not in the same way her father had always been so comforting. Tracy had bought her a puppy once, after her dad had passed, so her mother wouldn't be alone. But it didn't work out so Tracy had to find the dog another home. And she told the new family she would pay for the dog's therapy bills if the poor pup needed it. Now her mom lived with a friend of hers in Aberdeen. They looked out for each other which gave Tracy some peace of mind. And she tried to make it out of the city at least once a month to visit her mother and check up on her.

"Well, I'd like to see you," her mother had said sounding disappointed.

"I know Mom. I want to see you too."

"Mrs. Raccio's oldest daughter is here *every* weekend and brings along one of the grandkids. That busy woman finds time for *her* mother."

Argh. "I promise I will try to make it over as soon as I can. I need to go now. I love you Mom."

"I love you too. Good luck on your case."

Tracy had hung up the phone, put a Healthy Choice frozen dinner in the microwave, and then sat down to watch an old Sherlock Holmes movie — *The Scarlet Claw* — from her DVD collection. Luckily this had succeeded in keeping the dreams at bay, and her sleep had been deep.

Now it was back to playing Holmes herself, with Neal "Dr. Watson" Bennett at her side. She was anxious to hear if he had learned anything from last night's assignments. The news was not what she had hoped for.

"I'm sorry Tracy," he began. "But I couldn't find anyone that remembered Brian or his car. I talked to a convenience store employee, a few fast food restaurant workers, and some merchants at a strip shopping center, anyone who worked at anything in between the ride from Judds to the Shanes'. Nothing."

She frowned. "Did you talk to anyone at Judds?"

"The bartender on duty last night was not the one on the job Friday. The guy we want to talk to is named Ernie. He works Thursdays, Fridays, and Saturdays, 4:00 p.m. until close. No one else there would be of any help. The only thing that might be of use is that Brian couldn't keep an eye on his car while inside the bar. Not sure if it helps or not though."

The frown continued. "Just perfect. Well, one of us can talk to Ernie later. What about Barton and his Friday evening?"

Neal looked at his notes and then told her, "I was able to get over to the restaurant in Little Italy where Barton was one of the people welcoming some new locals to the bar Friday night. I found an employee who was working the banquet room that night, and she was able to put her hands on a copy of the program which had Barton's remarks scheduled for 9:30, during the dessert. I will try this morning to start tracking down at least a couple of names listed in the program so I can then hopefully trace Barton's movements."

Tracy looked at him. "Great work Neal. That's great work." She paused and said, "But my theory about Barton being involved seems to be losing its foundation. Not sure how he could swing it. But I do now want to talk to his driver. I know Barton has his own chauffeur. See if you can find out anything about him. His name is Bernard Cubbins. Maybe we'll find out something." She paused again and then asked, "Do you have any good news you can share?"

"Oh yes," he perked up. "I had an absolutely delicious General Tso Chicken platter last night with rice and wonton soup; and some cookies."

She laughed heartily even if his joke wasn't *that* funny. "I'm so jealous," she said. "Okay, Watson. Now that you're fed and rested go ahead and follow up on the banquet attendees and Cubbins, as well as digging for dirt on Barton's relationship with Shane like we talked about. And I forwarded that employee list from Brian to you this morning. That should be enough to keep you busy."

Neal smiled at her as he arose. "Are you doing okay, Tracy?" he asked.

"I'm fine, Neal. Really," she told him, and thought to add, "You and Beck have been great. It means a lot to me."

Neal nodded, and moved toward the door. Before leaving, he turned and said, "Whatever you need Tracy — whatever you need." She watched him go but couldn't think of anything to say to that. Tracy then picked up the phone and dialed Bill Ryder's phone number which Neal had previously obtained for her. Given the hour she expected him to be asleep, having just finished his shift, so she was not surprised when the answering machine picked up in his stead. She waited for the beep and said, "Good morning Mr. Ryder. My name is Tracy Brubaker. I am Brian Shane's attorney and would really appreciate if it I could talk to you about last Friday night." She left her office and mobile numbers, said thanks in advance, and hung up. Hopefully she'd be able to see him today. But that was up to him.

"Larry Waters is here," Rebecca told Tracy. "Do I send him back to you — or just back?"

Tracy sighed. He was a little early but, what the heck. "Bring him back Beck. I made the appointment with him last night. I'm sorry I forgot to mention it to you when I came in." Then Tracy added, "You better make sure we have smelling salts on hand, and 911 on speed dial."

"You got it."

Larry Waters was a small man, a nervous man, and a pain in the ass. Tracy was sympathetic to his situation — the bank should never have given him that loan to begin with — but he tested her patience something awful, and now he was probably her least favorite client. She didn't have the heart to drop him; at least not yet. But he was on the verge of being evicted by his own attorney.

At some point while being escorted to Tracy's back office Waters must have pushed his way past Rebecca — thereby taking his life in his own hands — because he came through Tracy's doorway so hurriedly he almost ran into one of the chairs in front of her desk. As always, he was sloppily dressed, this time wearing a blue pin stripe suit with wrinkles all over it. His white shirt had what looked to be tomato sauce stains on it. (Wasted tomato sauce—a minor crime.) The soles on his black shoes were so worn they were starting to break away. His graying black hair was uncombed, his eyes tired from being tired, and his teeth yellowed from his 10-pack-a-day habit. In fact, he started to take out a cigarette.

"You cannot smoke in here, Mr. Waters," Tracy said firmly and not for the first, and probably not for the last, time.

"Why not?" he whimpered.

"Because it's the state's law and it's my law. You are in *my* kingdom, remember?" She seemed to go through this with him every time he came in.

He looked at her bearing a hurt expression. "Well can I have a drink then?"

"I can offer you water or coffee, or I can have someone get you a soda from the vending machine down the hall," she offered.

"Do they have bourbon in that machine of yours?" he asked, with no hint or suggestion in his voice of how ridiculous his question was.

"They're still out," Tracy said flatly.

He started pacing. "Well I must have something to calm my nerves."

Tracy told him, "Well you could try biting your nails. I understand that's a very popular nervous habit."

He looked at her, and then at his nails, and then back at her. "Can I have a soda?"

Tracy buzzed Rebecca. "Beck could you please hop on down to the soda machine and get something for Mr. Waters—whatever soda has the least amount of caffeine and sugar, preferably."

"I'm on it," Rebecca said.

"Now Mr. Waters please sit down, or I'll charge you for new carpeting."

Again Waters looked at her. "Oh alright," he muttered. He squirmed a bit in his seat after sitting down and then continued. "They were outside my home last night. I heard them."

Not this again. "I doubt it Mr. Waters. You just heard something else. For example you may have been hearing tree branches banging on your house because of the wind."

"How could you know *that*? Were you there too?" Waters accused, his eyes widening.

"No Mr. Waters. I was prowling outside someone else's house last night," Tracy said, with no hint of sarcasm.

Rebecca heard what Tracy had said and guffawed as she entered with a Coke Zero. "Here you are Mr. Waters. Would you like a cup?"

He looked up at the towering Rebecca, accepted the can, and let out a barely audible, "No thank you." She left and gave Tracy a big smile on her way out.

Waters opened his soda and started drinking, or rather slurping, which gave Tracy the opportunity to deliver her usual sermon. "Mr. Waters—part of the agreement now in place with the bank while we work our way through this process, is that you are allowed to remain in your home even though you haven't made any payments for the past six months. Therefore, no one will be removing you from your home."

Slurp.

She gave him a brief stare. "You need to get yourself together so you can continue to work. You must have used up all of your vacation and sick days by now given how many emergencies you have had since you engaged me."

Slurp, shirt-spill. Now the tomato sauce had company.

"I want you to leave here, go home and make yourself presentable, and then go to your job at the toll booth, before they fire you, which will not help your case."

Sluuurp....

"Let me do my job and I promise I will do everything in my legal power to help you. Okay?"

He looked at her, and then he smiled. "Okay. Okay. I can do that."

Tracey smiled back. "I will call you as soon as I know anything. I promise."

Waters arose, emptied the remaining contents of the soda can, and turned to leave. "So you'll call me later today?" he asked her.

"Only if I have news to share with you. Do you understand that, Mr. Waters? Now you need to go to work."

He nodded and left. Tracy heard Rebecca offer to take Waters' empty beverage container as he hurried out. He must have seen it as a threat. "Here, take it. *Take it!*" Waters pleaded before she harmed him while attempting to retrieve the can.

Tracy let out a sigh and sat back in her chair shaking her head. "Did you hurt him Beck?" she called out to Rebecca.

"Not much," Rebecca answered. "I think I scared him though. Do you think he'll come back any time soon Tracy?"

Tracy answered, "Larry Waters is like the Terminator, Beck. He'll be back."

Bill Ryder returned Tracy's call and agreed to meet her at the apartment he shared with his wife. Their two children were living at out-of-state colleges, and his wife was at work, so the two could talk in private. Even though his 12-hour shift had ended at 6:00 a.m. he told her to come by around 11. He needed only a few hours of sleep so it would work out for both of their schedules. She found his apartment easily and rang the bell. He opened the door. "Please, come in, Miss," he said warmly. She smiled and entered.

The apartment was a three bedroom unit with a nice sized living area. The blinds were up so that the entire living room was bathed in sunlight. He led her over to what must have been the family dining table, a sturdy oak piece with four matching chairs, sitting atop light brown carpeting. He pulled out one of the seats and invited her to sit down. "What can I offer you: coffee, water, a soda?" Ryder began.

"Water, please," she said.

"Is tap okay?"

"Oh, sure."

"Ice?" he asked.

"Three lumps would be dandy," she told him.

Ryder smiled again and went to prepare Tracy's beverage and refill his coffee mug that said "World's Best Dad." He soon returned, placing Tracy's drink in front of her and putting his own on the table.

"Are those your kids?" she asked pointing to the picture on the mug as Ryder sat himself down across from Tracy.

"Yes, my sons, when they were four and two."

"They're adorable," she told him sincerely.

"I don't seem 'em much nowadays. But I do have this," he said raising his mug, toasting their existence.

"What are their names, if you don't mind my asking?"

"The older is William and the younger is Walter," he answered her. "Do you have children of your own?"

"No, not yet."

"Any nephews or nieces?"

"I'm an only child. But I have a seven-year-old goddaughter named Casey that I adore, Mr. Ryder."

Ryder smiled. He liked this young lady. "I guess we should start talking about last Friday," he said after a few sips of coffee. "I'm sure your time is more valuable than mine. And please call me Bill."

"As long as you call me Tracy," she responded.

Ryder began without further prompting. "I arrived at the Shane place around 5:00 in the evening, my usual time. Mr. Shane always had us—me and Doug I mean—eat with him and his family if we were working a night shift. I work five nights a week—Tuesday through Saturday. Anyway, Doug watches the gate at the foot of the driveway, and I have a booth behind the house near the center of the wall that surrounds the estate. I do a foot patrol every couple of hours or so. I come on duty at 6:00 p.m. so I do a circuit right away and then at 8:00, 10:00, midnight, and so on until 6:00 in the morning."

"What do you do when you're not patrolling?" Tracy asked.

"Well there's a small TV and radio in the booth. I bring books or crossword puzzles sometimes. There's plenty of lighting you see. It's not as boring as it may sound."

Hmm—next question: "Prior to Friday has anything ever happened on your watch? A break-in or a prowler, for instance."

"No, nothing. Truth is I don't know why Mr. Shane didn't just install security cameras and let me go." He took some sips of his coffee.

Tracy thought about that a minute while sipping her water. "Maybe he just liked having you around," she said. "There's something comforting about the knowledge some*body* is out there looking over you."

Ryder looked at her. "Yes, that may have been it. Both his kids lived at home so he wanted to play the protective father, I guess."

"So Brian got home around 10 that night?" Tracy asked.

"It was 10:07 p.m. when I looked at my watch. I was coming up to the house from the back when I heard the garage door slam. I looked over and saw Brian headed in the direction of the house."

"And you're sure it was Brian?" she asked, hoping her tone didn't make her question seem like a challenge.

"Yeah. He had on that green raincoat of his—we had some bad storms come through that night if you remember."

Tracy made some notes. "Mm; did you talk to him?"

"No. No reason to."

"And no one else came or went until Kurt Barton showed up?"

"Right. We use walkie-talkies to keep in touch throughout the shift. Doug radioed me close to 10:30 that Mr. Barton was on his way up the driveway. So I made my way back to meet Mr. Barton at the front door and let him in. Mr. Shane always had his staff out of the house by 6:30, after the help had cleaned up the kitchen from dinner, so I had to let anyone in who had an after-hours appointment with him. Anyway I let Mr. Barton in, called out for Mr. Shane, and…well, we both found him there."

Tracy, who had been furiously taking notes, stopped; a puzzled look on her face. She asked, "Doesn't the front gate call the house and let them know someone is on their way?"

"It depends. If you don't have an appointment they'll call the house and won't open the gate until someone gives the okay. If you are expected then you'll be let in. During the day when there are a lot of people about, the front gate will call the house and tell them the party is coming up. After 7:00 p.m., when there aren't too many people left and the house is locked, the front will notify me or who's ever on duty to meet the party and let them in. I mean, when the house is practically empty you can't be sure someone will hear the hall phone. And well, Mr. Shane would have been watching some baseball game last Friday. Don't want to disturb the man until you absolutely have to."

"I can understand that," she said nodding. "I wonder, did Doug radio you when Brian was on his way up?"

"No need for that," Ryder answered. "Brian has a key to the house. He wouldn't need me to let him in. Besides, he's usually coming in around 9:00 on Fridays when I'm back at the booth and not walking the grounds."

"I see," Tracy said. "And there was no other radio communication between you and Doug Stanz that night other than the announcement of Barton's arrival."

"That's right."

"You didn't hear the shot did you?"

"No; I didn't hear anything like that." His answer didn't surprise her. And his version of the night seemed to fit snuggly together with everyone else's. "Was Mr. Barton already at the door when you arrived to let him in?"

"I met him walking up the pathway to the main door. He had already gotten out of his car."

"Did you catch a glimpse of his driver at all?"

"No, I didn't. All the other times Mr. Barton was here his driver never left the car."

Tracy again stopped to drink her water. "Bill, the Friday before the murder, did you happen to hear the phone call Mr. Shane made to his attorney to set up the meeting?"

Bill had to think about that for minute, then his eyes widened slightly. "You know what—yes, I did hear it. Mr. Shane was in the living room pacing back and forth, shouting at Mr. Barton."

Tracy leaned forward a bit. "Did Mr. Shane sound angry, or maybe accusatory when speaking to Barton?"

"Umm, that's hard to say," Bill answered. "I guess I'd describe it as Mr. Shane being boisterous. I mean, every time I saw him angry his face got real red. You know, Irish temper and all." Bill stopped. "Are you Irish? Did I offend with that last comment?"

Tracy smiled at him reassuringly. "No Bill. I'm German on my father's side, Italian on my mother's. Two very head-strong personalities who could get into it every now and again."

"Oh, good. Well, when I looked at Mr. Shane that Friday I don't think he looked like he was angry. It was weird and uncomfortable is what it was."

"You're someone who likes to mind his own business, aren't you Bill?" Tracy asked him.

Bill looked at her a moment. "Yes, I would say that describes me."

"So you couldn't tell me if, during your years working for the Shanes, you ever knew anyone who might want to hurt Mr. Shane—a fired employee, for example."

Bill turned away from her while he finished his cup of coffee. As he made his way back to the kitchen for a refill he said, "No, no one like that. Mr. Shane was a good man. He didn't go around making enemies, unless you count all these healthy eating groups popping up all over the place." Bill returned to the table with a full cup.

Tracy knew it couldn't be an outsider because someone like that wouldn't know their way around the property much less know where to find the gun. There wouldn't have been time to go searching for it assuming they even knew it existed. But she didn't make these thoughts public. "Bill, going back for a moment to the night of the phone call, who else was there that probably overheard the call?"

He thought a minute and said, "Crystal and Doug were there, and Brian, and some of the day staff that was finishing up. I think that was it."

Tracy made some more notes. "Thank you," she said to him. She didn't have any more specific inquiries to make at this point, so it was now time for what Tracy called the "fishing net" questions.

"Is there anything else you can think of regarding that night, Bill? Or anything at all that happened during the week between when the meeting was set up with that unusual phone call and the murder—anything strange?"

Bill Ryder pondered the question; took a few more sips from his mug; and then jerked his head up. "There is something, but I don't see how it could matter."

"Please tell me, Bill," Tracy said excitedly.

"We seem to have a kleptomaniac at the estate."

"What?"

"Well some things have gone missing. I had a little flashlight I normally kept on my belt vanish. And Brian lost his watch. Doug had a tie clip Crystal gave him stolen. And I think Crystal lost a bracelet."

Tracy suddenly had knots in her stomach. How come no one else had thought to mention this? She would confirm Ryder's story of course but she had no doubts about it being the truth. "Do you know if any keys went missing?"

"Not that I've heard."

"So the items haven't been found and no one's been accused?" she asked.

"No to both questions. It's probably one of the day staff; lots of folks always mulling about—kitchen people, gardeners, housekeeping. It could be anybody."

"And these thefts all happened between the two Fridays?" she asked just to confirm.

"Yeah. My light went missing Saturday. I think Doug told me his tie clasp disappeared Monday. Then Crystal lost her bracelet on Tuesday, and Brian lost his watch on Wednesday. I haven't heard of anything else. But you should verify all of that because I could be mixed up about the whos and whens."

Tracy closed her notebook and said, "I'll do that. Bill, thank you *so* much. Thanks for everything."

Bill rose and escorted her to the door, where they shook hands. He opened his door for her and as she started to leave, he looked back at the mug sitting on the dining room table. "You know, I just can't imagine it." Tracy turned mid-exit to look at him. He was still looking at the mug. "I mean, shooting your own father. I hope I never hurt my sons so they would want to do that to me." He then turned back to look at Tracy.

"If it makes you feel any better, Bill, Brian did *not* kill his father. And I think you've put me one step closer to proving it." And with that Tracy left Bill Ryder to finish his cup of coffee and miss his children.

With Tracy interviewing Bill Ryder, Neal started making phone calls to Kurt Barton's fellow professionals listed in the program Siena had given him. The schedule helpfully listed each presenter's law firm so Neal was easily able to obtain phone numbers to go with the names. There were three other people listed as making remarks that evening: Carla Hardy, Wilson Crane, and Elizabeth Munsen, all partners in some of Maryland's most respected law firms. If Barton was going to stay around and speak with anyone, these three would be the most likely. Neal dialed the first number.

" Aspache, Hardy, Drake, and Summers," the voice said.

"Good morning, may I speak with Carla Hardy please?"

"Let me connect you with her secretary."

"Thanks," Neal told the helpful young lady. There was a brief wait and then a new voice.

"Carla Hardy's office."

"Good morning, may I speak with Carla Hardy, please?"

"She's not in at the moment. May I take a message, or would you like to leave a message in her voice mail?"

"Voice mail would be fine," Neal answered. He listened to Carla's greeting and then said, "Hello, my name is Neal Bennett, an attorney representing Brian Shane in the murder of his father. I'd like very much to speak with respect to last Friday evening's dinner as it relates to Kurt Barton, the Shane attorney." Neal then left his phone numbers, hoping for a return call before the July bar exam. The next two calls went exactly the same way. Neither Wilson Crane nor Elizabeth Munsen was in their respective offices, so Neal opted for voice messages in each case. He figured the odds were in his favor that at least one person would call him back.

Next he moved ahead with looking into Kurt Barton and Stewart Shane's personal financial relationship. A quick call to the Shane family accounting firm and Neal was able to obtain information regarding some of Barton's financial arrangements with Stewart Shane and his company, as well as some related philanthropic endeavors. Looking into Barton himself, Neal was having no luck finding anything they could use to their advantage: no local news stories indicating problems with the firm, no potential scandals hinted at in the business journals, no messy personal stories to show Barton as anything other than an upstanding citizen. In fact his firm was involved in rehabilitating homes in troubled sections of the city, and he was on the board of directors of several charities. His public persona was positively saintly.

What about Barton's more specific relations with Stewart Shane's company itself? Tracy hadn't turned up anything on the personal side when she talked to Brian. But Neal could check things out with respect to the business. But first he would have to get permission before asking his questions. He looked up the Shane home phone number Tracy had entered into the firm database and dialed.

"Hello," a female voice answered.

"Hello. Who am I speaking with please?" Neal asked.

A brief pause, and then she said, "Crystal Shane."

"Hi, Crystal. My name is Neal Bennett. I work for Tracy."

"Oh, hi," she said, her mood now clearly improved. "Tracy's not here."

"Yes, I know. I actually need *your* help."

"Really? What can I do to help?"

"I want to talk to some people at your company, basically nose around to be blunt about it. And I also wanted to talk to some people in the accounting department, who might have access to stuff like billing history, outstanding invoices; things like that."

"Oh," was all she said.

"Can you call someone over there like the COO, Controller, or anyone else you can think of that could clear me to ask my questions?"

She thought a moment and said, "Hold on. I'll call Steven Grossman, our COO. Stay on the line. I'm going to transfer you to another phone in the house, and then conference you in to my call with Steven."

"Thanks!" Neal said but he wasn't sure she heard him. Tracy had told him how upset Crystal had been, but the Crystal he was talking to seemed to be a different person. Suddenly he heard a phone ringing and Crystal ask, "You still there Neal?"

"Yes."

Another ring and then, "Hello; Mr. Grossman's office."

"Wendy, this is Crystal. I need to speak to Steven ASAP."

"Oh, hi Crystal. I'll find him for you right away."

Crystal wasn't taking prisoners, Neal thought. A few more moments passed. "This is Steve Grossman."

"Steve, its Crystal."

"Crystal how are…"

"There's someone with us on the call. His name is Neal Bennett."

She paused long enough to let Grossman say, "Hello, Neal."

"Hello Steve."

Then Crystal continued. "Steve: Neal has some questions to ask. He works for the attorney who is representing Brian. I want you to answer his questions, and make sure anyone else Neal wants to talk to knows to cooperate. Of course this is all privileged communication so you don't have to worry that anything you tell him will be posted all over the internet."

"Sure Crystal."

"Thanks Steve. I'm going to hang up now and let you and Neal start."

"Thanks and goodbye, Crystal," Neal said. But she was already gone.

Steve Grossman asked, "How can I help you Neal?"

"Just some general things. Was Mr. Shane having any problems with the company that you know about?"

"No. As you probably already know he wasn't as involved as he used to be. But things here are fine. Business is good in spite of the last few years."

Neal continued. "Specifically, do you know if the company's relationship with Kurt Barton and his law firm was still strong? Was Shane, for example, looking for new representation?"

Grossman was silent a few moments. "Not that I am aware of. Barton's been our attorney as long as I've been here. I think I would have heard if there was a problem. Certainly Stewart would have told me if something was wrong."

"Okay, thanks Steve. Could you connect me with someone in accounting, probably the accounts payable clerk would be best."

"Let me check my directory and then I'll connect you. I'm going to put you on hold while I talk to the AP person to let them know that it's okay to talk to you. It's been nice speaking with you. Goodbye."

"Thanks Steve." Neal waited a few minutes listening to the Shane SnackFoods Company jingles— *"Don't be ashamed to enjoy anything Shane — Shane, the snack food people!"* —that played while he was on hold.

"Rhonda Vasquez, accounting."

Neal introduced himself. "Rhonda, could you please pull the Barton, Lyons, and Rank invoice folder and pull up their payable ledger? I'm just checking to see if there are any large unpaid bills outstanding."

"I can grab the invoice folder and have someone print me the ledger while I'm doing that."

"That would be great Rhonda. Thank you." She put him on hold. The wait wasn't long.

"There are no outstanding payables to Barton, Lyons, and Rank," she told him. "I have the invoice file with me. What specifically do you need to know?"

"Could you look through the bills and tell me if there are any notes on them, the kind that indicate a problem with the work, or maybe a large reduction of charges, anything like that?"

"Let me see." He could hear her paging through the file. "Uh-oh, looks like we have a misfile," she suddenly said out loud.

"What was that?" Neal perked up.

"Somebody put a bill from the other law firm we use in this file by mistake."

"Other law firm?"

"Yes. Late last year we started using a different law firm to do some of our work," Rhonda told him.

Chapter 8

What to do next, Tracy wondered. See if Neal had found out anything regarding Barton? Go back to the Shane estate and talk to Brian, Crystal and Doug about the missing trinkets? Try to get Ernie's home address, or at least his phone number, from Judds? Stop for lunch lest her mother get wind of Tracy skipping meals as she is wont to do when working a high-pressure case (was there another kind)? Well, she could call Neal regarding Barton on her mobile phone. And she suddenly felt she needed to talk to Ernie face-to-face. Lunch? If she went to Brian's she could make a quick sandwich and follow up on Bill's revelation. Suddenly the decision was a no-brainer.

First thing, call Brian from the car and let him know she was on her way—and that she expected to be fed. And secondly; call her office to speak with Neal. He was there.

"How did the Ryder interview go?" he asked her as soon as he picked up her call.

"Supreme—might have something. But first, talk to me about Barton."

"Well, as far as his alibi goes, I left messages with the other presenters at the dinner. None of them have returned my call yet. As for brass tacks, Barton's management of the Shane estate will bring his firm millions over the next several years," he started. "There are several charitable organizations connected with Shane—one that fights childhood obesity, no less—that generate legal fees for Barton's firm, things like drafting grant proposals, and attending to general legal matters; big retainers. Barton also represents some of the executives with the Shane SnackFoods Corporation, so he's got lots of income coming in thanks to Stewart Shane."

"That's all great stuff Neal. Thanks; but how about any evidence of contention between Barton and Stewart? Something that could be construed as a motive?" she asked a little impatiently.

"Well, I was coming to that. I had a talk with someone in the accounts payable department at the Shane corporate office. Just to let you know: I first had to call Crystal to authorize me to talk to people over there. Anyway, I asked them to check the payment history on the Barton invoices, just to see if there happened to be some big unpaid bills out there, or any major disputes."

"And were there?" Tracy asked.

"No, but, the company has started using another legal firm in addition to Barton's. And when I did some follow up, turns out that in general their charges were lower than Barton's for comparative services. Now there's nothing official as far as I could find on Shane switching attorneys. And it's not unusual for a firm to see what's out there now and again, especially in this time of shrinking profit margins. Remember they did the same thing with their advertising agency. But we're talking a lot of money here that Barton's firm may have been about to lose if the company was going to do a full switch."

Tracy felt her heart beating faster — so much so that she didn't respond immediately to Neal's 'but.' "Tracy, you still there?" he finally asked.

"Present in body if not in mind — and the chauffeur, Bernard Cubbins?"

"He's been working for Barton for eight years. He drops Barton at his office in the morning, gathers him when summoned in the evening. Whether he has any free time during the day depends on Barton's schedule. Cubbins actually has a cottage on Barton's own estate."

"That sounds like quite a relationship they have."

"Tracy, the thing is: Barton doesn't drive. He doesn't have a license. I thought when I couldn't track it down that I was just doing something wrong but it turns out he let the license expire more than 20 years ago."

"Did you find out why?" Tracy asked.

"Not yet, but I'm still looking."

"Well, I definitely have to make time to talk to Bernard Cubbins," Tracy said. "No question about that now. Great work Neal. You get Sunday off."

"You are *too* good to me, Tracy. I am not worthy to…"

She cut him off. "See you later silly head. I'm pulling up to the gates now." She clicked off. The gates opened, and as she continued on she wondered if losing an income stream would really be a motive for Barton. Surely his firm didn't depend on just one client. But this client was a friend. Would Barton look at this as some kind of betrayal? She could see how someone like Barton might be greatly offended if he thought he was being betrayed. But Shane himself probably wasn't the one who sought out the other firm, most likely it was someone just trying to save the company some money. But would Barton see it that way? Maybe Crystal could tell her. More questions with no certain answers. Finally reaching the main house, she parked in the roundabout, jumped out, and ran to the front. Brian was there to greet her. Without even thinking she gave him a big hug.

"Are you okay?" Brian asked her, grinning.

"Supreme. Where's my food?"

He laughed. "This way." And he escorted her to her chow with his arm around her shoulder.

After finishing her sandwich—chicken salad on wheat with lettuce, dill spear on the side—in record time, she asked Brian to confirm the thefts. "That's right Tracy. Things have been disappearing. I mean, at first we all thought we just lost the stuff. But when Crystal's bracelet went missing after the light and clasp, well, we wondered."

"Was the bracelet valuable?"

"No, not really," he said quickly, but then thought better of it. "Well, maybe I shouldn't answer for Crystal. You should ask her that yourself."

Tracy nodded and said, "And I can ask Doug about the tie clasp too. How about your watch, you lost that Wednesday?"

"I think that's right," he answered. "But it was just a watch Tracy, nothing special. I'll get a new one eventually."

Tracy nodded again. "I need to talk to Crystal. Can you find her for me, *pleeeease*?"

Brian couldn't stand it anymore. He moved in and kissed her. She didn't push him away immediately, but she broke their embrace sooner than he would have liked. "Brian…" was all she could say. She didn't sound angry. He wasn't sure what she was really feeling.

"I'm sorry, Tracy," he said, though he really wasn't. "I guess I've wanted to do that since Friday. You and me in this kitchen, you there with that smile, and asking for something like the way you used to…I couldn't help myself."

"It's okay Brian; really." She backed away from him a little. "But I need to talk to Crystal now."

"Of course," he said quietly. "We both got back from making some funeral arrangements this morning, so she may be a little raw."

"I understand. I don't think what I have to ask will upset her. If she can't see me now I'll just talk to her later."

Brian led Tracy to the garden where Crystal was watering some of the flowers. There had been no additional rainfall since Friday night so Tracy wasn't surprised to find her here with hose in hand. She remembered how Crystal loved her garden. Doug Stanz was there helping, adorned in a brown, weather-proof jacket that would occasionally absorb some of the water from Crystal's poorly aimed hose. He laughed at the latest attack, at which point he saw Tracy and Brian approach, and informed Crystal. She seemed to be smiling as she turned off the nozzle.

"I'd give you a hug, Tracy, but I'd get you all muddy," Crystal told her, giggling.

Tracy smiled at her, and then put her hand on Crystal's arm. "I heard it was a rough morning for you, Crys. Are you okay to answer some questions?"

Crystal smiled back. "Sure, Tracy. It's fine. In fact I had to help someone out from your office today right after I got back from…"

Tracy interrupted so Crystal didn't have to finish her sentence. "Neal is his name. Yes: he told me he talked to you."

Doug broke some of the tension by pulling out a pack of gum and offering a piece to everyone. Crystal accepted; Brian and Tracy declined. Crystal leaned into her wet fiancé. "See how much this man loves me?" she asked Tracy.

"Uh, what do you mean?"

"I guess she's referring to the gum," Doug said. "I quit smoking a couple of weeks ago, and, well, started the gum to help me through it."

She instinctively looked at Brian. Even though Crystal and Doug certainly meant no dig at Brian, Tracy couldn't ignore the parallel. Neither could Brian. When Brian chewed gum it was to try and cover up his drinker's breath. And *he* couldn't give up the booze for the woman *he* supposedly *loved*. Brian turned away when their eyes met. But she wasn't going to dwell on it. They had been through this already. She turned her attention back to Crystal. "I wanted to ask you about the bracelet that you lost last week."

"Stolen, more likely," Doug said sounding agitated.

Crystal looked at him and then at Tracy. "I think I lost it last, what, Tuesday, Doug?"

"Sounds right," Doug answered.

"How did you notice it was missing, Crys?"

"I went to put it on Tuesday morning and it wasn't where I remembered leaving it. I was sure I put it on my dresser Monday night at some point."

"Did you go to put it on first thing Tuesday?" Tracy asked.

"No. I got up, had breakfast, showered, and then went to dress."

"So you don't know if the bracelet was still there first thing in the morning."

"No. Sorry. Is it important?"

"Well, anything unusual that happens during a period surrounding a crime is important to my mind," Tracy answered and then turned to Doug. "What's your tale of woe, Doug?"

"My tie clasp vanished," he answered. "It was a gift from Crystal, so I'm pretty ticked."

"When did the filching take place?"

"Last Monday. I showed up for dinner and took off my tie—you know: to avoid getting food all over it while eating. I had hung the tie up with the clasp attached to it on a coat hanger which I then hung up in the hall closet, along with my jacket. When I went back to put it on before starting my shift, the clasp was gone."

Crystal continued. "We checked the closet floor, under the dining room table—everywhere Doug had been since he arrived that night—nothing."

Doug nodded and then asked, "What does all this have to do with the murder? You think Stewart found out who the thief was and the thief shot him?"

"Doesn't sound likely, does it?" Tracy answered him. She looked at the three, who were looking at her, and continued. "When was Bill Ryder's flashlight taken?"

"Sometime Saturday," Doug answered. "He went to click it to his belt for his Saturday stint and couldn't find it. He kept it in his booth."

"Okay, that all checks out." At this point Tracy realized she hadn't seen the back security booth. "Could he have just dropped it, maybe? All the other items have some kind of value, as opposed to a mini-flashlight you can get anywhere."

"I'm sure he checked," Doug answered.

"Can I see the booth just to satisfy my curiosity?" Tracy asked.

"I'll have to unlock it for you," Doug said while reaching into his pants pocket for the keys. "We didn't used to lock the back booth during the day. It's only used during the night hours and there really isn't anything of value in there. But after my tie clasp went missing, I told Bill we should lock up anything we can." Doug motioned toward the direction of the booth, a small set of keys now in his hand. "Follow me."

All four of them moved toward the booth, which Doug unlocked. Tracy quickly scanned the floor to see if the flashlight was perhaps hiding. She didn't notice anything unusual. She saw the TV, radio, and puzzle books Ryder had mentioned. There was a single walkie-talkie there, whose twin she had seen the guard at the gate wearing the times she was personally greeted upon her arrival. Pointing to the two-way radio she asked, "You called Bill on this thing last Friday, right? To let him know Barton was on his way up."

"Yes."

"Do you know where he was on the grounds when he got your call?"

"No. I just let him know to meet Barton at the front door to let him in. Bill confirmed he was on his way and that was it."

"Okay. Thanks Doug." Tracy took one more look around.

"It's not a problem Tracy."

"I guess you can lock this place again," Tracy said, exiting the booth. Doug locked up the booth, shoved the keys in his jacket, and moved toward Crystal. They looked at each other, and then at Tracy.

"Do you need anything else from us Tracy?" Crystal asked her.

Tracy thought about it. "Crys: Neal found out that the company was using a new law firm? Is that true?"

Crystal thought a bit. "Well, I wouldn't go that far. One of our internal accountants who prepared the budgets thought we might be able to reduce legal costs. So we tried this other firm a few times. No big deal."

"What did Barton think about that?"

"Don't know and don't care," Crystal said firmly.

Yowza. Tracy switched gears. "Did you and Doug hear your father's call setting up Friday's meeting?"

They looked at each other again, confused. "What are you talking about?" Crystal asked her.

"When your father called Barton to arrange the Friday night meeting, did you hear him? Apparently your father was shouting on the phone. It would have been the Friday before last."

"Oh Tracy, Dad frequently shouts when he's on the phone. I really don't pay any attention to it anymore." Crystal stopped suddenly, realizing she had used the present tense regarding her father. She turned away from Tracy.

"Never mind then Crys. It's not important." Tracy gently touched Crystal's back. Crystal turned to face her friend.

"Oh Tracy..." Crystal started to say and then she found herself crying again. Tracy hugged her.

"I'm sorry Crys. I didn't mean to upset you." Tracy continued to hug Crystal until the latter pulled away. She had been putting up a brave front for everyone, but the accumulation of the day's events ultimately proved too much for her. She excused herself and headed for the house.

"She'll be okay, Tracy," Doug told her. "She hasn't been getting any sleep. You understand. Please don't blame yourself. Can I help you with anything else?"

"No, Doug. Thanks for showing me the back. Why don't you go and check on Crystal?" And without another word Doug moved hurriedly toward the home.

Tracy turned back to face the booth, and took a couple of steps forward. Then she turned around. She couldn't see the garage from the booth. Something was nagging at her—an idea was beginning to take shape in her mind. But it left almost as soon as it appeared. She made a fist with her right hand and gave her forehead a couple of gentle whacks. "Think you idiot, think."

"Tracy?" Brian prodded, interrupting her train of thought.

"Oh—sorry Brian..." She forgot he was still there. "...was living on planet Tracy for a moment. I just want to walk the path from the booth to the garage."

"Sure Tracy."

She took the most direct route she could to the garage, and then turned to look back where she'd just been. Nope, you can't see the booth from the garage either. Finally she told Brian, "We can go back to the house now." And without another word Tracy started marching toward the main home. Brian just looked on for a moment, and then followed Tracy's example.

Upon his return Brian found Doug getting Crystal a glass of water. When Brian approached him, Doug leaned over to him and whispered, "I think your girlfriend may be on to something." It had been a long time since someone had referred to Tracy that way in relation to him. But he dare not push his luck right now to test that implication. But he suddenly felt the best he had since the day she ended it. And he knew with her on his side, he hadn't a thing to worry about.

The Shane kitchen had intruders—at least as far as Tracy was concerned. The people scurrying about were no doubt charged with the preparation of dinner. But they had moved the box of Berger Cookies that Tracy swore was on the table next to the deli tray when she left the room earlier. After such a taxing Q & A she felt entitled to sugar. Now the box was nowhere to be found. Had the kleptomaniac struck again?

Never mind that though, she'd be big about it and forgo what was rightfully hers. She proceeded to the study where she had left her case and notes. With lightning speed she transferred her mental notes from the afternoon's interviews to her notepad. She had every confidence Rebecca would be able to translate her code. Eventually Brian joined her, but let her finish her writing before saying anything. He remembered the college days when Tracy would pour her brain out onto a page with frenzied fingers. You didn't interrupt that, lest you risk limping for a few days.

Realizing he was there, Tracy stood up and put the notes back into her bag. She looked at him looking at her as she walked toward the door.

"You're not leaving, yet?" he asked. "You might as well stay and have dinner with us. Doug has the night off so he'll be hanging around, and I don't really want to be a third wheel."

"Brian, I need to sally forth. I have a feeling I'm onto something. Little details I've come across the last few days are starting to form a picture—a picture, thankfully, you're not in."

He knew what she was trying to say, but he didn't think another couple of hours together would compromise her art. "Stay for dinner Tracy, and then I'll let you go; promise."

"Let me check in with Beck and Neal," she relented. "Then we'll see."

"I'll leave you to your calls, then," Brian said, a big smile on his face. Was it her imagination, or had Brian really not had a drink since Friday night?

"What's the report from the home front, Beck?" Tracy asked.

"All clear and dry," Rebecca assured her.

Tracy got the Waters reference. "Supreme."

"We got Brian's signed engagement letter back."

"Is he a great client or what? Can I talk to Neal please?"

"You bet. Are you coming back to the office?"

"I've been bribed with food and I am owed cookies; so probably not."

Rebecca chuckled. "Goodnight then." She transferred Tracy to Neal's extension.

"Offices of Neal Bennett, Attorney At Law," the voice on the other end said.

Tracy laughed. "When was I overthrown?"

"Hey: when the queen is absent from her throne long enough *anything* can happen. Seriously though: where have you been?"

"I'm on the trail of a notorious thief…and missing cookies, the two of which may or may not be connected."

"What? Oh, forget it, I don't want to know."

"Is everything under control? Any bombshells or even wet noodles?"

"You've got food on the brain, girl. No, we're OK over here. Still no call backs from those dinner guests, though. I may just call them back first thing tomorrow." He paused briefly and then added, "By the way, will *you* be gracing us with your presence tomorrow?"

"Sound those trumpets 'cause I'll be in tomorrow first thing. Neal, remind me of what time Ernie comes on duty tomorrow."

He checked his notes. "Four in the evening."

"Okay, please put on my schedule 'Judds at 4:00 p.m.' for tomorrow."

"Done."

"Thanks, boss," Tracy teased.

"Huh? Oh…"

"And I need to talk to Cubbins tomorrow too. Do you have any phone numbers for him?"

"Believe it or not he's listed," Neal told her.

"Okay — great. Just give me his number now and then I'll call him at some point to see if he's free to meet. Thanks as always, Neal."

"I live to serve," he responded before giving her the number, which she added to her notes. And with that the two said their goodbyes and hung up. Yes, she would stay for dinner. She had missed Crystal's company — and Brian's too of course. Crystal could use an old girlfriend right now to go along with the new boyfriend. Tracy wanted to be done with the questions for now. Enjoy a meal with friends and relax. She'd leave by 8:00 and still have a couple of hours to review the day's notes if she wanted to, and merge them with all the previously accumulated information. It had been a very rough, emotional five days, so a break — even a couple of hours — was a welcome relief.

Doug, Crystal, Brian, and Tracy sat themselves at the dining table while the wait staff brought them a nonstop parade of deliciousness including creamy potato soup, a garden salad, pork chops with asparagus au gratin on the side, and a way-too-small dish of vanilla ice cream. Pitchers of water and sweetened tea were passed about with regularity. The women shared stories that seemed to center around the men's fumbling attempts at romance. Doug and Brian shot back with tales of their women's strange dieting habits after experiencing how-will-I-ever-fit-into-this-whatever panic. Tracy threw in some legal tales that didn't violate any kind of ethics, and Crystal shared her account of the early days after assuming position of CEO: "If one other person had called me 'Crissy dear' I'd have fired the whole lot them." Crystal's audience laughed out loud. Watching Crystal fired up was probably the highlight of the evening. For the next couple of hours their worries seemed to leave them. Tracy was throughly enjoying herself.

When Doug left the table to answer the call of nature, Crystal asked Tracy, "So what do think of Doug?"

Tracy answered, "He seems nice. He's certainly cute. So do you guys work out together or what?"

Crystal giggled. "Tracy!"

"Hey, I meant at the gym or something. Gee whiz."

"Oh," Crystal said still laughing. "No, Doug isn't exactly a fan of exercise."

"What? No moonlit jogs together? No romantic bike rides by the harbor?"

"He lives in an apartment dear. He doesn't even own a bike. And as skinny as he is, if we were to jog I'm afraid he'd sweat himself away."

Tracy laughed. "Well, that will all change once he moves in here and has home cooked meals three times a day."

"Yeah, I guess," Crystal said. "Still, I'm lucky to have him during this time, like Brian's lucky to have you."

Tracy managed a smile but Crystal seemed to be jumping to conclusions. Brian said nothing. Tracy asked, "Crys, that bracelet you're missing, did Doug give that to you?"

"Oh, no, Tracy. I'm not sure where I got that." Then Crystal said, "I'm sorry we didn't think to mention those thefts earlier. There hadn't been any since last Wednesday so I just put them out of my mind."

"No worries, Crys. Bill filled me in. It's all good."

"Good ole' brother Bill," Crystal said pouring herself some tea. "I invited him tonight but he decided to pass. I guess he just wasn't up to it."

Tracy, who was herself drinking from her glass of tea, put it down and asked, "Why did you call him 'Brother Bill'?"

Crystal looked at her. "Oh, well you wouldn't know this of course, but I was married to Bill's younger brother for a while."

Tracy just stared at her. All she could think to ask was, "What?"

"Yeah, Bill used to be my brother-in-law. My Dad liked Bill, his brother Kevin not so much."

Tracy continued to look at Crystal, who wasn't picking up on Tracy's why-doesn't-somebody-tell-me-these-things vibe. "Details, girl!" Tracy almost shouted.

At this point Doug returned and saw the look on Brian's face. He just sat down next to Crystal without saying a word. Crystal said, "Bill came to work as a guard all those years ago. He said he had a younger brother who was good at landscaping. So Dad hired Kevin too. You know me and that garden, so I saw Kevin a lot, and then a lot of Kevin. Eventually Kevin and I started *formally* dating. Dad got mad, threatened to fire Kevin, so Kevin and I eloped."

Tracy waited for Crystal to continue, and when too much time had passed for her liking Tracy asked, "*AND?*"

Crystal looked at Brian and then at Tracy. "We were only together a few months. We had this prolonged honeymoon at a place near the ocean. Kevin kept hinting I should ask Dad for money and I kept telling him no way and, then, well, he told me he didn't want to be married to me anymore."

"What a jerk," Tracy said, genuinely angry. Crystal was a pretty girl with a head on her shoulders. But she had been sheltered growing up, and was far too trusting at times—a sitting target for the Kevins of the world. At least: she used to be; but not anymore, probably.

"Believe me Tracy: I'm over it," she assured her while starting to rub Doug's back.

"And your Dad had no problem letting Bill stay on?" Tracy asked.

"Why should he have? Bill was a good worker with solid references, and he had a family to take care of. Dad judged people individually. Dad and Bill became rather close because of all those dinners, talking about the things they had in common. Besides, Dad wasn't about to blame Bill for Kevin being such a creep."

Tracy found herself laughing at that. Only Crystal would choose such a quaint word as 'creep' when there were so many more colorful words around that would have been far more appropriate and descriptive. "Where's the creep now?" Tracy asked.

"Oh I don't know and I sure as heck don't care, do I Brian?"

Brian gave a "who-me?" expression, which had both Tracy and Crystal laughing heartily. Doug just grinned, not sure if he liked hearing about Crystal's ancient history. But the unexpected revelation stuck in Tracy's craw.

She should have known about this already. In hindsight, she should have allowed Neal to check Crystal's background. Hopefully that was the only error in judgment she had made thus far.

After dinner, Doug and Crystal said goodnight. Crystal was going to her office at the Shane SnackFoods corporate headquarters for a brief time tomorrow to catch up on things and wanted to turn in early, so the lovers wanted to have some alone time together. They smiled at Tracy and Brian as they left the dining room hand in hand. The two remaining diners looked at each other, not speaking for what felt like hours. Tracy broke the stare and looked around the room. "Where are my cookies?" she asked finally.

In an exceedingly poor attempt at a French accent, Brain said, "If zee lady wanz zee cookeez, zee lady shall have zee cookeez." Brian left the table and returned with the formerly missing Bergers — the thief had spared them after all. Brian also had a gallon of milk and two glasses.

After their second dessert the two went into the small living room and sat next to each other. Close. Brian put his arm around her. She took his other hand and put her head on his shoulder. "What are we going to do about us?" she asked him.

The question surprised him. He didn't have an answer. "So there is an 'us' then?" He asked her finally.

"The old answering a question with a question trick, huh?" she asked.

"Hey, you just did the same thing," Brian pointed out.

"Did I?"

"Hey, you did it again!" And he could feel her gently laughing. But the joke was on him. She quickly kissed him on the cheek and stood up. She moved toward the chair where her briefcase was now resting. She was clearly calling it a night. "Tracy you can't leave now."

"You promised me Brian I could leave after dinner," she reminded him.

She had him, so he threw up his arms in defeat and came over to hug her. After the embrace, Brian walked her to her car, when she stopped suddenly. "Brian, can I see the inside of the garage where you are parked again?"

"Sure Tracy. Wanna take another look at the wheels huh?"

"Yeah," she answered with enthusiasm.

Soon Brian was opening the garage's side entrance door located on the right, and turned on the inside light. There were three cars housed inside —

Stewart Shane's and those belonging to his children, including Brian's vintage auto. She moved to the back of the garage and looked through the centered window which gave a view of the backyard. "Could you turn out the light a moment?" she asked.

There was nothing suggestive about the way she asked, so Brian obliged without further comment. No sooner had he turned the light off then she gave him the OK to turn it back on. "What is it Tracy?" he asked.

"Not sure it's anything," she replied.

"You didn't even look at the car," he said, almost hurt. "What's going on?"

She smiled and moved past him. "Sorry Brian I really need to go." She continued quickly to her car but Brian caught up as she was ready to shut her door.

"Goodnight, Tracy," he said, and then he leaned in and kissed her.

When she was released, she said, "I'll call you tomorrow." He moved out of her door's pathway as she shut it, and then she pulled away to start her descent down the driveway. He stared off in her direction, and continued looking even as the taillights disappeared into the darkness. "I love you," he said, the words following the same path as the vanishing auto.

At her condo unit Tracy sat on her bed in her pajamas, crossed legged with her bare feet tucked under her knees, her notes spread out atop the comforter. It was almost 10 and she was tired, but she wanted to review the last three days work. The bombshell about Kevin Ryder would have to be looked into. Now she understood why Bill Ryder acted the way he did when she brought up past employees. Why hadn't he told her? She thought their rapport had been solid. In matters of family, though, things can get sticky. Tracy trusted that Neal could at least locate Kevin's whereabouts easily enough. She could call Neal now and ask him to use his home computer to start the search. But she didn't want to do that, not when she was reasonably sure Bill Ryder had nothing to do with the murder — unless of course he was keeping additional secrets. Someone had taken a shot at Crystal: an old lover maybe? But it was Stewart Shane who was murdered not Crystal. Tracy let out a grunt.

Still, she believed somewhere in her notes was the answer. She could feel it. But the answer wasn't coming. What question wasn't she asking? She had decided she would talk to the Barton limo driver herself to see if his story had changed since Friday. Maybe she could even get him to allow her an inside look into the limo. Barton would certainly not approve that if she went through him—she was sure of that. But Tracy could try to charm Cubbins into letting her sneak a peek. She hadn't been in a limo since her high school senior prom. Neal would hopefully hear back tomorrow from the attorneys at Barton's dinner, and see if his story checked out. Okay—revisit Barton as a suspect after tomorrow's answers, if they were received.

She didn't think talking to any more Shane SnackFood employees would do any good because the killer had to know where to find the gun. That meant it had to be someone close to the family and familiar with the household. Tanner had confirmed the alibis of the key employees. Were any of the Shane day staff potential suspects? Winnie had said Shane fought with lots of people but there wasn't any long standing animosity. So what would their motive be? According to Brian and Crystal, there were no rumblings suggesting unrest among the staff. Besides, they were all gone before Brian left. If someone had stayed behind their car would have been noticed in the staff parking area located a little further left of the family garage. Two employees in on it together who carpooled, and one stayed behind to commit the crime, his or her alibi supplied by the other? Okay; possible. Then how did the killer get out? Now we're back to that problem. Better wait for Neal's background reports on them before wasting anymore brain cells on the help. This eliminating the impossible stuff was tiring.

It was getting late and Tracy's brain was insisting on getting its beauty rest. She would try to talk to Cubbins in the morning, and then, before meeting with Ernie, she'd have most of the afternoon to bounce theories around with Neal, who might have some thoughts she hadn't considered. She wasn't sure exactly why but she thought a chat with an observant barkeep might prove useful. Bartenders observe behavior as part of their job—making sure they cut people off if they need to, knowing when to call for the bouncer. Ernie may have picked up on something and not consciously realized it. Maybe she would ask the right question that somehow answered all the others. Or was she just flattering herself? She wasn't a *real* detective after all. She didn't have the experience. Of course a fresh perspective can sometimes be just what a case needs.

She finally gathered all of her notes together, and placed them on her nightstand next to her alarm clock radio—almost 11 now. She set her buzzer for 6:30 a.m. and thought about the fact Bill Ryder would probably be getting home when she was getting up. She turned out the light next to her and stared at the red glowing numbers counting down the remaining hours of the day. She was drifting off…Suddenly she shot back up. What was it—did she just hear a noise? Was it something about the alarm clock? She wasn't sure. The notes sitting there on the table…something about that maybe; but what, she wondered. She lay back down. She looked at the clock again. She closed her eyes. Perhaps the solution would come to her in a dream. She sailed off to sleep, hoping that tomorrow would bring those elusive answers.

Fade in...

"Tracy?" the voice on the phone asked.
"Yes."
"It's Uncle Elias."
"Oh, hi. How are you?"
"Are you going to be at your dorm the rest of the night?"
Suddenly Brian's voice called out. "Come on Tracy we need to go."
"Just a minute!" she responded. Then she returned her attentions to her caller. "I'm going out in the next couple of minutes. What's up?"
There was silence on the other end. And it was loud. She started shaking. "Uncle El: what's wrong?"
"I want to send a car over to pick you up."
"Tracy, we gotta go! Come on already."
"Why? What's going on?"
More silence. "Tracy, I don't want to do this over the phone."
Tracy leaned toward the table that held the phone, and placed her hand on the edge for support. "You tell me what's going on. You tell me NOW!"
There was more silence, and then, "Tracy: your father. He…he's been shot."
"Oh dear God no!" She started crying. "Is he OK? He's okay, right?"
More loud quiet. "He's dead Tracy."
She started screaming, "No! No! No! NO!"
"Tracy, I'm sorry." Tanner paused, trying not to follow Tracy's example, and then quietly continued. "Look: someone is on their way to get you. Your mother's inconsolable. I think the two of you really need to be together now."
She slammed the phone down, and fell to her knees. Her body was convulsing as the tears poured out.

"Jesus Tracy can't you tell whoever it is you have to-" Brian stopped dead in his tracks as he came from around the corner. Tracy was on the floor, legs bent at the knees, her arms and chest resting on her legs, her hands covering her face. "Oh my God Tracy, what's wrong?" He went over to her and lifted her so that she was now leaning against him. He saw her red face. She was sobbing uncontrollably so Brian wrapped his arms around her to steady her. The two started rocking together. "Tracy what is it? You're really scaring me. You have to tell me what's wrong."

There were more sobs but she finally was able to speak. "Somebody killed my dad."

Brian felt the blood rush to his head. He looked at her, horrified. "Oh Tracy; oh my poor Tracy." And he started crying too. Not like him really, but he had had a few drinks before stopping to pick her up so his inhibitions were lowered. After about 10 minutes there was a knock on the door.

"Hello?" an unfamiliar voice called out.

"Back here," Brian answered. A uniformed officer, hat in hand, came around the corner. Brian looked up but did not let Tracy go.

"Awe, man," the escort said upon seeing the two on the floor. "This is Peter Brubaker's daughter?"

"Yeah."

The officer waited a few moments. "Can you help me take her to the car? I'm supposed to bring her home."

"Sure," Brian whispered. The officer—Carstairs—moved toward her and the two helped Tracy get to her feet. Tracy leaned on Brian and he walked her to the awaiting vehicle. Once there Brian eased her into the back seat. He tried to pull away.

"Brian, where are you going?" she asked, sounding alarmed. "He can ride with me, can't he?" she asked Carstairs.

"Yes ma'am, he can."

"Tracy," Brian started, "I have to go tell the guys what happened and why we have to cancel out. And I should let Crystal know."

"Can't you do all this from the phone at my house?" she asked between sobs.

"Tracy: I think I should tell people about something like this face-to-face. I also want to grab some extra clothes so I can stay with you at your house for the next few days. I'll be as fast as I can and meet you at your house. I remember how to get there."

Tracy looked at him pleadingly. "Promise me you'll be as quick as you can. I need you Brian."

He leaned forward into the car and hugged her. "I promise, Tracy. I'll see you soon. I love you."

"I love you too," she told him, and then she started crying again. When she finally let go Brian backed away and nodded to Carstairs, who closed the car door and then gave Brian a quick pat on the shoulder. Tracy was looking at Brian as the car pulled away. She put a hand on the window, and then rested her head on the backseat.

The Brubaker house was quiet, in spite of the many people who were going in and out and from room to room. Those who did speak did so in hushed tones. Elias Tanner's wife Rita was already there when Tracy arrived, and she moved quickly to help Tracy out of the car. "I've got you Tracy. I'm going to take you inside to your bedroom and let you rest for a while."

Tracy shook her head. "Where's Mom?"

"The doctor had to give her something to help her relax. He can give you something too if you need it. But we're all here to take care of you both. Now let's get you inside."

The next several hours remained a blur in Tracy's memory, missing pieces that could never be restored. She drifted in and out of consciousness until she finally decided to get out of her bed and see what was going on elsewhere in the house. She looked at the clock on the wall. It was just past 2:30 in the morning. Suddenly she realized Brian wasn't with her. She quickly made her way to the kitchen where several people, including Rita Tanner, were standing. Brian was not there.

"Did Brian call for me?" she asked aloud to anyone willing to answer.

Rita looked at her. "No one's called for you dear. Just the department telling us all what's going on."

"Oh," Tracy said. "Where's Mom?"

"Still resting," Rita told her. At that point a man Tracy didn't know moved forward.

"I'm Captain Tripp," he told her. "I want to tell you the man who killed your father is dead. Your father had wounded him and when he tried to make his escape he shot at other officers. I also want you to know your father saved someone's life tonight. Because of him a killer will most certainly be convicted. He died a hero, young lady. I know that means little now in your grief. But I wanted you to know that." Tracy just looked at him. Tripp then exited the Brubaker household. None of this really registered or mattered to her at the time. She learned later that a murderer many times over was on trial and the man who killed her father was supposed to eliminate the key witness in the State's case. Tripp was right though: the failure to kill the eyewitness resulted in a conviction—life in prison. A prison brawl years later resulted in the death of the man who indirectly murdered her father. The books had been closed.

But for now, Tracy was worried that something had happened to Brian. Every time the phone rang she jumped up. But they were just false alarms—until just after 11 in the morning. Tracy had, on this occasion, been the first one to the phone. "Hello?"

"Tracy. It's Brian."

"Oh thank *God*! Brian I've been so worried about you. What happened? Where are you?"

"I'm fine. I'm at home."

Tracy was confused. "You're fine? Then why aren't you here?"

There was a brief pause. "I just woke up."

"What are you talking about Brian? You said you would be here as soon as you could."

"I know; I know that. I went to tell my friends what happened, and they could tell I was upset. So they offered me a drink to take the edge off. And well, before I realized it I was in no condition to drive. So they called me a cab to take me home. I thought that'd be enough time to sober up. But after I got home I made the mistake of trying to catch a quick nap and…"

"I can't believe you did that." She said this with a ferocity that Brian had never heard.

"Tracy, I am so sorry. I didn't mean for any of that to happen."

Tracy didn't want to hear his pathetic excuses. She was in no mood for them. "How could you do this to me? You know how much I needed you to be with me."

"Tracy: I am so ashamed of myself. Please forgive me. This will never happen again."

"Of course it won't happen again you *idiot*! I only have one father for someone to *murder*!"

Brian gulped. Here was a side of her he had not yet experienced. But he was going to take his lumps. "I deserve that Tracy. But I still want to see you, to be there for you."

"No," she told him quickly. "I don't want to see you."

"Tracy: I'm coming over. And then if you tell me to my face to go, I'll go." He hung up the phone before she could answer. Less than half-an-hour later Brian was knocking on the front door. Tracy answered almost immediately. She let him in and quickly took him to the very same bedroom where Brian had promised Tracy's dad that he always would be there for his daughter.

She practically pushed him into the room and closed the door. She did not give him a chance to speak. "You son of a bitch!" she screamed. "You SON OF A *BITCH!*" And then she moved toward him, striking at his shoulders. But there was little strength in her flailing arms. Her actions were symbolic. He understood this and let her continue her attack, until he felt her strength weakening even further. Finally, he moved to embrace her. She made a feeble attempt to push him away, but he wouldn't let her. He kept holding on until she surrendered and hugged him back. She was crying again and Brian rested his cheek on the top of her head.

"Tracy: I am so, so sorry. I know what I did was inexcusable, maybe unforgivable. But I love you and I'm begging your forgiveness. I'm never going to drink again."

Tracy pulled her head away from his chest and looked up at him. "Do you mean that Brian? You'll stop drinking?"

"I promise. I love you Tracy. I'll do anything for you. I want to marry you someday."

Her anger left her. She returned her head to his chest and squeezed him. "I love you too Brian. Just hold me for a while. Let's just stay here and hold each other."

And so Brian Shane, love of Tracy Brubaker's life, had made a second promise in the spare bedroom of Peter Brubaker's home; another promise that too would shortly be forgotten and broken.

Fade out...

"Damnit dammit dammit DAMMIT!" Tracy sprung up from her bed shouting out loud as she tore her covers away. She turned and slammed her feet on the floor and started pacing, trying to catch her breath. She put her hands on either side of her head, massaging the areas just above her ears. She finally stopped moving and sat back down back on the bed. She knew this memory was going to replay itself. But she had been powerless to stop it. Fine then; now it was over with. A strange thought suddenly popped into her head: "If I could just blow up every distillery in the world..." And then she laughed at herself. "I'm losing my grip," she thought. And then she had another strange thought: "The police better find Stewart Shane's killer before I do, because if they don't, I'm going to beat that man to death." She pulled the covers back over her and forced her eyes closed. She felt the outrage leave her as sleep soon returned. Thankfully, there were no more dream memories featuring her failed romance to interrupt the remainder of her night's rest.

Chapter 9

Tracy woke up Thursday morning before her alarm sounded. Luckily, the previous night's involuntary trip down memory lane didn't seem to be affecting her this morning. She quickly brushed her teeth, showered, dressed, and grabbed two pieces of fruit on her way out the door. She was at her office before 7:30 a.m., beating Rebecca in by half an hour. She tended the coffee pot and put her written notes on Rebecca's chair to be typed up for the electronic file she kept for each client. She settled into her office chair and made her fruit vanish in mere moments. After a check of messages and emails—gosh darn spam wasting her time—she started making a list of things to do. It was over eight hours before she could see Ernie, so she started going through the notes Rebecca had made on the message pads; she updated some personal schedules based on Rebecca's notes, and decided which clients she'd call back or have Neal contact. Not the most exciting part of the job, but necessary. Her father used to tell her, whenever she snarled at having to write a paper, that paperwork was forever part of the deal. "Get used to it, love," he would tell her. "Paperwork is the third certainty in life that everyone seems to forget about." Weren't we now living in the electronic age—the paper*less* age?

Her musings were interrupted. "Mornin' boss." Tracy looked up and saw Rebecca standing there, already having poured her first cup of steaming liquid energy.

"Hey, Beck," Tracy said. "Just going through a few days of paperwork."

Rebecca walked in and handed Tracy some stapled reports—*Yay! More paperwork!* "Neal wanted me to type these up and give them to you," she told her boss. "This is the research on the case laws you asked him to look into."

"Oh, supreme; I can go over these this morning. Thanks bunches, Beck, as always."

"You bet." Rebecca exited, leaving Tracy to her growing pile of dreaded paperwork. At about 8:30 she heard Neal greet Rebecca. She stood up and went to her doorway. He was at the mini-kitchen pouring his coffee. He turned, saw her, and raised his mug. "Top of the morning to ya," he said. She smiled.

"Come to the principal's office after you're settled," she told him. "It's report card time."

"Gulp," he said aloud as he dropped off his belongings.

He caught her up on her various other cases the firm was presently handling. The suit against the foreclosure-happy bank was seeming to be leaning in their favor. Good news, especially if that meant Larry Waters would cease to be a fixture in her offices. One of her clients with a suspended sentence for shoplifting had completed his counseling and his public service hours, and had been crime free since his probationary release. It looked as if he was on the straight and narrow; more good news. And the discriminatory practices joint suit was moving toward settlement negotiations, but Neal was able to schedule those meetings for next week; still more good news.

"And as for the Shane staff, nothing came up on the backgrounds that are useful. They're hourly employees, some of whom have multiple jobs. I didn't find anything that screamed murder suspect."

"Well: I can't say I'm surprised." Tracy folded her arms and leaned back in her chair.

"And how does Brian's situation look from your end?" he asked her.

"Things are happening. I'll let you see my notes after Beck finishes typing them up. I found out that Doug Stanz is allergic to exercise. But the big news is that I need you to track down Kevin Ryder, former husband to Crystal Shane."

Neal blinked. "Let me guess—a relation to William."

"Brother."

"No kidding. Have you asked Bill about him yet?" Neal guessed correctly that Bill hadn't told her this bit of news previously since she didn't mention anything during yesterday's check-in.

"I will if I have to, if it turns out Kevin lives three doors down the road from the Shanes or something like that," Tracy answered. "I don't want to bring up something that happened so long ago unless I am reasonably sure it has bearing on the case."

Neal countered, "You don't think his failure to mention it at your interview is a red flag?"

She looked at Neal. "We only talked about the night of the murder really. I'm not sure I consider his not mentioning his brother as anything to get excited about. He may have been embarrassed by it."

Neal nodded. "Okay." He noticed Tracy staring off into space. "What are you thinking, Tracy?"

After a moment she said, "The puzzle is almost finished Neal. I can feel it." She paused. "It's like having a vague idea of what you're supposed to be seeing but still needing that final piece before you are absolutely sure."

Neal wasn't quite sure what she was getting at. "You think you're close then."

"Positive. I think I'll call Bernard Cubbins and see if I can meet him somewhere this morning after he drops his boss off."

"Okay. I'll follow up on my assigned callbacks, including those concerned with Barton's alibi."

"Thanks Neal."

He headed back to his office. He wanted to leave the puzzle master alone to figure out the solution.

Bernard Cubbins agreed to meet Tracy at a breakfast café on Cathedral Street. He would be there around 10 if she wanted to talk. "Don't know what I can tell you," he told her as they agreed on the rendezvous. She told him all she wanted was an account of the events of Friday night. Maybe she hadn't been completely honest with him. She described herself for his benefit and said she would be there as close to 10 as possible.

As Tracy approached the coffee shop she knew Cubbins was already there. The limo was parked illegally in a No Parking area right across the street from their meeting place. She parallel parked less than a block further than her destination, fed the meter *its* breakfast, and then headed for the café.

As soon as she entered, the smell hit her hard—flavored coffees, fresh baked muffins, *bacon*. Her stomach let her know in no uncertain terms it wanted samples. She turned to see a tall, mustachioed gentleman with a warm grin trying to get her attention. She smiled, nodded and headed in his direction, on the way purchasing a warm blueberry muffin and a caramel apple flavored cup of java. She seated herself at the two-person table where Cubbins was sitting, and put down her feast to pull out the notebook.

"Thank you for seeing me, Mr. Cubbins," she started.

"Bern or Bernie," he said, still smiling.

"Okay: Bernie it is."

He nodded. "You're a lawyer huh?"

"Yes I am."

"You gotta be pretty smart to do that."

"I tend to think working hard is the secret to success in anything you do, Bernie."

"Yeah. I guess you're right about that."

"I'm trying to work out a time line for Friday," she began. "I don't want to bother Mr. Barton about this again, so I thought, if you could just take me through the night's events from the time you picked Mr. Barton up from Marcelo's to the time you left the Shane estate, that should answer all of my questions."

"I can do that."

"So what time did you pick Mr. Barton up from Marcelo's?" she started, breaking off some of her muffin.

"I pulled up to the door just after 10. But Mr. Barton didn't make it to the car until about 10 after."

"Do you know what the delay was?"

"He said something about waiting for his coat, maybe they couldn't find it. I don't really remember."

"This muffin is supreme," she told him, washing her latest bite down. "And it was just the two of you in the limo."

"Yes," Cubbins answered, sounding as if he wasn't sure why she asked. "You married?"

"No, Bernie. Do you mind if I ask where you were before you left to get Mr. Barton?"

His smile left his face for a bit, but thankfully returned. "I ate at another place in Little Italy: Vincenzo's. I'm friends with one of the waitresses. I spent most of the night there. I had dinner, some cannolis and coffee afterward, worked some Sudoko puzzles to pass by the time."

She smiled and said, "Oh, you like doing those too."

"Yeah, they keep my brain working. That's important when you have a job like mine. You like playing racket ball?"

"I prefer swimming. How long have you been doing this for Mr. Barton?"

"Let me think; eight years almost. Swimming is cool."

"That's a long time. I guess you like Mr. Barton."

"He's fine; very business-like, not a sentimental type. But he pays more than other bosses for this work and the Christmas bonus is nice," he said, slightly chuckling. "You belong to a gym?"

She nodded while sneaking another bite. "My building has an exercise room and pool. I understand Mr. Barton doesn't drive."

Cubbins shook his head while having some of his coffee.

"Do you know why? — not that it has anything to do with the case." She hoped she asked that the right way.

"He never told me."

She was disappointed in his answer but said, "It doesn't matter anyway. So you left Marcelo's at 10 after 10. And then you went straight to the Shane meeting?"

"We had to. He wanted to be on his way by 5 after. So I did what I needed to do to get us there by half past; got there with almost five minutes to spare." Cubbins was clearly proud of himself. "You like Italian food?"

"I'm Italian on my mother's side. Then you waited in the car."

"Yup; pulled out my sports mag. But then Mr. Barton gets back in; says Mr. Shane's been killed; and that we'll be here a while, so he wanted me to call his wife and let her know he'd be late."

"Awful," Tracy said, shaking her head. "And you stayed in the car the whole time?"

"The police talked to me at one point. I told them pretty much what I told you. I know a lot of great Italian restaurants."

"And you never saw anybody else that night other than Mr. Barton and Mr. Ryder?"

He looked at her quizzically. "I didn't even see Mr. Ryder. I mean, I was reading my mag most of the night."

"Right." Traced paused, carefully choosing her words for her next question. "Is it in any way possible that someone could have snuck into your limo that night, and then maybe hidden themselves underneath a seat?"

He didn't answer immediately. Then his eyes widened a bit and he said, "Oh no, I don't see how. I keep the partition down so I can see the back of the limo. There's no way someone could just come in there without me knowing about it. My favorite Italian place to eat is a place called Bernardo's."

Tracy stopped writing and flipped back through her notes. "Bernie, this next question may sound strange, but, did you see a red, 1975 Mercury at any point that night? Maybe parked somewhere, or following you?"

Cubbins thought for a moment and then shook his head. "No, can't say I remember seeing any car like that around. You like sports cars?"

"Okay; I just thought I'd ask." She closed her notebook, finished off her muffin, and then asked, "Bernie, would you do something for me?"

He got very serious and said, "Well, I guess."

She leaned in a little bit and said, "I'd really *love* to see the inside of that limo. Do you think I could take a quick peeky weeky? I wouldn't touch anything."

He thought a moment. "I think I can do that. Let's go." He led her across the street to the car and opened up the back door. She went inside and sat down. Looking around, she noted the stretch limo could seat up to probably six passengers. It was equipped with a wet bar, LCD TV and DVD player. As the partition was down she could see what Cubbins meant about no one getting in there without him noticing. After enjoying the comfortable seat for an extra minute or two she exited.

"Thanks for being such a dear, Bernie," she said.

"You're welcome," he returned. And he watched her move quickly across the street and get into her Audi like a woman on a mission. He frowned; she hadn't even give him a chance to ask her out.

Tracy, once inside her car, looked at her phone, which she had previously silenced as she always did before a meeting, and noted the message indicator. It was from Neal, and it was short and sweet: "Tracy, this is Neal. Call me *immediately* when you get this message." And that was the extent of it. She dialed his number.

"Tracy?"

"Yeah, Neal. What is it?"

"Larry Waters is dead."

"WHAT?!"

"He was shot at his home sometime last night."

Dear God, Tracy thought. The little whiner got himself killed. And she suddenly and inexplicably found herself with tears in her eyes.

Tracy entered her office sullen faced and could not even muster a greeting for either Rebecca or Neal. A client of theirs had never been murdered before. Some had passed on due to natural causes, and there may have been a drug overdose; but this? Her stomach was in knots. Every inch of her was saying that Waters' murder was connected to the Shane case. But how could the two possibly be related? Nobody involved in the Shane case knew about Larry. How could they? She sat herself down on her swivel chair and leaned forward on her desk, hands over her face. She looked up and saw Neal staring at her from the doorway. She looked back at him. There were tears in her eyes but she wasn't quite crying.

"I got Larry killed, didn't I Neal?"

"No."

"This is why I don't get involved in murder cases. How could I have been so goddamned *stupid*?"

"Tracy, stop. You don't know for a fact one has to do with the other."

She looked at him as she stood up. He was about to be on the receiving end of her venting. "Oh, come on Neal. For four years we've been corpse-free and in less than a week I've got two murdered people in my sights. Do you really think Larry's death is a coincidence?"

"I'm not saying it is," Neal responded calmly. "But I'm not prepared to just say that it isn't, either."

She continued looking at him, her right hand on her hip. Then she turned away, and wiped her eyes. "Who can I talk to at BPD about this?" she asked, turning back to him.

Neal looked at the paper he had in his hand. "Detective Roche; he was the one that called here and told us what happened. They found several of your business cards at Larry's home. I explained what I could about his situation and told him I'd let you know about it right away. He does want to talk to you."

She sat down again, put her elbow on the desk and her right hand on her forehead. "I'm sorry, Neal."

"You don't owe *me* any apologies. You owe yourself one." She looked at him as he continued. "Even if Larry's murder is somehow connected to Brian Shane, you didn't kill him. The only person responsible for Larry Waters' death is the person who shot him. End of story." Neal now moved forward and gently placed the paper he was holding on Tracy's desk in front of her. He turned without a word and left her office. She looked at the number on the sheet and dialed Detective Roche.

Tracy arrived at Detective Roche's office before noon. He was a heavy-set man with graying hair and kind eyes. He was probably in his late 40s, she thought, and would make a perfect Santa for anyone's Christmas party. He just needed the white facial hair. He shook her hand and invited her to sit down. She turned down his offer for something to drink.

"A neighbor had noticed Waters' back door was kicked in and called 911. We found him on his living room floor. We arrived about 7:30. But the ME said he'd been dead for at least eight hours."

"So you think someone kicked in his door and shot him, maybe during an attempted burglary?" Tracy said quietly.

"That's the way it looks."

Tracy felt there was more to the story. "Looks?"

"Well," Roche said, looking at her, "there are some odd things about it."

"Can you please tell me?" She found herself getting upset again, which may have worked to her advantage as Roche obliged.

"The body had been moved. ME's certain of it. We think he was shot somewhere outside his house because there was dirt and grass under his fingernails and on his shoes, and there were similar stains on his pants. We still have a forensics crew going over the area around his house." He paused and then said, slightly lowering his head, "The poor bastard. He must have fallen or been knocked to the ground before he was shot, begging for his life, because the bullet passed through his hand before entering his skull."

Tracy jolted up out of her chair and turned away from the detective.

"Are you okay, Miss Brubaker?"

She gave him a slight wave, briefly closed her eyes, and then sat back down. "I'll be okay, thanks." She composed herself and asked, "Did you find the murder weapon yet?"

"No; still looking."

She nodded and then asked, "What can I do to help you?"

He gave her a warm smile and leaned back in his seat. "What exactly was your impression of this guy, I mean, without violating your lawyer oath?"

She returned his smile. "He was paranoid. I wouldn't be surprised if he had an actual medical condition, although I don't think he was on any medication. I guess that it's okay to tell you he was at risk of being evicted from his home because of missed mortgage payments. I was trying to help him with that. He got my name through a charitable organization that, among other things, helps people in his situation. My firm is one of the companies that the organization uses."

"I see," Roche said. "You said he was paranoid? What did you exactly mean by that?"

Tracy shifted in her chair a bit. "He thought that, at any moment, someone was going to come in and physically remove him from his home. No matter how many times I assured him that wasn't going to happen, he wouldn't believe me. Eventually he started calling me at all hours, showed up at my condo once demanding an update. I was trying to be understanding. But, to be completely honest with you, he was starting to wear on me."

Roche nodded again. "So he never thought somebody was out to kill him, just evict him?"

"Correct. He never suggested to me he thought he was in any other kind of physical danger."

Roche scratched his unshaven chin. "Well, in this day and age, people get shot for annoying the wrong person. But that doesn't seem to be the case here. I mean why move the body, unless of course you're afraid it will be seen?" Roche stopped thinking out loud and asked, "When was the last time you saw or spoke to him?"

"Yesterday morning," Tracy answered him. "He came for his usual—well for lack of a better description let's call it a pep talk. I told him I'd call him with any news. I think it was around 10 in the morning when he left my office. I didn't see or hear from him again."

"So you didn't meet him anywhere last night?"

"No. Why do you ask that after what I just said?" She realized how her response must have sounded and suddenly felt sheepish. But it didn't seem to bother him.

"Well we found his set of keys on the floor right next to the body. Figured maybe he walked in on somebody after coming back from somewhere, dropped his keys and ran, and then was killed outside. The killer brought the body back in to delay its discovery."

Tracy furrowed her brow. "That's strange. If Larry came in the front, why were his keys out of his pocket and on the living room floor, instead of on the key rack that's screwed into the wall by the door? That's where he usually put them. I visited him enough to know that."

Roche looked at her, and then offered, "Maybe he got distracted, heard something and went to investigate without hanging up his keys, then dropped them when he saw the intruder or his back door broken."

"I can't see that scenario, Detective," Tracy told him. "If Larry heard some strange noise he'd have turned and ran, *not* gone to investigate. That puts the keys falling by the front door or outside the house while he was running away, not close to where the body was found."

Roche thought a bit. "Well, maybe Waters never made it into the house after all—was shot before he could open his door. The shooter then picks up the keys and he lets himself in, then drops the keys by the body."

Tracy was getting a brain ache. She couldn't find a sensible theory that explained both the door being kicked in *and* the keys being where they were. "But then why kick in the back door if he has Larry's keys already?

Or if he's already broken in, why bother to retrieve the keys Larry supposedly dropped while fleeing?"

"That's a good point. Maybe the killer wanted the keys for a different reason: to open a trunk, or filing cabinet, or something else. Maybe there was a safe deposit box key the killer took. We are just beginning our investigation."

Tracy smiled apologetically. "I'm sorry Detective. I didn't mean to sound so standoffish. I just have this idea that refuses to leave my head that Larry's killing is related to my current murder case."

"The Shane thing," he said. "Yeah I found out all about that when I found your card and did some checking on you." He then smiled and said, "All good things." She returned his smile, and got up to leave. He said, "I'll keep an open mind and be in touch. Maybe it's a not a simple B&E like we thought. Thanks for coming in and for your help. And I'm sorry about your client." He moved around his desk to see her out and was unable to suppress a rather large yawn. Tracy looked at him sympathetically.

"Long day already, huh?" she asked.

"Well a sick kid keeps you up all hours. I'll be fine after I sack out in the lounge and get a little sleep."

Tracy's hand was reaching for the door handle when she suddenly froze, and the color drained from her face.

"What's wrong Miss Brubaker? You don't look so good," Roche said with genuine concern in his voice.

"What time did you say Larry was killed?"

Roche did some quick math in his head. "Latest would have been 11:30 last night. But he could have been killed as early as 10:30 give or take."

As calmly as she could she said, "Detective, you may want to get a forensics team over to my building and check out the grassy areas."

"Why do say that?"

"Because as I was drifting off to sleep last night around 11, something woke me up; it may have been a gunshot."

The BPD crime lab's mobile unit was at Tracy's condo building by one. And by half past they had found the scene of Larry Waters' murder; there was disturbed dirt and grass, as well as blood that had not only spilled onto the ground but also spattered on some of the hedges. "The killer probably wouldn't have seen all of this telltale evidence in the dark," Tracy thought. Or maybe he didn't care, instead figuring that by bringing Larry to his home and making it look like the murder happened there, no one would trace the crime back to here; wrong plan.

"We also found this," Roche said showing her. It was a cigarette butt housed in a small evidence bag. "We noticed a burn on one of Waters' fingers. Maybe this is his cig, and it burned him during a scuffle. Lab should be able to get DNA off of it I would think." She nodded. It looked like Larry's brand to her but, not being a smoker, she couldn't be sure.

Tracy's next move was to call Detective Tanner and ask him to meet her, along with Roche, at her living quarters to hear her theory of the crime. Even if, as a law enforcement employee, he would be skeptical about what she had to say, she knew, as someone who cared about her, that he'd want to know someone may have tried to kill her last night. When Tanner arrived, she told him and Roche her own theory of Larry Waters' murder.

"I think Larry came here last night to see me. He had been here before at least once that I'm aware of, maybe more times that I wasn't. He hinted very strongly when he left my office yesterday that he expected to hear from me last night. When he didn't, he came looking. Ever the paranoid he was probably moving about slowly, looking over his shoulder, when he saw someone, someone who was hiding in the bushes or just didn't look right to him. So, being Larry, he freaked and started running. The killer must have thought Larry saw him and, not wanting to take any chances, went after poor Larry. The crime team found a broken hedge branch that Larry must have tripped over. Larry fell and was shot."

Tanner and Roche looked at each other. Roche asked her, "How do you figure the rest of it?"

She obliged by continuing. "Well, since Larry's car was at his home the killer must have put Larry's body in the car and then driven Larry there. That should be easy enough to verify by going over his car; I'd bet there are bloodstains in it somewhere. There aren't a lot of parked cars along the street at the time the murder happened, so the killer could have pulled Larry's keys from his pocket, and then checked the cars that were there until he came upon Larry's. Probably wouldn't have taken too long. A look at the license or registration card would have told him Larry's address. He takes Larry home, uses Larry's key to open the front or back door, and then dumps the body in the living room, tossing the keys to the floor. He kicks in the back door on the way out to make it look like a B&E gone bad. He couldn't have known anything about Larry personally, didn't know he was my client. So the killer figured there'd be no connection to me and he'd be in the clear." She stopped and shook her head. "Poor Larry. My guardian angel was wide awake last night while his was asleep at the wheel."

Tanner and Roche exchanged more looks. Tanner finally said, "And you think the person who wanted to kill you is the person who killed Stewart Shane."

She looked at him intently. "It has to be."

Roche asked her, "How can you be so sure?"

"Because I don't usually get involved in murder cases Detective," she answered quickly. "I can't imagine anyone who would want me dead, except someone who has already killed at least once." Saying what she said out loud, hearing herself saying "me" and "dead" so close together, like new neighbors, rattled her in such a way that she found she had to sit down. She hadn't been this upset since…since someone else in her family was murdered.

Tanner went over to her. Roche followed him and said, "So I guess we gotta figure out how Waters' murderer got back to his own car. We'll start checking cab companies. It's an eight-or-nine-mile hike from here to Waters' place. Don't picture the guy walking back to get his own car." Tanner just nodded. Roche then moved to put a hand on Tracy's shoulder. She looked up at him, and he gave her a smile, and then he left Tanner and her alone.

"El, you *cannot* tell my mother about this."

"I wasn't going to," he said while rubbing her back. "But Tracy, if you're right about this, then maybe we need to sit down and go through what you've found out, let us pursue your leads."

She looked at him and said, "But I don't know exactly what I have yet. There are some possible alternate theories forming in my little brain but there's nothing concrete. I don't have any theory to present to you." Then Tracy started to feel her enthusiasm returning. She smiled. "You know El. I bet whoever killed Larry wasn't going to *kill* me, just try to scare me. Maybe fire a shot at my window from a tree or something. It's not like he would have come knocking on my door. I'm on the fourth floor so how would he have broken in, unless he was Spider-Man?"

"Tracy…"

"What this means is that I'm getting close. I'm making the killer nervous even though I don't have anything solid yet. I must be close. So there's no way I'm going to stop now. Be a little more paranoid, maybe, but not stop. Brian is innocent, and Larry died because a killer thinks I'm a threat.

No, El. I'm not backing off. If anything, I'm more determined than ever to find out who framed Brian for his father's murder."

Tracy had finally managed to convince Tanner to leave her to her own resourcefulness. She promised him she'd stay inside the rest of the afternoon and evening, pause her investigation—just to be on the safe side—and give the police the rest of the day to follow up on Tracy's new theory. Maybe they'd get lucky with one of the cab companies and it would all be over.

"Some detective *I* would have made," she thought. The death of Waters had really upset her, especially the image of his hand trying to block the shot. She didn't really like him that much, but she knew him. There had been some connection. But wait, that's just it. She knew the victim. That would rarely, if ever, be the case if she were a detective with the BPD. Her father had told her staying detached was the toughest, but most necessary, part of the job if you were going to *do* the job. So she was being too hard on herself again. The fact that she seemed to care less about the threat on her own life than Larry's death was something in her favor, right? "No time to feel sorry for yourself anyway," she thought; time to move forward.

The next thing to do was to call Neal and Rebecca and fill them in on the whole enchilada. Hey, she hadn't eaten lunch. She was hungry. But she wasn't ready to chow down just yet. She knew how her friends worried. It was after 4:00 when she phoned Neal, told him to get Rebecca, and then asked for the call to be put on speaker. She summarized the day's events, leaving out very little.

"Oh my God, Tracy. How are you holding up?" Rebecca asked.

"I'm great, Beck, really. Of course I feel awful for Larry. The least I can do is to help find his killer."

"Finding or helping to find killers is not your—or our—job, Tracy," Neal cut in.

"I know, Neal. I chose my words poorly. I only meant that by following up on Brian's case, we'll no doubt find out who killed Larry."

"You must have the murderer quaking in his boots," Rebecca said.

"Like a boss," Tracy enthused.

"I don't believe you two," Neal blurted out. "Somebody tried to kill you Tracy and you guys are acting like the prom king just asked you out."

"But Neal, this all means we're almost home."

"Or almost in a grave."

"Neal, really," Tracy said, irritated at his lack of enthusiasm. Honestly, he was starting to sound like a mother she knew.

"If it's no big deal, let's call your mother."

Was he psychic? Tracy didn't like where this was going. "Don't even joke about that, Neal."

"You think I'm joking? Maybe you'll listen to reason from her since I'm not doing a good job of it."

"Neal: I love you, but if you call my mother I will never speak to you again, which will make working together very difficult since I don't know sign language."

Tracy's retort got him, and Neal chuckled. "You are one-of-a-kind, Tracy Brubaker."

"They broke the mold."

"And buried all the pieces—hopefully."

Tracy laughed. "El's got me on curfew for the rest of today, if that makes you happy. I think I may have a bodyguard outside somewhere too. So I'll have to push my visit to Ernie the Bartender to tomorrow."

"Well, that's something at least," Neal said.

"Can you update me on what you've learned while the cat's been away?"

Neal didn't answer. "Neal? Are you still there?" Tracy asked finally.

"Kevin Ryder is dead." Now the silence was from Tracy's end. "He died when a man with a gun found Kevin in bed with his wife."

"Good Lord," Tracy said, genuinely surprised at the news. "When did *this* happen?"

"Thanksgiving weekend last year; a guy named Russ Taylor was supposed to be working the Black Friday shift all day but got sick and came home to find his wife and Kevin together. He left the bedroom, came back with his shotgun: killed Kevin, his wife, and then himself. At least he spared his two kids, I guess."

Tracy just let the silence remain for a few moments. This was the ugliness that depressed her. All she could do was say, "Thanks Neal—for telling me under the circumstances and all."

He asked, "Do you think it possible Bill blamed Shane for his brother's death?"

She pondered his question a moment. "I should probably talk to Bill about it. At the very least I should seriously consider it," she said, regret in her voice. "The simplest explanation could be that Ryder came in right after Brian did and shot Mr. Shane. He seems to have a possible motive—I mean, I guess, in some twisted way, I can see how Bill could hold Shane accountable: 'You drove Kevin away and now he's dead.' But why wait so long for revenge? And why do it that particular night?" Tracy paused and then thought to herself, no wonder police are so ready to believe that sons can kill their fathers. She told Neal, "The idea that Ryder did this depresses me though. He has kids."

Neal was quiet for a moment, thinking that plenty of murderers have offspring. But he opted not to share his thought. "Well, if you need me to do anything on this let me know."

"What about callbacks from our fellow lawyers?"

"I've been playing some phone tag. The match resumes tomorrow, I promise."

"Fair enough," she told him. "You and Beck close the office and go home. And be a little more vigilant, at least for tonight.

"Comforting thought," she heard Rebecca say.

"Good night guys. Stay safe. I love you two." She disconnected before she could hear their response, or before they heard her grumbling tummy.

Tracy ate heartily that night: a large plate of spaghetti, salad, an orange, and a generous dish of mint chocolate chip ice cream. A glass of milk helped wash it all down. But her mind was so busy trying to sift through the facts and find a workable theory that she really didn't *enjoy* it.

Who didn't have alibis for Wednesday night? She remembered Doug had off and left rather early because Crystal wanted to go into the office this morning. Barton? It all came down to Cubbins and just how loyal and honest a driver he was. Bill Ryder? He usually worked Wednesdays but wasn't at dinner last night. Did he take the night off in addition to turning down Crystal's offer to join them? She now had a potential motive for him and he had the opportunity to kill Mr. Shane; still no certainties, but certainly possibilities.

When her phone rang at 8:30 it startled her. Maybe it was Roche calling with news. She grabbed the receiver without even checking the caller ID. Oh dear, it was Brian on the line.

"Tracy are you all right?"

"I'm fine Brian."

"I've been trying to get a hold of you all day, at least, since I found out what happened."

"Sorry. I'd silenced my cell phone and haven't checked the messages yet." She paused and then asked, "I haven't made the news have I?"

"Not that I know of; Crystal started making some calls when I told her I couldn't get a hold of you and was worried. She finally talked to Detective Tanner. All he said was that one of your clients had been killed and that you were being interviewed. But Crystal—well she thought there was more to it than that and hasn't let up. You know how she can be when she wants something."

"I sure do," Tracy agreed.

"So?"

"So what?"

"*Is* there more to it than that?"

Tracy paused. She didn't want to lie to him. But she didn't want to tell him what she really felt either. He might fire her for her own protection. She had never been fired before. A no win situation, another fine mess; deep breath. "It's possible the man who was killed was murdered outside my building."

"No…"

"It doesn't mean anything. He may have been coming to see me and ran into a mugger or something."

"But what do *you* think this is about, Tracy?"

Crap. She'd hoped he wouldn't ask such a question. She would twist the truth just the teensiest bit. "I'm going to let the police do their jobs before I make any official statement."

"*Official statement*? Tracy what the hell?"

"Brian, don't get upset. There's nothing to be worried about."

"Why don't I believe you?"

Why couldn't he just leave it be, she thought. She did want to tell him the truth. In many ways it was good news, if she was right. But he was her client, not her boyfriend anymore, not entitled to make demands. She needed to shut this down. "Brian, I'll call you tomorrow. I have some more interviews I want to do and I need to get an early start. Please don't worry about me."

"You ask the impossible, Tracy."

Ouch—was *that* the right thing to say. Score one for Brian. "Goodnight Brian, and thanks for checking up on me."

"Should I come over? I promise no attempts at funny business."

"No, Brian. I want to turn in."

He sighed. "Well, okay. Oh, by the way, the reason I was trying to get a hold of you was to let you know Bill Ryder quit."

"What?"

"Yeah. Called just before his shift on Wednesday and said he couldn't make it in. And then called this morning and said he wouldn't be back. It was too upsetting for him to work here. Crystal told him just to take some time off and think it over. We consider him on paid vacation for now."

"Poor man; but that was sweet of you guys." She paused a moment and then asked, "Why didn't you mention last night that he called out?"

"I didn't know. Crystal was the one who invited him to dinner last night, and *she* took his call this morning before she left for the day. I only found out about all this later, when she got home from the office." He paused for a moment. "You know, I ought to put Crystal on the phone. She'd get the truth out of you. Hell, she'd be at your door in record time if she wanted to."

"I'll call you tomorrow, Brian. Goodnight." And she hung up the phone, feeling bad for not being completely honest, feeling good knowing he cared so much.

So Bill Ryder didn't have an alibi for last night either, except for maybe his wife. Ryder, Stanz, and Barton? All possibilities. But what had she asked that rankled someone enough to want, at a minimum, to threaten her? She could review her notes yet again. But by now she knew it all by heart: the timing, the alibis, the theories. Still, nothing was coming together for her.

Crystal. Yes, Crystal could be a force to be reckoned with if she set her mind to something. Tracy had seen it mostly when it came to academics, and maybe the occasional potential boyfriend. That brief marriage maybe shouldn't have surprised Tracy as much as it originally did. Crystal wanted Kevin, so Crystal got Kevin. And when she decided she didn't anymore, she moved on.

Tracy knew that Crystal loved Doug, seemed to love him deeply. And all her father could do was watch? Maybe not. What if Crystal was the one who was going to be removed from the will? She heard the call even if she pretty much blew off Tracy's question regarding same, conveniently (?) breaking down to avoid the question; and then what? Planned a girl's night out as an alibi? Snuck out of whatever movie they were seeing, unnoticed for at least an hour, while she killed her father? And then framed her brother, or at least arranged it so he was the best candidate? Nonsense; couldn't be. But now all the estate would be hers. Poppycock. Crystal never seemed to care about money. But, duh, Tracy you never saw Crystal having to do without. What might she have done if faced with *that* dilemma? Not possible. Her father had made her CEO. Plus the police had talked to her friends, probably in the hopes that Crystal may have told her companions something incriminating about Brian. And Tracy told Neal to make their interviews low priority. Still, it's silly to think Crystal, as awesome as she is, could get all those people to cover for her. Tracy believed most people were decent, and would not be easily swayed to help cover up a murder. And she didn't buy the "all rich people are evil bastards" school of thought either. She found this sudden train of thought without any merit.

Crystal didn't have an alibi for last night. Maybe she was acting the part of the supportive sister this whole time when she really had finally had enough of the controlling father and drinking brother, the two men in her life who were holding her back or pulling her down. Good Lord. Tomorrow she would have to tell Neal to follow up with that list Crystal had provided. She was, after all, Brian's attorney, not Crystal's. And she wouldn't be doing her job if she played her "I know this person couldn't have done it" card one too many times. As she got ready for bed, as much as Tracy hated to admit it, Crystal Shane had to be added to the list of possible suspects.

Fade in...

Tracy had just poured the pasta into the strainer when she heard the knock on the door. "Just a minute Brian," she called out. She put the strainer into the sink, dried her hands, and then went to welcome her guest.

"Finally," was all Brian said as he came into the small foyer.

Trying to remain cheerful, she apologized. "Sorry Brian. I'm running a little behind."

He turned. "Oh, Tracy, I should be apologizing. I didn't mean to snap at you."

She went to hug him and their lips met briefly. Then she took him by the hand. "This way to *Chez Tracy*." Brian smiled and willingly followed.

"Smells great in here; what's on the menu?"

"Nothing too fancy: spaghetti and sauce, garlic bread, lettuce and tomato salad."

"It sounds perfect to me, Tracy." He looked around. "Where's your mother?"

"At church with some friends. Then she'll be with them for a while after that."

"I see."

After Brian sat down Tracy placed a glass of water in front of him. She backed away, and touched her lips. She looked at Brian and frowned. "How much have you had?"

He tried to feign ignorance. "What are you talking about?"

She was in no mood for Brian's "Let's Play Dumb" game. "You know damn well what I'm talking about."

He sighed. "Look: Dad's been on my case about my grades again, and the fact that I didn't show up at the offices last Saturday. I just needed to relax a little bit. No big deal. I'm fine."

"Uh-huh." Tracy turned her back on him and then mildly slammed the salad and bread bowls on the table. She went back to the stove to prepare his plate of pasta and sauce, and then dropped it in front of him, saying nothing.

"This is great Tracy. Thanks." She just glared at him, and then she made a plate for herself and joined him at the table. They ate mostly in silence. Finally Brian said, "So do you have anything besides water to drink around this place? It's pretty tense all of a sudden."

"No," was all Tracy said.

"So we're just going to sit here then?" he said tersely.

Tracy looked up at him. "You promised me."

"What?"

"You promised me you'd quit drinking."

Brian looked at his plate. "Look, I'm sorry. It helps with the stress."

"You always say you're sorry but you keep on doing it."

"You don't understand."

"Then help me understand."

Brian was now agitated. "What's the big deal Tracy? I haven't gone out drinking with the boys since that night. I've been there for you, haven't I?"

Tracy now was feeling agitated. "You've been coming by, sure—after you've had a few drinks. And don't think I don't know that you have some more after you leave. I've called your house several times over the last few weeks to see if you got home okay. All I ever get is an answering machine."

"Everyone's asleep," he said weakly.

"And when you *are* with me you're nervous and jittery, going on about how your father is on you and that you're mad about this or that. Then you decide you want some action. This isn't you Brian. You were never like this before you started drinking so much. This isn't the man I fell in love with."

Brian stood up. "What do you want from me, huh, Tracy? You don't understand the pressure I'm under. I'm not smart like you. Good grades don't come to me easily."

Now Tracy stood up. "You think my grades come *easily* to me?" she asked angrily. "Let me tell you something. I worry and sweat over every point I earn. I study my ass off. And it doesn't matter how well I've done in the past because the potential for future failure is always there. You have no idea the pressure *I'm* under. If I don't keep up my grades I lose my scholarship and then it's bye-bye college. My father isn't rich like yours." She paused and gulped. "I mean, wasn't."

"Ya know: I'm *really* tired of hearing about your sainted father; like I'm supposed to live up to him or something."

"That's not true."

"No? Then why lately is it that every time you open your mouth it's, 'My father' this or 'My father' that?"

"Because I just lost him and I miss him!" she yelled, tears welling up in her eyes.

"Well I lost my mother and you don't hear me going on and on about it. Just admit it Tracy. The reason you keep bringing him up is to rub my face in it; to keep reminding me of not showing up that night."

"Brian I forgave you for that."

"You're a liar!"

"BRIAN! How can you say that to me? Why are you being like this?"

Brian finally realized how much he was upsetting her and tried to calm down. "Tracy, why can't it be enough that I love you, huh? Why are you making such a big deal out of a few drinks?"

"Because you're an alcoholic Brian and you need help."

"I am not."

"You are! And I don't want to be with an alcoholic whether he loves me or not!"

That did it. "So, you want to break it off huh? As soon as it gets tough for you then that's it."

"No," she said through tears. "I want you to get help so we can be together like we talked about."

He shook his head. "No, you want me to be perfect and do what you want me to do. I love you. You love me. That should be enough, right?"

"If you loved me you'd stop drinking."

"Oh, so you want me to *prove* I love you do you, is that it?! Love you like your dad did, huh?! I'll tell you what, Tracy. Why don't I go out and get myself shot like dear old dad huh? Then I'll be *just* like him!"

Tracy straightened up. She felt the flush in her cheeks. She glared at Brian so intensely that he knew he just crossed a line. "Get out," she told him sternly.

"What? What did you say to me?"

"I said: get out. O-U-T."

Brian didn't move. He hadn't expected this. This wasn't the shy, somewhat insecure young woman he met almost three years ago standing in front of him. No; this was a confident, self-assured woman who knew what she wanted and, more importantly, what she didn't. Ironically, he knew his love for her had helped her become this person. And now it appeared he was being dismissed.

"Are you still here?" she asked since Brian remained standing. "Fine. Now it's your turn to listen to *me*." She paused briefly to regain her composure. "Brian: I have tried to be as understanding as I can be. I'm sorry you lost your mother to such an ugly disease. I can't imagine how you feel. And I'm sorry your father doesn't understand how hard you try because your grades are not what he wants. I know you do your best. I wish he understood that. And I am so sorry about what he said to you about that false charge. I cannot begin to imagine how that made you feel. After you dropped me off that night I cried for you, because I knew you were hurting; the man I loved was hurting and there was nothing I could do to help. I am sorry about all of these things. They are not fair. And you did nothing to bring these on. And because of that, I have tried to be patient and understanding, tried to see things from your perspective. But it's gotten out of hand and my patience is at its end."

She paused as he continued to stare at her. "Don't you understand I'm under pressures too? If I don't do well in school I'm out. And my father was *murdered*, Brian—gunned down. He won't be there to walk me down the aisle or bounce his grandkids on his knee. And now I have to help take care of my mother and the household because no one else can do it, all the while keeping up with my classes. Do you think that's easy Brian? *Do you?* But I don't wallow in self-pity and turn to alcohol to make it all better—

because it *doesn't* make it all better, Brian. That's why you and I are where we are now.

"I love you Brian. You've made me feel so loved and cared for that knowing these things has made me a stronger person. You've brought out the best in me. I could tell you anything. I could be silly, be serious, be anything I wanted to be when I was with you. I never had to pretend with you. We've had such a special time together and I want that back. I want the man I fell in love with *back!*" She briefly lost her composure but just as quickly regained it. She moved toward him. He backed away not knowing what was coming. She continued on to a small shelf near the kitchen entrance wall and removed the push button phone, which she then took and placed on the kitchen table. Next she went to the counter and took a pencil and pad of paper, both of which she placed next to the phone. She then turned and once again faced Brian. She cleared her throat.

"So this is what we're going to do. You have two options. Option one: You pick up this phone right now and you dial 411. And when that friendly operator comes on you ask for the Baltimore City chapter, or whatever they call it, of Alcoholics Anonymous. And then you're going to write down the phone number they give you. You're then going to call this number and ask when the next meeting tonight is, and you're going to write down the time and address of that meeting. Then the two of us are going to get in your car and drive there. You will go to that meeting and I will wait in the car for you. And you will get any and all information you need so you can start going to meetings. And you will continue to go to meetings until you are at the point where you no longer drink. And if and when the urge hits after that point, you'll go to another meeting.

"If you do this, if you pick up that phone and make that call, I promise to stand by you and help you anyway that I can. I will go with you to each and every meeting and wait for you, if that's what you want. I will stay with you all night any night you want if that will help you when you find it hard to fight the urge to drink. I will go to meetings for loved ones of AA members if that's what you want. Whatever I can do to help you beat this, I will do, *if* you make that call."

She took a deep breath and then continued. "Option two: If you don't pick up this phone and make that call, then I want you to leave. Don't call me, don't stop by, don't try to see me. I don't want to see or hear from you again until you're ready to make that call. But you better not wait too long, Brian. I'm quite a catch, you know?"

She was finished now. He looked at her, still speechless. Why wasn't he moving toward the phone? This decision was a no-brainer. Pick up the phone and make the damn call. But then the twins showed up; that pesky duo that call themselves Ego and Pride. They told him, "You can't give in to her. If you do, then it's over. Anytime she wants something she'll go through the same song and dance. You want to be with someone like that?"

"I love her and she loves me," he mentally countered. "I want to be with her and this is the only way."

"If she loved you she'd understand you can handle this by yourself."

As if she sensed his internal struggle, Tracy picked up the phone and brought it to Brian. She lifted it up so that it was in front of him just below his throat. He looked into her eyes; those pleading eyes. Ego and Pride spoke again. "Look! She's weakening! Just stand here a while looking at her, and she'll put the phone down and apologize and beg your forgiveness for having spoken to you like that."

He was about to promise that he'd get help. But what were his promises worth? Nothing, that's what. So he just stood there. Finally, she stepped back and returned the phone to the table. She turned her back to him and was now facing the kitchen stove, her arms folded in front of her.

Tracy was feeling panic. She knew she was doing the right thing for both of them. He needed help and she still wanted him in her life. But he was being more stubborn than she anticipated. If he loved her the choice should be an easy one. Disconnected words circled her brain like a stock market ticker tape. "Please Brian pick up the phone I love you and I want to help you" and "please pick up the phone we can still be happy if you just please pick up the phone I love you don't you know that…"

The sound of the screen door closing made her swing around. She sprinted to the front in time to see Brian yank open his car door, slam it shut, and pull away. She stood there briefly, staring at the empty street, before she finally closed the door. She went back to the kitchen and stared at the table; remnants of the last meal served on the day of execution of a relationship. She quickly put the uneaten food in storage containers, washed the dishes, and cleaned up the table. She turned out all the lights except for one in the kitchen so her mother could see when she finally got home, and then she made her way to her bedroom. She lay down fully clothed, turned on her side and clutched her pillow. Eventually the tears came again, but this time she wasn't mourning her father or even Brian. She was crying because of another casualty, the future—the future she was once so sure of that was now a thing of the past.

Fade out...

Tracy opened her eyes. Another visit from the Ghost of Relationships Past had come to an end. She fought the urge to look at the clock. Instead she thought about the broken promises from years ago. Then she remembered Brian's promise to her the other night, to let her leave after dinner. A promise to let her leave, now *that* was a promise she wished he'd broken.

Chapter 10

Tracy's troubled sleep was not over: images of Larry Waters being shot, sometimes his face would be replaced with hers, a hole in his hand and in his head, *"They're coming to get me, to throw me out in the cold...;"* slurp — then blood spilling out of a soda can, Tracy pulling the trigger, a scream. Tracy woke up. Was the cry from her dream or from her own throat? She looked at the clock. 5:52 a.m. So she *had* gotten some sleep. She certainly didn't want to go back to bed. Since her home imprisonment was over, she wanted to get back to the case. Still lots to do, lots of people to talk to: another sit-down with Bill Ryder, the calls due back from the other attorneys regarding Barton, talks with Crystal's Friday night chums, a face-to-face with Ernie, the Judds' bartender. This all had to be done. She decided she would try to talk to Bill first.

For the second time this week Tracy arrived at the office before Rebecca — a record. She put the coffee on, cleared out her new voice mail messages and emails, and then took to the dreaded pink pile on her desk. She heard Rebecca unlock the front door at 7:45 and then make her way toward the back. "How are you doing Tracy?"

"I'm fine," she fibbed. "My sentence has been served and I am once again a free woman."

Rebecca studied her. "Well I'm glad you're alright and in good spirits."

"Thanks."

Rebecca left Tracy to her business. The attorney was putting up a brave front, Rebecca thought. But the idea that someone wished Tracy harm would be the elephant in the office until the Shane case was over.

While Tracy didn't like to call people before 9:00, unless specifically receiving approval to do so beforehand, she was officially impatient. At 8:00 she dialed Bill Ryder, planning to leave another message. But she wasn't much surprised when he picked up.

"Bill, it's Tracy Brubaker."

"Oh, hello," he answered without much enthusiasm.

"I heard you quit yesterday."

"I tried to. Ms. Shane told me I was just on vacation for now."

"Can we meet again? I'd like to talk with you once more if I may."

There was silence. "I guess that'd be okay," he answered finally. "I'll be here all day. My wife leaves for work in half an hour, so any time after 9:00 should be fine."

"I'll try to be there around 9:00 then. Thank you Bill." As she was ending her call she heard Neal enter and exchange some words with Rebecca. Tracy just sat looking at the doorway knowing Neal would be filling the empty space shortly.

"Change your mind yet?" were the first words out of his mouth.

"About what?"

He looked at her sternly. "I guess not then."

She returned his look, but then said, "Neal, I don't want to fight about this anymore. We have clients and we have a lot to do and I need your help, your full attention."

"You have it."

She smiled. "Supreme! While you're waiting for your callbacks start contacting the names on Crystal's list."

Neal left the doorway and seated himself in front of her desk. "You having second thoughts about Crystal Shane?" he asked.

"I'm covering all bases, even if I think I know the answers."

"Okay."

"Neal, in all seriousness, if you think you're not getting the truth from one or some of them, let me know yesterday. I may want to talk to them too."

"I'll do that."

He was giving her short answers, with none of his usual jabs thrown in. It hurt her feelings a bit, even though she tried to take it as his great concern for her being the reason. "Thanks Neal. I'd also love it if you can find out why Barton doesn't drive. It may not mean anything, but I have to admit I'm seriously curious." Another nod. "I've made an appointment to see Bill Ryder at 9:00. He quit his job yesterday so that, along with what you found out about his brother, pretty much necessitates another talk."

"Quit, huh? That's curious."

"Then I'll call Detective Roche and see if he has anything regarding Larry Waters' murder he can share. Ernie's on target for 4:00."

"Sounds good," was all he said.

"Okay, well, I guess that's it for now. You can go now, unless you have something else you want to say to me."

He looked at her. He knew he could tell her what he was thinking without fear of reprisals. They had that kind of relationship. That's why he enjoyed his work with her so much. But maybe some self-editing was called for here. "Tracy, I'll be honest with you. I'm worried about you, worried *for* you. And I can't pretend that I'm not. Yes, you could be close to an answer. But will you be around to find it?" He paused to study her reaction. She said nothing. "Just promise me you'll be extra, extra careful from here on out."

"I promise you, I will be." She smiled at him. "Can I get a hug now?"

He finally smiled back at her. "Is that an order?"

"Yes."

"Harassment."

"Sue me."

"I'd rather hug you." And the two got the darn thing over with and he left her. There was a call from the front.

"Tracy: Arthur Pankow is here to see you."

"Okay Beck, show him on back." Tracy rose to greet Pankow as he entered.

"I heard about yesterday," he started.

"Good morning to you too, " she greeted him. He just looked at her. "So, I guess it looks like Larry was killed outside my building."

"Lab hasn't gotten the DNA results back yet on the butt, but the brand matches what Waters smoked. Yeah, I'd say he was killed outside your building alright."

She looked at him. "Why are you here, Art?"

"I'd like to know what you've found out. Somebody may have tried to kill you."

"I don't think…"

"Forgive me Tracy but I don't care what you think. If you know something about Waters' murder you need to tell us."

'Us'? So that's how it was. Tanner didn't get anything out of her so now it was Pankow's shot. Okay, her turn. "First of all, I don't know of any reason why someone would want to kill me, and by extension Larry Waters. I'm not holding anything back. Second, if I *did* know something, in all likelihood I would have found it out during my work with a client. That would make it work related—all privileged." He looked at her shaking his head.

"So for now, I'm going to continue with my case until I find out who killed Stewart Shane."

"*What?*" Pankow roared. "I don't believe you. Who do you think you are Penny Mason?"

She fired back, "Who do you think *you* are: Franklin Furter?"

More disbelief on Pankow's part. She didn't think he got the Hamilton Burger joke. "You know, Frankfurter, Hamilton Burger, it's a joke."

He continued to stare at her. "So it's just business as usual for you then, just pretend like nothing happened?"

"No, I'll definitely be paying more attention to my surroundings. But whoever this guy is, he's a coward. He hides in the dark and is easily panicked. I should be safe in the daylight hours."

"Unless he decides to try and run you off the road or something. Being easily panicked makes him *more* dangerous and unpredictable, Tracy."

She was getting tired of this. "Why does everyone think I should be playing the frightened victim here? That I should crawl into a hole somewhere and let other people take care of me? You guys are convinced Brian's guilty, so if I skedaddle where does that leave him? I'm going ahead with my work on the Shane case; end of story. Okay?"

Pankow relaxed his shoulders. Was he there because he really thought she was holding back on Waters' murder, or because he was concerned for her safety? "Okay Tracy. I hope you know what you're doing. Just be careful. I respect the hell out of you for standing your ground. But I hope that doesn't cost us one of the best attorneys I know." And with that he turned and left.

Well gosh golly gee. She wasn't expecting *that*. She would have to buy him a root beer after this was all over. There was another buzz from Rebecca: "Kurt Barton is here to see you."

"I love a parade and all but this is ridiculous!" Tracy thought. "Okay," Tracy said, slightly exasperated, throwing up her arms. Rebecca entered Tracy's domain shortly followed by Barton. "Can I get you something to drink Mr. Barton?" Rebecca asked.

"No. I won't be long." Rebecca left the two attorneys. "Ms. Brubaker, it has come to my attention that you are questioning people about my activities Friday. My driver said he talked to you yesterday."

"Yeah, Bernie. Nice guy."

Not amused he continued, "And a colleague said he got a message to call back one of your associates. I thought I answered all of your questions when I made time in my *busy* schedule for you earlier this week. Just what is your game, Ms. Brubaker?"

"No games, Mr. Barton. I'm just trying to get corroboration on everyone's version of events last Friday."

"*Corroboration? Version?*" Barton asked sounding offended.

"For the defense I'm building sir, I need to fully understand everyone's movements Friday. I'm constructing a time table, nailing everything down as best I can. That's all."

"I don't think that *is* all, Ms. Brubaker." He glared slightly. "You obviously think I had something to do with Stewart Shane's death."

"Well his company was using other law firms for work your firm historically did for them."

He looked taken aback. He wasn't expecting that. "It's not unusual for people to think they can get the same quality work for less money."

"So you knew about it then?"

"Of course; I understood."

"But couldn't that have led to your losing more and more work?"

"We were not in danger of losing our position as Shane's primary attorney, if that's your implication."

"I see," she said sounding as skeptical as she could.

"Now look. I did not come here to answer any more of your questions."

"Oh? Why did you come here then?" she asked. She also thought: "Maybe to see if I was still on the case? See what I knew, if anything, about last night?"

He regained his composure. "Be careful that your questions do not imply anything that could be construed as libelous, Ms. Brubaker. If you attempt to besmirch my reputation in any way I *will* take action."

Besmirch? "I'm not looking to besmirch. I'm just trying to gather all the information I can to help represent my client; nothing more."

That seemed to satisfy him for the moment. "Good day to you then," he said as he turned to leave.

"Back at ya," Tracy mumbled. And with that thankfully out of the way, Tracy exited to find out if Bill Ryder was likely a murderer.

When Ryder opened his door for her this time, he merely nodded and extended his arm to the familiar dining table. He was obviously a sad man based on his facial expression. Why that was, Tracy couldn't be sure. Part of her brain leapt to the conclusion he felt guilty about killing Larry Waters. But if she *really* believed that, why was she here, alone with him? She had mace in her case, and was a first degree brown belt in judo. Her father had made sure that his daughter could protect herself, although he always said her mouth was her most lethal weapon. She approached the table and saw a glass of ice water was awaiting her at the same place she sat down the last time she was there. She turned to give him a smile as she took her seat. He moved slowly to join her.

"What's wrong Bill? Can I help with anything?"

He shook his head. "I've just been real tired lately. Don't feel like doing much right now." He managed a small smile and said, "But my boys will be back with us soon for the summer. It will be good to see them again."

She nodded. "I guess once you're a parent you're always missing your kids when they're not around. I know my mom still wishes I lived with her."

He smiled a little wider. "True; too true."

"Can I ask why you want to quit, Bill?"

He hesitated. But she was giving him that sympathetic look of hers, making it seem like she *was* there to help. "I guess I liked Mr. Shane more than I cared to admit even myself. With his killer still out there I don't feel comfortable working at the estate."

"But that feeling could certainly change once the killer is caught."

"Maybe; I'll have to see how I feel when that happens."

She paused. "Bill, can I ask you, do you think Brian killed his father?"

He looked at her, surprised by the question. "All I know is they argued a lot. But killing him? Hard to say. But then again he was drunk, and maybe he did something stupid. I don't know."

Now the difficult part. "Bill, can we talk about your brother Kevin for a minute?"

He looked at her and then turned his head to the side, uttering some noise that sound like "Sheesh" without the 'sh' on the end. "I knew it," he said. "I figured you'd find out about him eventually."

"I'm sorry Bill. But I think it may be important background for — well it may tell me something about Mr. Shane."

"And me too," he said, some anger sneaking into his voice. "You think I killed Mr. Shane over Kevin?"

"No Bill, I don't. At least not in here," she said pointing to her heart. "But I have to follow up on this if I'm going to be doing my job to the best of my ability."

He seemed to believe her since he nodded, although without meeting her eyes. "What can I tell you about him?"

"How did he come to be employed by Mr. Shane?"

"Well, it was Crystal that hired him. That garden of hers—well, it used to be her mother's pride and joy. So she looks at that garden as some connection with her mom. Mr. Shane let her work in it, and also let her hire the people she liked to help her."

"I see." Tracy did understand Crystal's attachment to the garden, that maybe she could find her mother's presence hidden amongst the beautiful flowers. It was the same as Tracy's feelings about the small room that she had turned into a mini-home theater, and how it kept her father alive and vibrant. Just walking into that room could be enough sometimes to make her feel he was still with her. Maybe he even haunted the place: Peter Brubaker the Friendly Ghost.

Bill continued. "After I got the job, she asked me if I knew anyone who was good at gardening. I knew my brother used to have a landscaping gig, and he was out of work at the time. So I gave her his number, never thinking for one second what happened would happen."

She stopped her note taking to ask, "How long did it take Kevin to move in on Crystal?"

Ryder snorted. "You make him sound like a…like an opportunist."

"You mean he wasn't? Crystal told me he dumped her when it was clear there would be no more money."

Bill was getting agitated. "That's just *her* story. Kevin told me they broke up because of what a control freak Crystal was. She wanted what she wanted when she wanted it. That's bull about the money. She knew she had daddy eating out of her hand. She could get the money when she wanted. All that, *and* he thought she was just using him to piss off her father."

Bill didn't seem to like Crystal very much, and he was certainly making it sound like Kevin was the sympathetic party here. And Tracy might have been willing to believe it, *if* Kevin hadn't been found in bed with another man's wife. She asked Bill if he knew anything more about his brother's recent death.

"That lady probably seduced him. He comes over to do the yard work, hubby's out, and she makes her move. He's weak so he doesn't say, 'No'." He then added, "He didn't deserve to die for it."

She certainly agreed to that. Kevin *was* probably the snake as described in Crystal's version, not the innocent in his brother's take. But being gunned down like that? Even if Tracy had had her choice of punishments for Kevin

Ryder and his ilk, *that* option would not have been on her list. "But Mr. Shane never took revenge against you for Kevin?"

Bill shook his head. "No. Never. He never asked about it. I tried to tell him how sorry I was and how I didn't know what was going on with Crystal, but he'd just shut me down."

"Maybe he too felt Crystal was the instigator here," Tracy offered, which Bill seemed to like hearing.

"Yeah, I guess that might have been it. But I can't express how much Mr. Shane's loyalty meant to me."

"I can tell it meant a lot to you."

Bill started talking free form, sharing what he was feeling. "He had a strong work ethic, Mr. Shane did, and he liked people who shared that quality. I worked hard to support my family and Mr. Shane respected that. But Brian didn't, so they fought." Tracy didn't like hearing that but she wasn't about to interrupt. "That Crystal's got a head on her shoulders when she uses it. But she's used to getting what she wants. That Doug fella that's gonna marry her, well, the jury's still out on him. He could be another Kevin."

Tracy knew that Bill meant that to be in Doug's favor. It was interesting to get another person's perspective on these two friends of hers. For all their flaws she thought them decent people. Wasn't their willingness to give Bill time to work through his feelings proof of that decency? Tracy had one more question for him, and his answer would be telling. But she had to phrase it correctly. Bill shouldn't have known that the murder of Larry Waters last night had anything to do with her or the case, and that was assuming he even knew about it to begin with. "So, what are you going to do for the next few days while you ponder your future with the Shanes?"

He shrugged. "Just stay here. Spend time with my wife. Catch up on my reading. I used to build models with the boys. Maybe I'll go visit a hobby store and get some kits."

"What did your wife think of having you home the last two nights?" She thought that sounded nonthreatening.

He didn't hesitate to answer her. "She went to bed at 9:00 so I don't think she thought *anything* of it." He laughed a bit.

Tracy laughed too. This seemed like a good place to stop. She finished her notes and told him, "I think that's all I need Bill. Thank you for your time and honesty." He gave her a smile and led her to the front door. She added, "I hope you go back to the Shanes. I think they like having you there partly because you're a connection to their father." She then turned and went through the open door. She heard nothing further from Bill Ryder, just the sound of the closing door.

So Bill Ryder's wife went to sleep at 9:00. He could have left her and been at Tracy's building in time to kill Larry. But why? Tracy couldn't figure it. She had only talked to Bill one other time before today, and he didn't resist sharing what happened to his brother. She wasn't ready to cross him off yet. But he didn't seem her most likely candidate.

In her car Tracy phoned Detective Roche. "Sorry Ms. Brubaker," he started. "Nothing to report yet; we're still tracking down cab drivers working in the area that night around Waters' and your places. No witnesses have turned up who saw anything. No murder weapon. We're running all the prints we took at Waters' house but so far there haven't been any hits."

Roche couldn't see her frowning. "Are you showing pictures of anyone in particular to the cabbies you're talking to?"

"Just the one Tanner gave us, the one of Brian Shane." Tracy felt her face getting warm as Roche continued. "Some cab companies offer discounts or free rides if you're drunk—will take you wherever you want." Now she was positively hot. "Do you have anyone else in mind?"

"I hope to have a for you soon. But right now I've got a list of three or four."

Roche was quiet a moment. "Well, if we find someone who had a fare matching our MO we'll let him look at all those you have in mind. Fair enough?"

"Yes, fair enough Detective Roche." She was cooling down now. "Thank you. And please let me know if I can return the favor and help you out."

"Sure thing, Ms. Brubaker; you have a good day. Bye now."

Tracy pushed the hang up button on her GPS and thought about Tanner's fixation on Brian. She was getting angry again. How could he think Brian would want to hurt her? Or was she looking at this the wrong way? Maybe Tanner picking only Brian's photo was his way of doing a quick elimination of Brian as a suspect? Well, that's the half-full approach anyway. It was almost 10 now. She was anxious to find out what Neal had learned, if anything, with respect to his assignments.

Rebecca said, "Neal, there's a Carla Hardy on line one for you." Neal swung his chair away from his computer screen, picked up the receiver, and pushed the pound and one keys.

"Neal Bennett speaking."

"Mr. Bennett, this is Carla Hardy returning your call."

"Thank you for getting back to me, Ms. Hardy. I just had a couple of questions about last Friday night's dinner you attended with Kurt Barton; shouldn't take long."

"What is it you want to know exactly?"

"I know Mr. Barton made his remarks starting around 9:30. I have a copy of the program. Did you see him after he was done?"

She paused before answering. "I think we had a few brief words. But since he was at the front table with me and the other speakers we did most of our talking during dinner."

"Would you be able to tell me what time he left?"

"No."

"Do you remember about what time it was when his speech ended?"

"Oh, it wasn't very long, less than 10 minutes. Shall we say 9:40?"

"Thank you. One last question, did he talk to anyone that you know of about his scheduled meeting that night at 10:30?"

Another brief moment of silence and then, "Well: I know he mentioned he wouldn't be able to join us for some cocktails after the dinner like he's done in the past. Yes. I do think he said he had a late meeting. But that was the extent of it."

"Thank you so much for your time, Ms. Hardy."

"Goodbye then." And she was gone.

No help really. She didn't remember seeing Barton after his speech; didn't prove anything either way. Better luck hopefully with Wilson Crane or Elizabeth Munsen. Next up: making his way through Crystal's list. There were four names on it, no doubt all good friends. He chose to start alphabetically with Darci Brewer, who worked at a travel agency. It was past 9:00, so she should be in by now. He dialed her number.

"Hello this is Darci. Where would you like to go?"

He had some answers for that but thought better of sharing them. He introduced himself, told her he was trying to help Brian Shane, and that Crystal had given him her name to call about Friday's activities. Did she have time for a few, quick questions?

"Oh sure," she said pleasantly.

"What did you ladies do last Friday?"

"Went to a movie and then to the harbor for dinner. Walked around a little bit. Then Crystal checked her phone and got that horrible message."

"Did you guys travel together or meet separately?"

"We met at Karen's house and then took her minivan."

"What time did you gals get to the movie?"

"Seven o'clock at Harbor East."

"What did you see?"

"*The Other Woman.*"

Neal paused. "Isn't that one about a guy who cheats on his wife *and* his girlfriend?"

"That's the one."

They took an engaged woman to a movie about a married guy who has multiple mistresses? That just didn't sound right. "And you left right after the movie to go to dinner."

"That's right. We got to Phillip's just after 10."

"How long were you there?"

"Not sure. I know it was past 11. They close at 11 but we were there after that. And then we walked around the harbor for a bit like I said, and then headed back to Karen's. Crystal was checking her messages in the van when she suddenly got upset. Pretty scary."

"So you guys were a group all night; didn't go off on your own at all, or even in pairs."

She thought a moment and then said, "Not unless you count restroom breaks."

Neal decided not to comment further. "Did Crystal talk about her father at all? For example, did she say if Brian and he were having problems?"

"Oh no, nothing like that," Darci quickly answered. "She talked mostly about her job and Doug, about the wedding. I don't recall her talking about her dad at all, or Brian for that matter."

Neal took that as good news. "I think that's all Darci. I really appreciate your time."

"Hey, no sweat." She asked, "So did Brian really do it?"

"We don't think so."

"Well that's good; for Crystal's sake. I'd hate to think she wouldn't have any family at her wedding."

Neal rang up the other three names on the list, including Karen Lone, the designated driver for the evening. The group was supposed to spend the night at her house, which they did, except for poor Crystal who had to leave suddenly. With only the slightest variations, the other women's accounts matched Darci's. Crystal seemed solid.

Just about 10:30, the time Tracy was returning to the office, Elizabeth Munsen returned Neal's call. Yes, she spoke with Kurt Barton during the dinner. Yes, she thought Barton ended his remarks at about 9:40. No, she doesn't remember speaking to or seeing him after the speech. Thank you, you're welcome, goodbye. That left just Wilson Crane. Neal would talk to Tracy and then call Crane again.

Neal entered Tracy's office. "I have some things to report, Tracy," Neal said sounding much less standoffish than he did this morning. "I talked to two of the three attorneys at the Barton dinner. To cut to the chase Tracy, Barton finished his presentation about 9:40 p.m. Neither of them could be sure when he actually left the event. There was a lot of mingling, a lot of drinking. He could have left when he said he did, or he could have left as much as 15 minutes earlier. I'm not sure if 15 minutes really matters in this case."

Tracy looked at him and said, "Neal: I think timing has *everything* to do with this case, even if I'm not quite sure exactly how yet. Thanks for the follow up."

He nodded. "Also, Tracy, just to let you know, you were absolutely right about Crystal. I talked to those friends on the list you gave me, and Crystal seemed to be with someone the entire evening. I mean, she was even accompanied to the bathroom..."

Tracy continued looking at Neal, waiting for him to make some crack about the sisterhood of the potty palace or some such thing. Instead he just asked, "How did your talk with Ryder go?"

She sighed. "He was still upset about Shane's murder. He seems to think Crystal is the villain in his brother's marriage. But I still don't see him having a strong enough motive to kill Mr. Shane."

Neal shook his head. "Okay. Let me go bug Wilson Crane." He turned and went back to his office.

Now where was she on Stewart Shane's murder? Crystal and Barton seemed to have alibis, Stanz didn't have time to commit the crime and be back at his gate to meet Barton, and Bill—well she really didn't have anything on him other than opportunity and a dead brother; in other words, she had nothing. But somebody must have thought she had *something*. No way was she wrong about a connection between her and Larry Waters' murder. And the Shane murder had to be that connection. What *about* Larry's murder? Crystal couldn't have lifted the body and carried it to the car. That left Stanz, Ryder, or Barton. But why would one of them want her dead? Maybe she was wrong. Maybe she just had a stalker or something. Oh what a cheery thought *that* was.

Two o'clock: Neal entered Tracy's office. "Got time for me?"

Tracy looked at Neal hopefully. "You've solved the case!"

"You're setting yourself up for disappointment."

Tracy frowned. "Depressing man; what's up?"

"I just talked to Wilson Crane: Same story as the other two. He can't be sure if he talked to Barton after 9:40."

"Great."

"But I may be able to tell you why Barton no longer drives."

Tracy leaned forward. "Out with it."

"It looks likes Barton and Brian have something in common—a fondness for the grape."

"Oh no…" Tracy started.

"Barton had only been married for about a year. He and his wife were on their way back from the anniversary dinner when they were involved in a near fatal accident. Barton's wife lost a lot of blood and almost died. The other driver was clearly drunk—the story I found said over .1%. Barton wasn't charged, even though he and the wife shared some champagne at the restaurant earlier. Now, that was over 30 years ago. Ultimately he just let his license expire."

"So Barton felt some responsibility for almost getting his wife killed and couldn't deal with being behind the wheel anymore, is that what we're saying?"

"That's the best I could come up with. Missed it the first time since the story was so old; the internet wasn't around in the 1980s like it is today."

"It would certainly explain his attitude toward Brian, redirecting the anger at himself he must be carrying around." She paused and then looked at Neal. "I think you've got it George!"

He grinned. "I'm not having any luck in finding out if Stanz was into anyone for heavy dollars. I don't have any contacts with vice, and this isn't the sort of stuff that shows up on Google."

She nodded. "I'll reach out to El on that one then. Couldn't hurt, right?"

"Guess not. Other than that, I think I've cleared up all of my loose ends. Where does that leave us?"

She tilted her head back. "I'll let you know after I've tied up my own loose end, one who goes by the name of Ernie."

At 3:40 p.m. Tracy exited her office for her meeting with the Judds' bartender. She told Neal not to leave the office tonight until he had heard back from her just in case she got some information she needed him to follow up on, or at least something that might help solve the riddle of Brian's missing time. She opted to bring a purse with her instead of a briefcase to look less—officious. When she arrived at Judds just past 4:00, the parking lot across the street was mostly empty, so she parked there. Of course it was early on a Friday, so regulars would be the most likely clientele there now. She pushed through the heavy doors and headed to the barstool closest to where the bartender was already standing. She hopped up on the stool, put her purse on the bar, and made herself at home.

"What can I get for you young lady?" the bartender asked her.

"Ale," she answered resting her arms on the counter. "Ginger. Three lumps."

He gave her a strange look and then grabbed a glass, added three ice cubes, and filled the container with Canada Dry. "One ginger ale, three… lumps," he stated, placing her order in front of her.

"Thank you kindly," she said. She took a sip and then asked, "Are you Ernie?"

"Yes, I am," he told her.

"I'm Tracy. I'm a friend of Brian Shane's. I'm trying to help him out on this murder charge against him."

He looked at her curiously for a moment. "Oh, yeah—Brian," he finally said. "The cops asked me about him—what he did here last Friday night, stuff like that. You a cop?" he asked her.

"Lawyer," she answered.

"Oh," was all he said. "I didn't think so." Ernie continued talking as he started gathering some empty glasses, and wiping down the bar. "I couldn't really tell the cops anything though. Brian just came in, drank, and went." Ernie paused and then said, "The whole thing is really unbelievable."

Tracy looked at him, perhaps in a mildly flirtatious manner and said, "I was hoping *we* could talk about last Friday when he was here."

Ernie looked at her grinning at him. She *was* pretty. He was suddenly feeling a little flushed. "Right—like I told the cops, he was here last Friday," Ernie finally said.

"Yes, you said that already," she said, mildly teasing him. "Brian got here around 7:30 p.m., right?"

"Sounds right."

"And he left a little before 10," she stated.

Ernie briefly considered her last comment and then said, "No, I don't think so. He usually leaves around 9:00. I'm pretty sure that's when he left on Friday." Ernie stopped what he was doing suddenly and added. "Yes—he did leave at 9:00 because he didn't have his watch with him and he asked what time it was a couple of times."

Ah yes, the stolen time piece. "Did he tell you where he was going as he was leaving?"

Ernie thought a moment. "No," he answered, and then added, "I think he usually just goes home."

Tracy took a couple swigs from her glass, now having given the ice ample opportunity to chill the contents. "Did you notice if he met anyone here? Maybe he struck up a conversation with someone? Maybe someone followed him out when he left? Maybe he even got in some sort of altercation, exchanged a few heated words with another patron?"

Again, Ernie considered her questions. "No, not that I recall; he pretty much has this 'leave me be' vibe going when he drinks here. And besides, it was early. We don't get real busy here until after 10 on Fridays."

Her enthusiasm was starting to melt, just like the ice in her glass. Then she had another thought. "Was there, maybe, a disturbance in the parking lot or outside the bar? Or something that might have grabbed some attention; something that might have delayed a person trying to leave: an argument, an accident, a fight—anything?"

He tilted his head back as if he were searching the ceiling for an answer. "Uh, no; sorry," he finally answered. But then he added, "There *was* a near fender bender or two later on, but I'm pretty sure that was after Brian left."

"Oh really; what happened?" she asked, more out of curiosity.

"Well, when the cable went out some of the folks who were watching the game kinda' freaked out being the score was so close. Suddenly everyone wanted to pay their tabs and go find a place to watch the ballgame. People nearly clipped each other boltin' from the parking lot."

"The cable went out?" Tracy asked, her enthusiasm returning with a vengeance.

"Yeah. They've been messing with the cable lines in this area. I think we're finally getting high speed internet or something. Anyway we had a bad storm come through and that shorted out something or other, affected most of the places around here. Most of the night the rain was pretty light;

I mean they didn't have to delay the game or anything. But that sudden downpour…wow."

"When did the cable go out? How long was it out?"

Ernie paused and then said, "Not sure exactly when it went out, but I think it was before 10. Can't tell you when it came back on because we turned off the TV and just forgot about it."

Tracy thought a bit. Then she thought some more. And then Tracy Brubaker slammed her hand on the counter, getting looks from those who weren't already observing the conversation she'd been having with Ernie. "That's it! *That. Is. IT!*"

Ernie stepped back a bit. He hadn't seen this show before.

"Ernie — you are now one of my most favorite people in the whole wide world ever. How much do I owe for the drink?"

Ernie relaxed again and smiled. "Ah, well, seeing as I'm now one of your favorite people, I guess it's on the house."

She looked up from her purse, through which she had been looking for cash, positively beaming. She took the $5.00 bill she already had in her hand and put it on the counter. Then, she turned abruptly, her feet moving almost as fast as her mind. And when she was pulling open the exit door she swore she heard someone ask, "What in the hell did she have to drink, Ernie?"

"Ginger ale!" Ernie answered preplexed.

Tracy barreled through her office doors like a freight train, full steam ahead. It was just after 4:30 and things had to be done and done now. She had debated calling Neal from her car phone while on the way. But she was so wound up now she was afraid she wouldn't be able to split her concentration. Now was *not* the time to have an accident. So when she did finally arrive back at her workplace, she whisked past Rebecca and just called out "Neal!" as she passed him. Both Neal and Rebecca rushed to her office. She didn't give them a chance to open their mouths.

"Neal," Tracy started, "I need you to find out what cable company serves Judds. They had an outage there last Friday so I need you to find out what time it happened and how long it lasted. And I need to know if the area affected by the outage includes the Shanes. Get started on it now because those cable offices probably close at 5:00 p.m. and it's a Friday and if you need to contact them you'll need to do it now. *Go!*"

Neal turned without saying a word. "Beck," Tracy continued, "I want you to check on the weather for, say, the last three—no, four—weeks in the area covering the Shane estate, working back from this past Friday. I want to know if it rained at all prior to Friday's storm, and if so, how badly, and all that. Okay?"

"Righto."

Tracy picked up the phone and dialed the BPD hoping to speak with Detective Tanner. He was unavailable so she asked for Officer Banks.

"Banks," he said when he finally picked up.

"Ted, its Tracy."

"Oh hi, Tracy. What's up?"

"I need you to connect me with someone nice and friendly in the crime lab that has access to the raincoat Brian was wearing the night of the murder."

"What do you need from them?"

"I just want to verify some lab results. Nothing fancy."

Banks thought a bit and then said, "I guess that'd be okay. I'll connect you to Cheri. Just tell her that you're Shane's lawyer and I'll stay on the line with you to let her know that it's okay. It shouldn't be a problem though. Talk to you soon."

"Thanks bunches Ted." As she awaited the pickup, Neal and Rebecca re-entered her office. That was fast, she thought.

"Crime lab; Cheri Alabaster speaking," the voice that clicked on said.

"Hi Cheri; my name is Tracy Brubaker and I'm Brian Shane's attorney. Officer Banks told me you could help me. I understand you have access to the Shane evidence."

"It's okay, Cheri," Banks added.

"What can I help you with?" Cheri asked, sounding bored.

"I'm curious about the raincoat that was tested for powder residue. I know the test came back negative but that's not what I'm interested in."

"What *are* you interested in?"

"Was there anything in the pockets?"

There was a brief pause. "Give me a moment."

Tracy looked at Neal and Rebecca looking at her. Her heart was racing. This is where she had to be lucky. If not, even though she was sure of who, why, and now how, it would mean nothing without…

"Yes, there were some items," Cheri said upon her return.

"Please tell me what they were." Tracy listened to Cheri's answer, pen and notebook in hand.

Neal and Rebecca observed some strange phenomena in the next few moments. First, Tracy's face broke out into a smile so big it forced her own eyes shut. Then she jumped up and down, at least twice. Then she made some other noise before settling down. Finally she asked, "Cheri, will anyone be in the crime lab that could assist me within the next 20 minutes or so? I'd like a quick test done that should be easily OK'd by Detective Tanner, the primary on the case." Tracy waited for the answer, then said, "Thank you!" and promised she'd be there as soon as she could. She hung up the phone and looked at her two pals.

"You yelped," Neal said.

"Sounded more like a squeak to me," Rebecca countered.

She looked at them quizzically. "I neither yelped nor squeaked," Tracy challenged.

"Oh, you yelped alright," Neal countered.

Tracy wrinkled her nose at him. "I need to go. Did you guys get those answers yet?"

"I have the weather info right here," Rebecca said as she handed the printouts to Tracy. Oh beautiful, wonderful paper!

"9:48 p.m.," Neal told her. "Back on at 12:37 a.m. And yes, the outage affected several private residences that included the Shanes'."

"Group hug!" Tracy shouted and quickly embraced her associates before bolting out the door.

She left Neal and Rebecca standing there utterly confused and more than a little concerned. Finally they looked at each other and Rebecca asked Neal, "Do you think we can go home now? Or maybe I should call someone?"

Neal pondered the questions and finally said, "Well I'm outta here. I think I need to see a doctor about whiplash."

Tracy was usually a conscientious and courteous driver. But she was fighting hard to keep her inner aggressiveness from rearing its ugly head as she drove home. "Please God," she said aloud. "Just let me be right. *Just let me be right.*" If she *was* right, then she might have what she needed to prove Brian's innocence. If her guess *was* correct, she couldn't help but appreciate the irony that the police had had the evidence to exonerate Brian in their possession this whole week.

She was so excited that sleep did not come easily. Her mind kept retur-
ing to the past.

Fade in...

Brian Shane opened his eyes; it was morning already. Tracy had her
back to him. She was breathing softly; he saw the blanket that was covering her rise and fall slowly. Part of him wanted to move the covers away
and gaze, with the full light of morning, at her naked body. But instead he
moved closer to her, brushed the hair away that was covering her neck,
and kissed her softly. She must have already been awake because she immediately turned to face him. She smiled at him, and then he moved in to
kiss her lips. When he pulled back, her smile returned. "Good morning,"
Tracy said finally.
    "It certainly is," Brian responded.
    "What time is it?"
    "Early, not even 7:00 yet."
    "That's good. Lots of the day left." He moved in to kiss her again. She
could tell he wanted an encore. Together they gave a bravura performance.
Afterward they lay side by side looking into each other's eyes. Ever the
student, Tracy decided to review what she had learned the past eight-or-
nine hours. "It wasn't like it is in the movies," she said.
    "What do you mean?"
    "They always seem to know what they're doing the first time."
    "Yeah; I get you now."
    "It felt like we were putting a bookcase together or something: put this
here, move that there. I didn't realize noses could be such a problem."
    He laughed. "It wasn't as romantic as you thought it would be, huh?"
    "Not the very first time."
    "That's why we..."
    "And this morning?" she asked slightly chuckling.
    "Third time's the charm," he chuckled back. And then he kissed her
again.
    It wasn't true exactly that it hadn't been romantic. Last night was the
culmination of both an exciting day in the academic career of Tracy Brubaker and their now almost two year courtship. She had scored a 97 on her
history exam (highest grade in the class) and received an A on her creative

writing assignment. She also learned she'd be exempt from two finals as she had aced the courses. She was feeling euphoric. Easter had passed a few weeks ago but she was hopping around like a bunny rabbit waiting for Brian to pick her up for their Friday dinner date. The smile hadn't left her face the entire evening. When they left the restaurant they returned to Brian's home, and to his room. The kissing had been passionate; mutual arousal obvious. But she had always been the "good girl" and not let things go too far. Brian had never pressured her. He made it clear he didn't want her to do anything she wasn't comfortable with, even though he had asked her to sleep with him several times before.

But last night had been the perfect storm. She was riding a high the entire day. She recalled the dinner with her parents, where Brian all but asked her father for his daughter's hand. He had been on top of her on the bed. "Tracy I want you so much," he had whispered several times. She wanted him too. She was excited, full of desire as well as curiosity. So when he had started unbuttoning her shirt she didn't stop him. When he had realized what was going to happen, he had stopped and pulled back, looking at her to make sure his assumption was correct. Then his lips and hands had resumed their mission.

Now they were looking at each other, having learned things about each other few, if any, other people would ever know. "You're so beautiful Tracy," he said. "I love you so much."

"I love you too," she responded quietly. After a bit she asked, "Brian, can I ask you something? And I want you to be honest with me."

"What is it Tracy?"

"Now that we've, well… What I mean is, are you going to expect this all the time now?"

Brian looked at her. There was concern in her face. "I *will* be honest with you Tracy," he started. "I would certainly like to do this again with you — many times. But no, I don't want you to feel like this is going to be how I expect every future night we have together to end. I was serious when I told you I don't want you to do anything you're not comfortable with."

Right answer, so she leaned in and kissed him again. She pulled back to look at him. His eyes started moving in a southerly direction from hers. Perhaps because she still had her history test on her brain she grinned and asked, "Exploring again?"

He looked back at her. "Definitely; it's a beautiful world in here."

And then she started laughing. Not mildly, but the kind that turns one's face red, causes tears to make their escape. "Tracy what is it?" Brian asked mildly alarmed.

"Exploring..." she managed to say. "Brian Shane's going to explore and plant..." she trailed off, her laughter preventing the words from coming out.

"What?"

She finally continued. "He's going to explore and plant his flag." And she rolled over moving from side to side in a fit of hysterics.

"Flag?"

She nodded. She still couldn't speak. Finally he understood. "Oh, I get it," he said. "We're using nicknames already." She nodded again. He started laughing too and joined in on the fun. "Yes: I'm going to explore and plant my flag on Planet Tracy."

Suddenly she stopped, and looked at him. She closed her mouth, reopened it, and then said, "Wrong preposition," and lost her composure again.

"Tracy made a dirty joke!" Brian laughed. And it took a few more minutes for both of them to calm down. These were the humorous moments that only lovers would find funny. After they settled down, Brian looked at her, his body practically quivering. "My God I can't believe this."

"What do you mean Brian?"

"This is only the beginning. We've got—what—60 more years together? I mean: I just can't imagine being any happier or more in love with you than I am right now."

The smile left her face, and then it left his. And she moved toward him and started kissing him. When her stomach let out a growl she stopped long enough to look down and say, "Shut up," and then started her own exploration. It was going to be a while before breakfast.

Fade out...

Tracy opened her eyes and saw the unoccupied space next to her. She sighed and then rolled on her back. She saw the cross that hung on her wall and then turned away from it. Yes, according to her faith she had sinned, partaken of something meant for married couples. They sinned four times between dinner and breakfast that Friday and Saturday. And they would sin some more before it would stop because of outside forces.

Is that why what happened, happened? Were they being punished? Did God send a ruthless ex-lover and a trigger-happy thug to punish them for what they had done? Male and Female—He created them. Male and Female—He destroyed them? No, she didn't believe that. If that were the case daughters would be losing their fathers at an alarming rate. But there was some ugly poetry here. They slept together, and then Brian sleeps through Tracy's suffering and his father's murder. She shook her head at the thought.

Brian had set the bar. No one else had even come close. "Come on baby, what are you saving it for?" is what she started hearing after three or so dates with a guy. Sometimes even before that. "Saving it for someone I know really loves me," she'd think to herself. It had taken a few years after the breakup to even try the dating scene again. And she didn't like what she found when she re-entered it. Finally she had just stopped being pro-active. She shook her head again. If things had worked out as they should have, she'd probably be celebrating a wedding anniversary this month. She always wanted a May or maybe June wedding. She turned on her side in the direction facing the clock.

Being married, that was at the root of it. Tracy had taken it for grant-ed that she and Brian Shane were going to be husband and wife. Mr. and Mrs. Brian Shane. So why not then get a sneak peek at what their future held? She had given the gift a woman can give only once to only one man because she thought…How could she have foreseen? In her mind, she and Brian became one that night. And that's why she couldn't stay away. They were soul mates. Evil forces had divided them: false witness, mur-der, demon rum…the Three Stooges of evil. She was getting angry. Let no man tear asunder what God has joined! Asunder—what a powerful word. That's what she and Brian were right now. But if she had truly sinned, then she could be forgiven, and by extension, so could Brian. What was torn can be mended. Nothing is impossible with God!

Right. Tomorrow she would make at least one thing right. She'd get Brian out from under this latest evil attack. And then they could perhaps start rejoining themselves together. It wouldn't be easy, and it would take time. But if Brian were willing she'd be willing. Would he be willing to pick up that phone, to make that call? Enough. She had to get some sleep. Tomorrow was going to be an exhausting day. But it was going to be worth it if all worked out like she hoped. Tomorrow, *she* would be tearing some-one's future asunder.

Chapter 11

Saturday afternoon. Tracy arrived at the Shane estate, just over one week after the murder of Brian's father, ready to lay it all out on the table. She thought she had it. She had briefed Detectives Tanner and Lucas last night after the results of the test she asked for came in from the crime lab. Tanner thought her evidence was provocative, but not necessarily conclusive. Lucas wasn't sure either. She convinced them to arrange a meeting with the people who had been at the estate the night of the murder. Brian, Crystal, and Doug would be no problem. But getting Bill Ryder and Kurt Barton over there might be a little trickier. "I guess it couldn't hurt," Tanner had finally said. It was now two, an hour before she asked everyone to be there. The Shane children and Doug were ready and waiting. She wanted to talk to Brian alone before her presentation. She had carried out plenty of defenses in court before. And she would try to look at this in the same way. But that was much easier said than done.

Brian noticed Tracy was nervous and wound up. She confessed she hadn't eaten anything since dinner yesterday and slept little the night before. It was like exam week, Brian thought. And he knew Tracy's feelings about that—failure was not an option. Heck, neither were B plusses.

They were seated next to each other in the study, while Crystal and Doug waited in the large living room outside. "Brian," Tracy began. "I've tried my best over the past week or so to find a way to prove you didn't kill your father."

"I know that Tracy."

"It now all comes down to this. I know who killed your dad. But that doesn't mean anything if I can't back it up. So I'm going to do this the only way I know how."

"As if you're in court."

"Yes; exactly. Frankly, I don't want your case to go that far, put you through any more than you've already been put through. Detective Tanner has done us both a huge favor and agreed to be here today to indulge me. I think even Lucas might show up. I don't know if an arrest will be made or not. But I'm going to present what I have to an abbreviated jury. I want you just to sit there and listen, like you're at the defense table in a court room. Just listen and resist the impulse to interject. That might distract me. I need to *sell* this to Detective Tanner today." She paused and then added, "I hope I did what you needed me to do for you."

Brian took her hand, and she looked down at their clasped fingers. "Tracy, you already *have* done what I asked you to do—help me; maybe even almost got killed for doing it. You stopped your life to be there for me. I can't ask for any more from you than what you've already given." He started stroking her hand and fingers gently. "And I got to see you again. I know it hasn't been easy for you. I caused you so much pain that I still can't quite believe you're here helping me."

She looked at him. "I'm here because I don't think you're a killer. And because I need to know for myself if it really is over for us. I mean, in spite of everything, I still treasure those early times we were together, the time when I believe I knew the real Brian Shane. Maybe I'm just a romantic, but I've always believed in second chances."

He listened to her and nodded. "Looking back I can't believe how awfully I treated you in those last months. I replay those moments all the time in my head and I still do not understand why I did what I did, said what I said. I so wish I could go back in time, take the pain I caused you away. I'd give anything to be able to do that. Oh Tracy, how I hate myself for how I treated you." She didn't say anything so he continued. "Anyway, if it doesn't work out the way you hope today, I don't want you to think for a second that I would hold you responsible for anything that happens to me. I know you did your best. If I had listened to you all those years ago I wouldn't be in this position. We both *know* that. You tried to help me, to save me once. And I treated you horribly. But here you are to try and save me again…"

Tears started coming down her cheeks, the accumulated stress of the past week and the accompanying memories showed on her face. And Brian's mea culpa didn't help matters either. "I don't want to let you down, Brian."

"Not possible for you to do. You never have before." And they leaned in and kissed briefly, and then she put her head on his shoulder while embracing him. "I still love you Tracy. No matter what happens this afternoon, please believe me when I say I still love you."

Detectives Tanner and Lucas arrived about one half-hour before showtime. What surprised Tracy though was another, unannounced party guest: Arthur Pankow. "Tanner informed me of what was going on," Pankow told her. "I thought I'd get a sneak peek of how you were planning to make your case. Take some notes, maybe."

"Hey, that's cheating," Tracy told him.

"Maybe; but I had nothing better to do today."

She looked at him. "Okay you can stay. But you can't object to anything or interrupt me. You'll make me lose my place."

He smiled. "Fair enough."

Kurt Barton was the last guest to arrive. He had been told three and so that's when he planned to be there. It was a great inconvenience of course, what with it being such lovely golf weather, on a Saturday, no less. But Detective Elias Tanner had strongly suggested he attend. Besides: how would it look to the Shane children if their lawyer seemed disinterested in the heirs to the company and the mystery surrounding their father's death? But it wasn't a mystery; the police had arrested Brian. So what was this all about?

Officer Ted Banks, who had arrived with Detectives Tanner and Lucas, led Barton to the large living room — the scene of the crime — where several others were already seated and waiting. Of course *they* had nothing pressing on *their* schedules. Brian Shane was sitting by himself on a corner chair, his hands clasped together, perhaps in prayer, while he stared at the floor. Crystal Shane and Doug Stanz sat together on the couch opposite the end where Stewart Shane had been sitting when he was shot. Bill Ryder sat on the seat that brought the 'L' together. Detective Tanner was on his mobile phone moving about the room. Another Detective was there, as well as State's Attorney Pankow. And there was that woman who practiced law and was, rumor had it, Brian Shane's former girlfriend. She was doing some pacing herself. "Sit anywhere," Banks told him. So Barton sat, since there really was nowhere else to sit, next to where Stewart's body sat dead one week ago.

When she saw Barton park his tush, Tracy walked over to Officer Banks and whispered something in his ear. Banks nodded and left the room for a minute. He returned escorting Bernard Cubbins, and told him to stand anywhere he wanted. Barton raised an eyebrow. Tracy then walked over to Barton and said, "I thought it would be nice to have him come in, stretch his legs. I hope that's okay." There was no response from Barton. She then went over to Brian, and put a reassuring hand on his shoulder. He looked up at her and then squeezed her hand.

When Tanner finally hung up his phone, Tracy left Brian's side and went over to the detective. "It's on its way Tracy," he told her reassuringly.

"It will be here at any time now." She turned and continued to pace. She had brought only a water bottle with her for sustenance, so she pulled it out of her briefcase, which was leaning against the chair where Brian was sitting, and took a few swallows. She capped it and placed it on the center table. Then the doorbell rang. Banks moved toward the direction of the front door with Tracy not far behind. On the other side of the entrance was a uniformed officer holding a large, brown paper bag. She handed it to Banks, who turned and nearly ran into Tracy, who was mere steps behind him.

"Is this what you've been waiting for Tracy?" he asked while handing her the bag.

"Yes," she said as she peered in, looking to make sure what she needed was in there. A smile came over her face. Giving Banks a big grin she just said, "Thanks, Ted."

"You're welcome, Tracy," he responded with a smile of his own.

"I have to have my props, Ted. Even though I'm not in court I have to have my props."

"Just like Columbo," Banks teased.

Tracy said, "*Thank you very much*," in a poor Peter Falk imitation and then turned and headed back toward the living room. "Here I am," she thought. "All my suspects gathered together just like in the movies and Agatha Christie's books." She took a deep breath. "I just hope I can pull this off. On with the show…"

Upon entering she delivered her opening lines to her audience. "I'm sorry to keep everyone waiting. The fact is I was waiting for something myself that just now arrived." She placed the bag she was holding on the floor against the wall and continued. "I promise to make this go as quick as I can. I know most of you have better things to do." She directed her gaze at Barton.

"You all know of course I'm representing Brian in the murder of his father. In conjunction with this I've been investigating anyone who might have had a reason and/or opportunity to kill Stewart Shane. Several things have come to light over the last several days that have the potential to cast suspicion on people other than Brian. If I were in court I would try to present these things to a jury in the hopes this would create reasonable doubt. I suspect everyone here, especially Mr. Barton, knows that a lawyer zealously represents her client. Part of such representation is to have the jury looking at other people."

Tracy paused and looked at Kurt Barton. "Mr. Barton, you are an attorney of great repute. I know we haven't spoken much but I get the feeling you are a man that takes things such as honor, loyalty, and friendship very seriously. I can't help but wonder if you felt betrayed when the Shane Company, a company that you have helped in immeasurable ways for many years, started looking elsewhere. Mr. Shane was not just a client, he was a friend. You had to be somewhat offended. I know I would have been. Enough to kill him though? You seem to have a good alibi. But Doug Stanz never saw who was in your limo that night. We only have Bernie's word that you were in there and that no one else was. And Bernie's been with you a long time, he understands loyalty. I wonder if you had an extra passenger in the limo that night when you exited the estate, someone who originally entered by hiding in Brian's car."

She didn't give Barton a chance to respond, as she quickly switched her attentions to Bill Ryder. "Bill, it would have been easy for you to enter the home after Brian did and then shoot Stewart Shane. You could have been anywhere on the estate when Doug radioed that Barton was on his way up. Perhaps you blamed Stewart for the death of your brother; it was Stewart Shane's attempt to control his daughter that drove your brother away. I don't have any siblings myself but I have lost someone very dear to me to violence. But my father's killer was himself killed too early for me to contemplate revenge. If that had not been case, I wonder what I'd have done.

"Doug," she started as she moved in front of him, "you said it yourself that you know how it looks, a man of meager means engaged to a wealthy woman. I find it hard to believe that Stewart Shane would have let this wedding go through. By killing him you would have removed that threat. You seem to have a solid alibi. But since you know the security routine and the inner workings of the estate, you could have planned in advance, like sneaking a bike onto the property to help you get to the house and back in a seemingly impossible time frame."

Tracy took a deep breath as she moved slightly to her right. "And Crystal, you and I were once like sisters. I wish I'd have made an attempt to keep our relationship, even after Brian and I ended ours. You're smart, ambitious, and know how to get what you want. These traits are no doubt why you are where you are today. But I can't help but wonder how someone like you felt living with a father who still treated you like a child, trying to control your life. Or living with a brother who had become a drunken annoyance, an older brother who you felt you had to watch over, instead of the other way around. You knew Brian's schedule that night. Maybe the person hidden in Brian's car, if there was one, found a hiding place not in Barton's limo but in your car when it finally arrived. Alternately, you could have given anyone the keys to anywhere on the estate to serve as a hideaway."

Tracy moved back to the center of the room, noting the expressions of indignation, confusion, and horror on some audience members' faces. "Now please don't misunderstand me," she continued. "I'm not saying these things to hurt anybody. If we were in court, these very private matters could become a matter of public record. Despite what you may believe, I don't want that to happen, to cause any more pain to innocent people. So I hope that you will all cooperate today, help me walk through the night of the murder and answer some of the lingering questions that, despite what the police may think, need to be answered. If you all are willing to do that, perhaps we'll all agree on who Stewart Shane's murderer really is when all is said and done."

Tracy re-surveyed the onlookers. There were some nods, and everyone remained seated. She looked over to Elias Tanner who nodded himself. She then pulled out her small notebook, flipped open its cover, and began. "Okay. Let's start around 7:00 in the evening two Fridays ago," she said while staring at the page in front of her. "And if I say anything with respect to the facts — or rather the perceived facts — that is incorrect I hope someone will correct me." She looked up at Tanner again, and then surveyed the rest of the room to see if she still had their attention. She did.

"Brian Shane leaves the estate about quarter after 7:00. Any and all household employees are by now gone. Crystal has left for the evening for her movie and dinner with friends. Mr. Shane is alone in the house, presumably watching a baseball game. Brian heads to Judds as he typically does on Fridays and arrives at his destination around 7:30 p.m. I confirmed the arrival time at Judds with my pal Ernie, best bartender *ever*. Brian leaves Judds around 9:00 and arrives back home at 10:05 p.m. This arrival time is confirmed by both security guards and Brian himself, who noted the time, more or less, courtesy of the grandfather clock in the hall, when he entered his house." She paused, and then said, "Question number one — Where was Brian Shane between 9:15 p.m., the time he normally gets home Fridays, and 10:05 p.m.? Where did he go and what did he do for that 50 minutes, give or take?" Again she paused. She looked up. "But we'll come back to that."

She continued. "Brian parks his car in the garage, enters the house, hangs up his raincoat in the hall closet, at which point he sees his father watching television—'some sports thing on ESPN' I think is what Brian told me. His father turns, sees Brian, but doesn't say anything. Brian heads upstairs to his room." Tracy looked up and stopped moving about the room. "Question number two—how is it that Stewart Shane was watching a cable television program past 10 when the cable in the area went out at 9:48 p.m.?"

Pankow spoke up. "The cable went out?"

Tracy turned to him. "This area is undergoing an upgrade and the storm impacted the construction location; knocked out the signal for a while." She turned back to face her onlookers. "But we'll come back to *that*. Brian now enters his bedroom—let's say it's about 10:10 p.m.—and basically collapses on the bed after removing his shoes. He falls asleep, and is awakened just after 10:30 by Bill Ryder and Kurt Barton, who arrived earlier at the gate at 10:26 p.m., and is told his father has been shot. They demand to know what happened. Brian says he doesn't know a thing." Tracy looked up from her notes and moved her head from side to side to alleviate the stiffness that was starting to form in her neck. Looking back down at her pad she asked, "Question number three—why was there a stack of books and magazines blocking the view of the alarm clock radio on Brian's nightstand?" Again she looked up and around. "No takers?" she asked them. "Well, we'll come back to that then too."

Tracy closed her notebook and moved closer to where Tanner was standing. "Does that sound like an accurate summary of what happened here Friday night a week ago, Detective Tanner?" she asked him.

He looked at her. "Yes, I would say so."

"And to you, Detective Lucas?"

"Sure."

She scanned her jury trying to gage how she was doing. Hard to tell, but no one was yawning—yet. Time to move on.

"Okay. Then let's briefly touch on the other crimes that have plagued the Shanes recently, thefts of small personal items." Tracy went over to Crystal. "Crys, we need to share this information with the rest of the class. What was the first item hoisted by the thief? Was it Bill Ryder's mini-flash-light?"

Crystal nodded. "I think so." Tracy looked over at Ryder. He nodded in agreement.

"And when did *that* theft take place?" Tracy asked her.

"The Saturday before Dad was killed, right Bill?" Crystal answered.

"I'm sure I had it during my Friday shift, but couldn't find it when I was prepping for Saturday's work," Bill affirmed.

"So you kept the flashlight in the security booth, which was, until recently, left unlocked?" Tracy asked.

"That's right," Ryder told her.

She turned to Brian. "Brian, when was your watch taken?"

He looked up from the floor where his eyes had remained up until now. "The following Wednesday," he told her.

"And that was the last item that was taken?" She looked to Brian, then Crystal, then Stanz, and then Ryder. They all looked at each other.

Finally Crystal said, "We think so. At least, we haven't noticed anything missing since then and no one's said anything about other thefts."

"So the thefts, still unsolved, started the day after Stewart Shane arranged the meeting with Kurt Barton and ended the Wednesday before the murder," Tracy said while moving closer to Barton. "Mr. Barton: I just want to briefly revisit what you and I discussed in your office when you so kindly made time for me." Barton nodded slightly. Tracy almost chuckled when the image of a Barton Bobblehead popped into her mind. Would it sell well? Oh the effects hunger and lack of sleep can have on the brain.

"You told me," she continued, "that when Mr. Shane made the call he was shouting, but not in an angry way. Rather: as if he thought you couldn't hear him. Correct?"

This time Barton actually opened his mouth to answer her. "Yes, I thought maybe he was having phone trouble."

"And the call came in just as you were leaving the office for the day, so it would have been around 5:00 p.m.?"

Barton was back to nodding his answers—a bobble for yes.

"Thank you, Mr. Barton." She moved away from him and back to the center of the room. "I asked the police to check the phone company's records for the Friday of the call just to verify the time. According to those records the call was placed from Mr. Shane's mobile phone at 5:02 p.m. Sound right Mr. Barton?" Affirmative bobble. Tracy looked around her. She took a breath. Her heartbeat started to accelerate. Here we go, she thought.

"Now let's go back and answer those previously posed questions, shall we?" Another brief pause: "Let's start with the second question. How is it that Stewart Shane was watching cable TV at 10:10 p.m. when the cable signal was lost at 9:48 p.m.?" She looked around the room; silence. "Answer, he couldn't have been." Tracy moved toward Brian, putting her hand on his shoulder. "So either Brian is lying when he says his father was watching the tube when Brian came in after 10, or he isn't, and someone else is." She noticed several people straighten their postures. She quickly continued. "But why would Brian lie about such a thing? What would be the point? What's always bothered me is that had Brian shot his father — had the presence of mind to find the gun, return to the living room to commit the murder, and then toss the weapon out the window — why wouldn't he then just lie and say he came home and found his father dead? He told the police right from the get-go he knew about the meeting with Mr. Barton, so he knew the body would be found very soon. So if he didn't lie about that, why would he lie about his father watching television when he couldn't have been?" She paused again. "Conclusion: Brian is telling the truth."

Tracy moved toward where Bill Ryder was seated. "Mr. Ryder — Bill — you told the police you saw Brian leave the garage and enter the house at 10:07 p.m. and that you're sure of the time because you checked your watch when you saw him."

"That's right," he answered.

"But that can't be right," she countered, "because the cable signal was already out, so Brian couldn't be walking into a home with no signal and see a man watching cable TV."

There was silence now. And Tracy noticed Bill Ryder had become the focus of the small crowd. He looked around, not quite sure what to say. Was she accusing him of something?

"I tell you I saw him!" Ryder finally said, defensively.

Without raising her voice, she asked, "Well, how do you know for sure it was Brian?"

He stared at her a bit, having calmed down. "Well, he was wearing that green raincoat of his. Look: I heard the side door to the garage slam shut and saw him..."

Tracy interrupted. "So is it more accurate to say you saw someone in a green raincoat exiting the garage and then heading toward the house? You were coming from the direction of the back booth and garden so you would have seen only the back of the person coming out of the garage. You told me you didn't call out to him. Did he have his hood up?"

Ryder looked at her. He thought for a moment. The room remained quiet. He looked around and then answered her. "Yes, I suppose you're right. I thought it was Brian because of the raincoat. I never did see his face."

Tracy smiled at him. *"Thank you, Bill."*

And now it was time; another deep breath; a quick prayer. Tracy had seen this sort of thing played out in plenty of Agatha Christie movie adaptations. How would she fare? Finally she said, "And that brings us to you, Doug."

It was his turn to stare at her now. And the look she was giving him was not a friendly one. He gulped and then said, "What do you mean?"

"You signed Brian in at the gate as arriving at 10:05 p.m." She briefly stopped. An image of Cindy-Lou Who interrogating the Grinch made a brief cameo in her mind. "Why did you sign Brian in at 10:05 p.m. when he really arrived home at his normal time, close to 9:15 p.m.? Why did you do that Doug?"

Stanz just looked at her. His mouth went dry. All he could think to say was, "I didn't. I mean, he *did* arrive just after 10. Bill saw him. Brian saw the clock in the hall."

"Bill saw someone in a raincoat. A clock can be changed," she challenged.

But he wasn't about to back down. "Oh, I get it. You're just coming up with a scenario to save your boyfriend. You've got this all wrong!"

A strange mix of indignation and excitement boiled up in her. She wasn't about to back down either; the hell with it then. "Here's what I think happened the night of the murder," she said while breaking eye contact with Stanz and moving back to the center of the room. "After everyone had left for the evening, including Brian, you went back up to the house, quietly entered, and moved the hall grandfather clock ahead about 50 minutes. You knew Brian got home normally around 9:15 p.m. and you knew the punctual Mr. Barton was due at 10:30 p.m., but was more likely to arrive a few minutes earlier. You had to create a window of time that was too narrow for you to be able to run up to the house after Brian arrived, kill Mr. Shane, plant the gun, and then return to meet Barton. So you figured moving the clock ahead 50 minutes would do the trick. Detective Tanner himself made the point that 20 minutes was not enough time to make the round trip and commit the crime. So you wanted it to look like the murder happened between 10:10 p.m. and 10:30 p.m. or, as it turned out, between 10:05 p.m. and 10:26 p.m." She stopped and looked at Doug. Stanz said nothing.

"After moving the clock ahead, you went upstairs to Brian's room and stacked some books and magazines on his nightstand so he wouldn't be able to see his alarm clock when he got home. He would just go to his room and crash like he always did. You figured there'd be no reason for him to fool with the clock. And you had already stolen his watch. You took the flashlight and bracelet, and faked the theft of your own tie clasp just to cover up the theft of the watch, because you feared if only Brian's watch vanished, it could ultimately arouse suspicion as to the nature of your plan. The watch was stolen last, to give Brian the least amount of time to replace it. And we both know that while Brian's car is super-sweet and has an awesome sound system, it, like most cars of that vintage, does not have a clock in it." Stanz still remained stone faced. She was hoping for a crack; something. But no such luck. She took quick looks at Tanner and Pankow. At least they were paying attention; onward then.

"Anyway, you moved on to Mr. Shane's room and took his gun from the unlocked bureau drawer. I thought it was funny how you insisted Bill lock his booth up after the thefts started but didn't think to try and secure the gun. Anyhoo, now with the gun in your possession, you returned to your booth. It was still early enough that Bill wouldn't have started his 8:00 rounds yet so there was little risk of you being seen."

At this point Tracy paused, her eyes searched for—there it was. She found her bottled water and took a couple of quick swigs, capped it, and returned to her previous position. "At about quarter after 9, as usual, Brian came home, and he did exactly what he said he did. Again, you knew Bill would be back in his own booth by this time so there was little risk he'd have seen Brian arrive. He never had before. The back booth is too far away from the garage for someone to see the inside light turned on if the garage door is opened." She paused briefly to look over at Brian. He smiled at her. That's just what she needed right now.

"Shortly after Brian arrived you returned to the house, again quietly entered, and shot Mr. Shane. You moved the grandfather clock back to its correct time, grabbed Brian's raincoat from the closet, went outside and tossed the gun on the ground beneath Brian's window, and then went to the garage to await the arrival of Bill Ryder for his 10 o'clock rounds."

At this point Stanz sprung to his feet and shouted, "You're wrong! You're *crazy*!"

"About what exactly Doug?" she immediately asked. "I saw mud near the grandfather clock myself—it's probably still there if you want to take a look—so someone with muddy shoes was near there that night. The police wear those footy things to protect the crime scene, so that narrows down who could have been so close to the clock to only a handful of people, you being one of them. The gun could easily have been tossed from anywhere, not just out of Brian's window. But I'm not finished yet."

He sat back down. He hadn't prepared a rebuttal in advance.

She continued. "You watched for Bill through the garage's back window. When you saw him and he was close enough, you exited the garage, making sure to slam the door as hard as you could so he would hear you and then look in your direction as you made your way back to the house. You also mentally noted what time that was. You quickly returned the raincoat to the closet after entering. And at this point you must have seen the TV screen was full of digital snow. Time was crucial so you quickly found the remote, shut off the TV, and tossed the remote back on the couch. You didn't notice that the remote bounced off the couch and onto the floor, which is where the police found it. That's what the crime scene photos show and what I noticed that Friday night.

"You waited for Bill to be far enough out of sight before you headed back to your booth. It would have taken you less than 15 minutes to get back there since you're running downhill all the way. It took me about 11. After you got there, you subtracted a couple of minutes from the time you noted Bill saw you, and entered *that* time as Brian's arrival time so that your and Bill's accounts would match up. And of course you were there in time to greet Mr. Barton, who courteously showed up close to 10:30 as scheduled. As for Brian also being a party to his own frame, you weren't worried about the grandfather clock in the grand scheme of things because Brian most likely wouldn't take a close enough look to know the exact time of his entrance, if he even noticed the time at all. It was a precautionary measure on your part. As long as it appeared to Brian like it was after 10, then that would be good enough."

There was silence in the room. Eyes shifted attention from Tracy to Doug and back again. Crystal was near tears but Tracy could see the anger building in her facial muscles. If this were a chess game, he had just been "checked." But it wasn't mate; not yet.

"You have absolutely no proof of this...ridiculous fable," he said, not quite growling, but close to it. "Your case against me is lamer than the one against lover-boy over there."

But she smiled at him. Why was she smiling at him? The more she continued that smile the more nervous he became. She finally showed mercy. "Well: I might have something. The police and SA will have to decide its value."

Tracy gave quick glances to Tanner, Lucas, and Pankow, who all watched her now moving toward the brown bag on the floor. She then stopped and turned to face Doug again. "You see, the way I figure it, my murderer is a first time killer. He's had no practice in murder and has concocted a scenario whereby everybody has to do exactly what they always do and when they always do it. It requires almost split-second timing in certain areas. It's a very ambitious plan. Any number of things could go wrong. As a result, time must be moving very slowly for the killer. So there you are Doug, a nervous man in a three-car garage. You have just shot someone. If some poor traveler gets lost and comes to your empty booth looking for help, your careful plan is toast. If Bill makes his rounds too early to allow for your manufactured time window to work, or too late so that you can't make it back to the booth to meet Barton, your goose is cooked. Or if Barton, heaven forbid, gets there too early and you're not back yet, your beans are baked."

She paused again. Yes, she was enjoying this, for a lot of reasons. And boy was she hungry. Moving on... "So I figure you're in that garage, nervous, really nervous. What can you do to ease the nerves? If you're a nail biter you bite your nails. If you're a smoker you take a puff. But you don't smoke anymore, Doug." Again, Tracy paused. She went back to the large bag that had been sitting on the floor since its arrival. She picked it up and moved it to the glass table. Grand finale time...

"At the risk of sounding immodest, Doug, I figured it was you early on. The old rich-girl-with-poor-boy story is either the stuff of fairy tales or murder motives. And I was skeptical. That Friday Mr. Shane called his attorney, you would have been arriving for dinner around the time of the call. It was *you* Mr. Shane wanted to overhear that call, probably because he had confronted you before about marrying Crystal, and you just ignored him. Mr. Shane couldn't appeal to Crystal because the last time he did that she ran off with the guy." Tracy made no glance toward Bill Ryder. "So his phone call was basically his way of letting you know you had a week to clear out, or Crystal would be out, so to speak. Instead, you came up with this imperfect plan to murder him." Tracy again needed some refreshment from her bottled water. Then she continued.

"So I started paying close attention to you, seeing if you would give yourself away somehow." She stopped and moved in a little closer to Stanz. "And I noticed something. On two occasions you put something back into your right front-most pocket regardless of where you took it from. You took your handkerchief from your back pocket to wipe the mustard off of Crystal's mouth after lunch, but you put it back into your front pants pocket. When we went to look at Bill's security booth you took the keys from your pants pocket but you put them back in the front pocket of that jacket you had on. I guess it's a habit of yours."

Tracy stopped and returned to the bag, reaching in and pulling out the raincoat, still sealed in an evidence bag. She then moved slightly away from the table and continued. "You were wearing this in the garage for, what, almost half an hour? You: the former smoker; the nervous first-time killer. The police took this into evidence the night of the murder to test for gunshot residue. Of course there was none. But I called yesterday to see if they had found anything in the pockets." Tracy dropped the raincoat on the table and pulled out her notebook again while moving back toward the brown bag.

Tracy flipped to the appropriate page in her book. She started reading. "Contents of pockets as per Cheri Alabaster from the crime lab: one crumbled tissue, 69 cents in change, the ubiquitous lint, and…" Tracy stopped and reached into the open bag to remove its only other item. She pulled it out—a small closed bag whose contents were not immediately viewable to those attending. She continued, "…this; one opened, partially used pack of chewing gum."

She again turned to Doug. "And so I wondered: what if this wasn't Brian's gum like the police assumed it was? Gum he might chew to cover up the smell on his breath from drinking. What if this was the killer's gum? What if the killer had the habit of putting things in his front pocket by reflex? You were chewing gum the night I first saw you on the gate. When exactly did you start chewing that gum? Why not earlier while in the garage?"

She moved closer to Doug, who knew *exactly* where this must be going. "So I asked the kind people of the lab if they could fingerprint the gum wrapper. And they did." She moved in closer still. "They got a nice thumb print off the outer-wrapper. And they were able to match it to a thumb print from a certain person's fingerprints that were taken when he applied for his gun permit—your fingerprints, Doug." She was almost in his face now. "Tell us: how, why, and when did your gum get into Brian's pocket, Doug?"

She had been bending over to meet Doug's defiant glare. She straightened herself up and went to return the items to their container. Doug again stood up. "You call that proof? That gum could have been put there any time!"

But she was ready for that. "No Doug. You only stopped smoking a couple of weeks ago, so you weren't chewing gum until then. Crystal will confirm that. And I checked the weather: no big storms had come through here in more than three weeks prior to the night of the murder. So there'd be no reason for you to wear a raincoat since you started your gum-chewing. And only *your* print was on the gum, in somebody *else's* raincoat, which has been in an evidence locker for a week now."

Checkmate. No, no way. "You can't charge me with murder based on… *that!*" Doug screamed.

Tracy was losing her patience. It was clear from the way she said, "You just don't get it yet, do you Doug? This whole desperate plan of yours was so you could secure Crystal's inheritance so you'd have cash flow to pay off old debts and live a prince-charming life. In fact, it wouldn't surprise me to learn that the shot taken at Crystal and you last month was some kind of warning from people you owe money to, people you've been promising to pay off once you can get your hands on the Shane fortune. But the police can look more into that. Regardless, do you really think Crystal's going to marry you now—the man who killed her father and framed her brother for it?" Tracy again moved toward him. "So your whole plan has been for naught, because I think you're going to lose your Crystal. And what do you think is going to happen when your creditors find out the wedding is off? You might actually be safer in police custody. Bottom line is Crystal won't be marrying you now, whether I can prove anything or not." There was some anger in her last words. But he had no more words for her. She backed up from him, and regained her composure. "Besides: I'm not the police or the SA. It's not my job to prove anything anyway. Just to offer another possible scenario in the murder of Stewart Shane, which I think I've done. I'll let the law decide whether they have enough to charge you." He just glared at her. "Look around you Doug. Why don't you ask my mock jury what they think?" He looked around. He didn't like the vibe he was getting.

"Oh, as for Larry Waters—the man you shot and killed Wednesday night—I don't know if you know this yet or not, but Larry was a client of mine. He was there that night to see me, meaning more bad luck for you, I'm afraid. They were able to trace him back to me regardless of your efforts not to have that happen. I'm sure when the police start showing your picture to the cab drivers on duty that night in the area between my building and Waters' house, you're going to be identified sooner or later. Maybe you already have been. That would be enough for a search warrant I think. The cops may even find some blood on the clothes you were wearing that night and match it to Larry's. Heck they may even find the murder weapon in your residence." She paused and moved in toward him, meeting him face to face and eye to eye. "Any way you look at it, I got you, you son of a *bitch*."

Tracy was now again the center of attention. She suddenly became aware that all eyes were on *her*. She caught a glimpse of Kurt Barton and could swear he had a slight smile on his face. But she suddenly felt very self-conscious, and as much as she wanted to shout, "Book 'im, Dano!" what she actually said was, "I'm done." Doug sat back down on the couch, shaking his head.

While Officer Banks moved in to remove the bagged raincoat and gum, Detective Lucas approached Doug Stanz and suggested they should discuss things elsewhere. Tanner announced a car was on its way to supply the transportation. Stanz turned to Crystal with pleading eyes, and as he started to speak, Crystal cut him off saying, "Don't you even…" with as much anger in her voice as she could muster. He rose and let Lucas escort him outside to await the forthcoming police car.

Tracy approached Crystal, who was still seated, and put her hand on her friend's shoulder. "I'm so sorry, Crys. I really feel bad about all of this."

"I sure can pick 'em, huh?" Crystal said with a bitter laugh. Then she arose, now slightly sobbing, and hugged Tracy. "I wish you *were* my sister," she whispered to the attorney. Then Crystal went over to her brother, who was now standing up, observing what had just transpired. Crystal gave Brian a hug too, while Tracy gathered her belongings and started making her way to the door. Along the way she found herself behind Kurt Barton, who turned to her. "Ms. Brubaker," he said while slightly bowing. Then he went out the door. She wasn't sure if bowing was more or less of a sign of respect than bobbling in Barton's world. She hoped it was more.

"Tracy," Crystal called out before Tracy had fully exited the Shane home. She turned and Crystal said, "I am going to call you in a few days and you and I are going to have a nice *long* talk."

"Crys, that'd be supreme." And the two shared another hug. Crystal pulled away and went back to her brother, who was engaged in some conversation with Detective Tanner. Tracy decided to head outside and get some air. The adrenaline was starting to drain. She wanted to get back home, maybe call Neal and Rebecca and let them know what happened.

Tracy was outside now, watching Doug Stanz being driven off to what would most likely prove to be his new home for a while. He was staring out the car window, his eyes fixed on the driveway, not risking meeting anyone's stare.

"Tracy!" Brian called out while moving toward her. "You weren't just going to leave like that were you?"

She looked at him. She wasn't as well prepared for this face-off as she had been for her most recent one. But she had given the matter a lot of thought—maybe too much.

"I don't want to stop seeing you just because this is over, Tracy," Brian began.

She quickly corrected him. "It's not exactly over yet Brian. You're still technically charged. They still have to follow up on Stanz. But I can probably get those charges dismissed with some prodding. If I'm right about Doug owing dangerous people, he may end up making a deal with the SA."

He looked at her curiously. "What about…"

"Us?" she said finishing his question.

He presented his case. "Tracy I haven't had a drink since last Friday. I have my first AA meeting on Monday. I'm going to go back to school. Hopefully be someone who can work his way up in Dad's company. Crystal has said she'd support me and give me a chance."

She placed her right hand flat on his chest, looking at him. "That's wonderful Brian; all of it. But it *has* been only a week. What will happen next week, now that this is pretty much all over?"

"But Tracy with you—us—as my goal…"

"But I cannot be your 'goal' Brian. I can't be a reward. You need to do this for yourself and only yourself. Things are going to happen that will test you and you have to rid yourself of any scapegoats. I mean: what happens if we have a fight? How will you handle it? What happens if I go away for a week on business and you find yourself lonely looking for something to do? Or, Brian, what if we do give it another whirl and it doesn't work out between us? Will you hit the bottle harder than ever? Do you understand my point?"

He wasn't expecting to be turned down. The tender moments they had shared: embraces, kisses. Had they been nothing more than two former lovers comforting each other? It certainly now seemed like he had allowed himself to make incorrect assumptions. "Tracy, I…"

She moved her hand to his cheek. "You need to do this for *you*, not me. I don't want to go through what I went through before, watching you…I can't do it. I can't go through it again. It was too much the first time." She was now fighting back tears. "A lot of time has passed Brian. I have responsibilities now. I wouldn't be able to stand by you the way I could have when we were in school.

"And while we're not the same people we were, I still stress and worry like I used to. But the stakes are bigger now. I guess what I'm saying is that I know myself, what I'm capable of, and what I want. I want you to get the help you need. You're only going to know who you are and what you *really* want when you get and stay sober."

He nodded. Maybe she was right. But she wasn't saying they had no future together. He said, "So, maybe after a while on the wagon, I can call you? Maybe we can have dinner together?"

She smiled at him. "You know me, never say never to anything. You know how to get in touch with me. And you know I'll be cheering for you from the sidelines. Besides, we'll be seeing each other soon anyway, when they arrange dismissal of the charges, if that's in the cards."

Arthur Pankow approached Brian Shane and put his hand on his shoulder. Brian turned to face him. "Mr. Shane, why don't you go with Officer Banks? We can talk about getting these charges dropped."

Brian turned back to Tracy who was smiling at him, one of her irresistible smiles. He hugged her, and then kissed her on the cheek. She allowed this. She really would be cheering for him; she wanted him to overcome his demons. This was his new beginning. And maybe a new beginning for her too.

Brian followed Officer Banks. And Pankow turned to Tracy, who was still smiling. She said, "So you are already going to move forward with dismissing the case against him?" she asked with a hopeful smile.

"After what I just saw in there? Tracy, if I had been on the jury I'd probably have let Brian off," he said smiling also. "I think you may have something with the gum, and the cable going out. Maybe you're even right about the car shooting incident. I can talk to our people at vice to see if they've heard anything about Stanz, reach out to Delaware and Jersey too. Regardless I want to hold this Stanz guy while Roche's people are out circulating his picture to the cab companies. Maybe we already have enough to get a warrant to search his place. Either way, I'm not sure I can move forward, or want to move forward, with a trial against Shane until we clear all this up. I can always re-file if need be." Pankow gave her another smile and turned to leave, just as Tanner was making his way toward her. Tanner just smiled at her, and the two started moving in the direction of Tracy's car.

"Poor Doug, he got too clever for his own good and it tripped him up," Tracy observed.

Tanner asked, "What do you mean?"

"Well, Doug couldn't have foreseen the rain being a factor, so using the raincoat had to be an improvisation—a better choice because of the hood than a windbreaker or whatever he was originally planning on wearing. And it might have worked out for him if the storm hadn't also knocked out the cable," she explained. "The Lord giveth and taketh—and will be takething Doug to the slammereth."

Tanner laughed and said, "Tracy Brubaker: mind of a lawyer, heart of a detective."

She laughed herself. She liked that—a lot. Maybe she should have that put on her office door. "I am Peter Brubaker's daughter, after all," she said.

The smile left Tanner's face. "Yes. Yes you are. I wish he could have been here to see you today. He would have been so proud of you—and I never would have heard the end of it." Tracy laughed at that. And then Tanner added, "*I'm* proud of you."

Now it was her turn to give out hugs. She embraced Tanner, kissed him on the cheek, and again started to move toward her vehicle. Tanner called out, "Don't forget to call your mother." She turned and he was smiling again, a bit mischievously this time.

"First thing I'll do after I get something to eat. I promise."

Then Tanner asked, "So, when are we going to do this again, Tracy?"

Tracy Brubaker thought for a moment, and then she answered him, smiling mischievously herself. "Why El, I don't know *what* you're talking about. You know I *never* get involved in murder cases." And with that she entered her car and headed for home, imagining with great delight what kind of meal she would reward herself with for a job well done. Hmm, steak was suddenly a definite option.

Tune in for the next exciting chapter in the Tracy Brubaker mystery series, Cross-Stitched!

Visit www.midmar.com
for a complete list of titles!